As Maggie walked to the director's private office, a flicker of anticipation skipped through her.

She tried to tell herself that her suddenly erratic pulse was due to her imminent mission. *Herself* wasn't buying it. She knew darn well what was causing the shimmer of excitement in her blood.

He was waiting a few steps away.

Maggie paused outside the door to draw in a deep, steadying breath, but it didn't do any good. As soon as she walked into his office and saw the man standing at the window, her lungs forgot to function.

He turned and gave her one of his rare smiles. "Hello, Maggie."

She forced the air trapped in her chest to circulate. This was her boss, for heaven's sake, and she was too professional to allow her fascination with Adam Ridgeway, the man, to complicate her relationship with Adam Ridgeway, the director of OMEGA.

Unfortunately.

Dear Reader,

Happy Valentine's Day! And as a special gift to you, we're publishing the latest in *New York Times* bestseller Linda Howard's series featuring the Mackenzie family. Hero Zane Mackenzie, of *Mackenzie's Pleasure*, is every inch a man—and Barrie Lovejoy is just the woman to teach this rough, tough Navy SEAL what it means to love. There's nothing left to say but "Enjoy!"

Merline Lovelace concludes her "Code Name: Danger" miniseries with *Perfect Double*, the long-awaited romance between Maggie Sinclair and her boss at the OMEGA Agency, Adam Ridgeway. Then join Kylie Brant for *Guarding Raine*. This author established herself as a reader favorite with her very first book—and her latest continues the top-notch tradition. *Forever, Dad* is the newest from Maggie Shayne, and it's an exciting, suspenseful, *emotional* tour de force. For those of you with a hankering to get "Spellbound," there's Vella Munn's *The Man From Forever*, a story of love and passion that transcend time. Finally, Rebecca Daniels wraps up her "It Takes Two" duo with *Father Figure*, featuring the ever-popular secret baby plot line.

Pick up all six of these wonderful books—and come back next month for more, because here at Silhouette Intimate Moments we're dedicated to bringing you the best of today's romantic fiction. Enjoy!

Yours,

Leslie Wainger
Senior Editor and Editorial Coordinator

Please address questions and book requests to:
Silhouette Reader Service
U.S.: 3010 Walden Ave., P.O. Box 1325, Buffalo, NY 14269
Canadian: P.O. Box 609, Fort Erie, Ont. L2A 5X3

MERLINE LOVELACE

PERFECT DOUBLE

Published by Silhouette Books
America's Publisher of Contemporary Romance

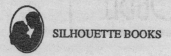

SILHOUETTE BOOKS

ISBN 0-373-07692-4

PERFECT DOUBLE

Books by Merline Lovelace

Silhouette Intimate Moments

MERLINE LOVELACE

As a career air force officer, Merline Lovelace served tours of duty in Vietnam, at the Pentagon and at bases all over the world. During her years in uniform, she met and married her own handsome hero and stored up enough exciting tales to keep her fingers flying over the keyboard for years to come. When not glued to the computer, she goes antiquing with her husband, Al, or chases little white balls around the golf courses of Oklahoma.

Perfect Double is the fourth book in Merline's "Code Name: Danger" series for Silhouette Intimate Moments. Look for her next sizzling contemporary romance, *Beauty and the Bodyguard*, which is Book Three in Silhouette's exciting new "Fortune's Children" series.

Merline enjoys hearing from readers and can be reached at PO Box 892717, Oklahoma City, OK 73189.

To Dee and Betty — friends, treasured in-laws, and two people who know what romance is all about! With bunches of love...

Prologue

She had to die.

That was the best solution.

The only solution.

He stood at the window and stared, unseeing, at the winter-grayed streets. The thought of killing her, of snuffing out her vibrant essence, twisted his gut. But there wasn't any other way. She didn't know she held a tiny scrap of information that could bring him and his world tumbling down. She had no idea she possessed the power to destroy him.

She had to die before she discovered she held that power.

And a part of him would die with her.

Chapter 1

Softly falling snow blanketed Washington, D.C., adding a touch of lacy white trim to the elegant town houses lining a quiet side street just off Massachusetts Avenue. The few residents of the capital who weren't glued to their TV sets this Superbowl Sunday scurried by, chins down and collars turned up against the cold. Intent on getting out of the elements, they didn't give the town house set midway down the block a second glance. If they had, they might have noticed the discreet bronze plaque set beside the entrance that identified the offices of the president's special envoy.

Most Washington insiders believed the special envoy's position had been created several administrations ago to give a wealthy campaign contributor a fancy title and an important-sounding but meaningless title. Only a handful of the most senior cabinet officials knew that the special envoy secretly served in another, far more vital capacity.

From a specially shielded high-tech control center on the third floor of the town house, he directed a covert agency.

An agency whose initials comprised the last letter of the Greek alphabet, OMEGA. An agency that, as its name implied, sprang into action as a last resort when other, more established organizations, such as the CIA, the State Department or the military, couldn't respond.

Less than an hour ago, a call from the president had activated an OMEGA response. From various corners of the capital, a small cadre of dedicated professionals battled the snow-clogged streets to converge on the scene.

Maggie Sinclair unwrapped the wool scarf muffling her mouth and nose and stomped her calf-high boots to remove the last of the clinging snow. Stuffing the scarf in her pocket, she hurried through the tunnel that led to OMEGA's secret underground entrance. At the end of the passageway, she pressed a hand to a hidden sensor and waited impatiently for the computers to verify her palmprint. Seconds later, the titanium-shielded door hummed open. She took the stairs to the second floor and scanned the monitors set into the wall. Satisfied that only the special envoy's receptionist occupied the spacious outer area, she activated the sensors.

Gray-haired, grandmotherly Elizabeth Wells glanced up in surprise. "My goodness, Chameleon, you got here fast."

"I took the subway. I wasn't about to try driving through this mess." Shrugging out of her down jacket, Maggie hooked it on a bentwood coat tree. "Besides, I wanted to leave my car for Red. Just in case."

Elizabeth's kind face folded into sympathetic lines. "What a shame you were called in right in the middle of your father's visit. He doesn't get back to the States all that often, does he?"

"No, he doesn't."

Actually, Red Sinclair was lucky if he managed a quick trip stateside once a year. As superintendent of an oil-field exploration rig, the crusty widower traveled continually from one overseas job to the next. He might be drilling in Malaysia one week, Saudi Arabia the next.

"And when he does come home," Maggie added with a grin, "he usually times his visits to coincide with the Superbowl. I left him and Terence ensconced in front of the TV, alternately cheering the Cowboys and cursing the Redskins."

"You left the poor man with Terence?" A ripple of distaste crossed Elizabeth's face. Like most of the OMEGA team, she actively disliked the bug-eyed blue-and-orange-striped iguana a certain Central American colonel had given Maggie. The one time the receptionist had been pressed into lizard-sitting, the German shepherd-size creature had devoured her prized water lilies.

"Honestly, dear, I don't understand how you can keep that...that creature as a house pet. I find him utterly repulsive."

"Dad does, too," Maggie replied, laughing. "Unfortunately, the reverse doesn't hold true. Terence hates this cold weather. He's been trying to climb into Red's lap to share his warmth, not to mention his beer, all afternoon long. I left them just before halftime, tussling for possession of a bottle of Coors."

"Perhaps I should give your father a call," Elizabeth mused. "If you're going out of town, he might like to get away from that disgusting reptile for a while. Maybe have dinner with me."

Maggie's brows rose. "*Am* I going out of town?"

Elizabeth gave a little cluck of disgust at her uncharacteristic slip. Having served as personal assistant to OMEGA's director since the agency was founded, she knew when and how to keep secrets. She also knew how to use the Sig Sauer 9 mm pistol she kept in her upper-right-hand desk drawer. She'd fired the weapon only once in the line of duty, to deadly effect.

Maggie grinned to herself. This kind, lethal woman had a background and a personality as intriguing as her father's.

"I wish you would give Dad a call, Elizabeth. I'm sure he'd enjoy having dinner with someone who doesn't prefer bugs as an appetizer."

The receptionist grimaced and reached for the intercom phone. "I will, I promise. Right now, though, I'd better tell the chief you're here. He's waiting for you."

While Elizabeth announced her arrival, Maggie raked a hand through her snow-dampened, shoulder-length brown hair. A quick tug settled her faded maroon-and-gold Washington Redskins sweatshirt around her jeans-clad hips. This wasn't quite her standard professional attire, but the coded message summoning her to headquarters had signaled a matter of national importance, and she hadn't taken the time to change. Oh, well, OMEGA's director had seen her in worse rigs than this. Much worse.

Now all brisk efficiency, Elizabeth nodded. "Go on in, dear."

As Maggie walked down the short corridor leading to the director's private office, a flicker of anticipation skipped through her, like a tiny electrical impulse darting across a circuit board. She tried to tell herself that her suddenly erratic pulse was due to her imminent mission, whatever it might be. Herself wasn't buying it. She knew darn well what was causing the shimmer of excitement in her blood.

He was waiting a few steps away.

Maggie paused outside the door to draw in a deep, steadying breath. The extra supply of air didn't do her any good. As soon as she walked into his office and caught her first glimpse of the tall, dark-haired man standing at the window, her lungs forgot to function.

After almost three years, Maggie thought wryly, she ought to be used to Adam Ridgeway's effect on her respiratory system. The sad fact was that each contact with this cool, authoritative, often irritating man left her more breathless than the last.

He turned and gave her one of his rare smiles. "Hello, Maggie. Sorry I had to drag you away from the game."

She forced the air trapped in her chest cavity to circulate. Okay, the man looked like an ad for *GQ* in knife-pleated tan wool slacks, a white oxford shirt and a V-necked cashmere sweater in a deep indigo blue that matched his eyes. And, yes, the light from his desk lamp picked up a few delicious traces of silver in his black hair, traces he claimed she herself had put there.

But he was her boss, for heaven's sake, and she was too mature, too professional, to allow her growing fascination with Adam Ridgeway to complicate her relationship with the director of OMEGA. Unfortunately.

"Hi, Adam," she replied, moving to her favorite perch on one corner of his massive mahogany conference table. "I don't mind the weather, but if the Skins lose this game because I'm not there to cheer them on, Red's going to gloat for the rest of his visit. He still can't believe I've transferred my allegiance from the Cowboys."

"That is a pretty radical switch for an Oklahoman," the Boston-bred Adam concurred gravely.

"No kidding! A lot of folks back home think it ranks right up there with abandoning your firstborn or setting fire to the flag."

Actually, Maggie's move to Washington three years ago had resulted in far more than a shift in allegiance in football teams. Until that time, she'd chaired the foreign language department at a small Midwestern college. An easy mastery of her work and a broken engagement had led to a growing restlessness. So when she received a late-night call from the strange little man Red Sinclair had once helped smuggle out of a war-torn oil sheikhdom, she'd been intrigued. That call had resulted in a secret trip to D.C. and, ultimately, her recruitment as an operative.

From the day she joined OMEGA, Maggie had never considered going back to sleepy little Yarnell College. What woman could be content teaching languages after leading a strike team into the jungles of Central America to take down a drug lord? Or after being trapped in a Soviet nuclear-missile silo with a brilliant, if incredibly clumsy, scientist? Or dangling hundreds of feet above the dark, crashing Mediterranean to extract a wounded agent from the subterranean lair of a megalomaniacal film star? Not this woman, at any rate.

Although...

If pressed, Maggie would have admitted that the life of a secret agent had its drawbacks. Like the fact that most of the men she associated with in her line of work were either drug dealers or thieves or general all-around sleazebags.

Oh, there were a few interesting prospects. A certain drop-dead-gorgeous Latin American colonel still called her whenever he was in D.C. And one or two operatives from other agencies she'd worked with had thrown out hints about wanting to know the woman behind the code name Chameleon. But none of these men possessed quite the right combination of qualities Maggie was looking for in a potential mate. Like a keen, incisive mind. A sense of adventure. A hint of danger in his smile. A great bod wasn't one of her absolute requirements, but it certainly wouldn't hurt.

So far Maggie had only met one man who came close to measuring up in all categories, and he was standing a few feet away from her right now. The problem was, whenever they came face-to-face, it was generally just before he sent her off to some far corner of the world.

As he was about to do now, apparently.

"So what's up, Adam?" she asked. "Why are we here?"

"I'm here because I got a call from the president an hour ago," he said slowly, his eyes on her face.

"And?" Maggie prompted.

The tingling tension that always gripped her at the start of a mission added to the fluttering in her veins that Adam's presence generated. Anticipation coursed through her, and her fingers gripped the smooth wood as she focused her full attention on his next words.

"And you're here because you're going to impersonate the vice president for the next two weeks."

Maggie's jaw dropped. "The vice president? Of the United States?"

"Of the United States."

"Taylor Grant?"

"Taylor Grant."

Maggie's astonishment exploded into shimmering, leaping excitement. In her varied career with OMEGA, she'd passed herself off as everything from a nun to a call girl. But this would be the first time she'd gone undercover in the topmost echelons of the executive branch.

"Now *this* is my kind of assignment! The vice president of the United States!" She shoved a hand through the thick sweep of her brown hair. "What's the story, Adam?"

"For the last three months, the vice president has been working secretly on an international accord in response to terrorism. According to the president, the parties involved are close, very close, to hammering out the final details of an agreement. One that will send shock waves through the terrorist community. When this treaty is approved, all signatories will respond as one to any hostile act.''

''It's about time!''

In the past few years, Maggie had seen firsthand the results of differing government approaches to terrorism. Depending on the personality of the people in high office, the response could be swift or maddeningly slow, strong or fatally indecisive.

''The key players involved in crafting the treaty are gathering at Camp David to hammer out the final details,'' Adam continued. ''No one—I repeat, no one—outside of the president, the VP herself and a few trusted advisors know about this meeting.''

Maggie eyed him shrewdly. ''So I'm to deflect the world's attention while this secret meeting takes place?''

''Exactly.''

She chewed on her lower lip for a moment. ''Why me?''

''Why not?'' he countered, watching her face.

''Mrs. Grant has at least half a dozen women assigned to her Secret Service detail,'' Maggie said bluntly. ''They know her personal habits and routine intimately. They wouldn't need the coaching I will to double for her.''

''True, but none of them matches her height and general physical characteristics as well as you do.''

Maggie composed a swift mental image of the attractive young widow. Tall. Auburn-haired. Slightly more slender than Maggie herself. A full mouth that quirked in a distinctive way when she was amused, which was often. Stunning violet eyes that sparkled with a lively intelligence.

Far more important than any physical characteristics, however, were the vice president's personality traits. Taylor Grant was totally self-assured. Gracious, yet tenacious as a pit bull when it came to the political issues she championed. And she carried herself with an easy confidence that Maggie knew she projected, as well. With a flash of insight, she sensed that was the key to this assignment.

She'd earned her code name, Chameleon, because of her ability to dramatically alter her physical appearance when going undercover. But she'd survived in the field because she knew that a successful impersonation came from within, not from without. The trick was to believe you were the person you pretended to be—if you did, you could convince others. This mission would take intense concentration and all of Maggie's skills, but she could do it. She would do it.

"Imagine," she murmured, her brown eyes gleaming. "I'll be presiding over joint sessions of Congress. Just think of the bills I can push through in the next couple of weeks. The bloated bureaucratic budgets I can slash."

"I'm afraid you won't have much opportunity to exercise your political clout," Adam said dryly. "To cover her absence, the vice president has announced that she's taking a long-overdue two-week vacation to her home in the California Sierras."

With real regret, Maggie abandoned her plans to ruthlessly streamline the entire federal government.

"Okay, what's the catch?"

One of Adam's dark brows rose.

"A two-week vacation in the High Sierras is too easy. I've got this tingly little feeling there's more to this role than what you've told me so far."

The ghost of a smile curved Adam's lips. "Your tingles are on target."

"They usually are," she said with a trace of smugness.

His smile faded as he studied her face. "Early this morning, Taylor Grant received a death threat. Your mission while you're undercover will be to discover the source of this threat."

The fact that Mrs. Grant had received a death threat didn't particularly surprise Maggie. A Secret Service contact she'd once worked with had mentioned that the White House switchboard screened upward of fifty thousand calls a day. A battery of skilled operators separated disgruntled voters from dangerous malcontents and forwarded the "sinisters" for investigation. Maggie had been amazed at both the number and the content of the wacko calls that came over the switchboard. One, she'd been told, had ended with a long-drawn-out shriek and the sound of the caller blowing out his brains.

But in addition to outright kooks and psychotics who might target Taylor Grant, Maggie could name at least half dozen ultraright-wing groups the vice president had outraged. An intelligent, outspoken woman with strong liberal leanings, she'd been chosen as the president's running mate to balance his more conservative platform and to guarantee California's huge block of electoral votes. No, Maggie wasn't surprised Mrs. Grant had received a death threat.

Still, the Secret Service was charged with investigating such threats. Once again, Maggie puzzled over the reason for her involvement in this mission. She knew Adam too well to suppose that he'd called her in just because she resembled Taylor Grant in general size and shape.

"So what was different about this threat, that it activated an OMEGA response?" she asked.

"The call came in over the VP's personal line. Whoever made it knew how to bypass the filters that protect her from such calls, and how to electronically synthesize his voice."

"His voice? If it was electronically disguised, how do we know the caller was a he?"

Adam regarded her steadily across the half acre of polished mahogany that constituted his desk. "Because the nature of the call suggests it was made by someone who knows Mrs. Grant well. *Very* well. Well enough to mention her husky little gasp at moments of extreme passion.''

"Extreme passion?" Maggie's jaw sagged once more. "Good grief, are you saying the vice president of the United States is being threatened by... by a former lover?"

"So it appears."

While Maggie struggled to absorb this astounding information, Adam rose, a sheet of notepaper in his hand.

"This is a list the VP supplied of the men she's known intimately."

Eyes wide, Maggie glanced down at the list he handed her. To her surprise, she saw that it was very short. *Amazingly* short, for a charismatic, dynamic woman who'd been a widow for over ten years. A woman who kept the press and the public titillated with a string of very handsome and very eligible escorts.

There were only four names on the list:

Harold Grant, the vice president's husband. The California sculptor had died from a rare form of bone cancer more than a decade ago.

Peter Donovan. Maggie couldn't place him, but the notation beside the name indicated that he had managed the VP's first campaign for governor.

Stoney Armstrong. That name she recognized immediately! The handsome, square-jawed movie star had escorted then-Governor Grant one whole, tempestuous spring. Their pictures had been splashed across every tabloid and every glossy magazine on several continents.

And...

Maggie's eyes widened. "James Elliot?" she gasped. "The secretary of the treasury?"

Adam nodded. "Elliot met Mrs. Grant after the president named him to head Treasury. Their liaison was reportedly short, but passionate."

"So that's why OMEGA's running this show instead of the Secret Service!" Maggie exclaimed.

In addition to his responsibilities for the fiscal policies of the United States, the secretary of the treasury also directed the Secret Service. The idea that the supervisor of the very agency charged with protecting the vice president was one of three men suspected of threatening to kill her boggled Maggie's mind.

"Elliot himself suggested OMEGA take the lead in this case," Adam said slowly. "He recognized that his liaison with Mrs. Grant, as brief as it was, compromised him in this case."

"No kidding!"

Her forehead wrinkling, Maggie studied the short list once again. Four names, three suspects—one of whom was a close personal friend of the president, and a member of his cabinet. Whew!

"There's another name that should be included on the list," Adam added in a neutral tone.

"Really?" she murmured, still absorbing the implications of James Elliot's involvement. "Whose?"

"Mine."

With infinite care, Maggie raised her eyes from the paper in her hand. As she searched Adam's face, a wave of conflicting emotions crashed through her.

Instinctive denial.

Instant awareness of the staggering impact this had on her mission.

And jealousy. Sheer, unadulterated jealousy. The old-fashioned green-eyed kind that was embarrassing to own up to but impossible to deny.

Taylor Grant was just the kind of woman who would attract Adam, Maggie admitted with painful honesty.

Polished. Sophisticated. At ease with politicians and princes. She moved in the same circles Adam did. Circles that Maggie, content with herself and her world, had never aspired to...until recently.

Summoning every ounce of professionalism she possessed, she sent him a cool look. "Well, that certainly puts a new twist on this mission. Suppose you tell me why the vice president didn't include your name on her list."

A glimmer of emotion flickered through his eyes at her tart rejoinder. It might have been amusement or irritation, but it disappeared so quickly, Maggie couldn't tell. With Adam, she rarely could.

"Because I'm her future, not her past, lover," he replied evenly.

For the space of several heartbeats, silence blanketed the spacious office. Maggie fabricated and rejected a dozen possible interpretations of his statement. Only one of them made any sense, and she wouldn't let herself believe that one.

"Come again?" she asked.

Navy cashmere contoured Adam's well-defined shoulders as he crossed his arms. "Until this point, I've enjoyed only a casual friendship with Taylor Grant."

Maggie fought down a ridiculous rush of relief.

"That friendship is about to deepen."

"It is?"

"It is."

She cleared her throat. "Just how deep do you intend to take it?"

"As deep as necessary."

She refused to acknowledge the slow curl of heat his words generated. "I think you'd better give me something more specific."

"For the duration of the time you're undercover, I'll be your sole contact. We'll be together night and day for the next two weeks. As far as the rest of the world is concerned, we're in love. Or at least in lust."

Right. As far as the rest of the world was concerned. Maggie bit down on the inside of her lower lip and forced herself to concentrate as Adam continued.

"We'll debut this new relationship at the VP's last official Washington function before she leaves for California."

"Which is?"

"A special benefit performance at the Kennedy Center tomorrow night."

"Tomorrow night?"

Maggie jumped off the corner of the conference table, her mind racing. She had less than twenty-four hours to transform herself into the person of the vice president of the United States. And into Adam Ridgeway's latest companion/lover.

At that moment, she wasn't sure which role daunted her—or thrilled her—more.

Chapter 2

The next hours were the most intense Maggie had ever spent preparing for a mission.

A quick call to her father glossed over the reason for extended absence. Although she'd never told Red Sinclair about her work for OMEGA, he knew his daughter too well to believe that her civilian cover as an adjunct professor at D.C.'s Georgetown University occupied all her time.

Grumbling something about making clear to a certain reptile who was in charge during Maggie's absence, Red hung up and went back to the Superbowl.

After that, the OMEGA team moved at the speed of light.

Jake MacKenzie, code name Jaguar, arrived to act as headquarters controller for this operation. Since his marriage last year to a woman he'd rescued from a band of Central American rebels, Jake hadn't spent much time in the field, but he was one of OMEGA's most experienced agents. There wasn't anyone Maggie trusted more to orchestrate the behind-the-scenes support for this mission than the steely-eyed Jaguar.

With Jake beside her, she listened to the chilling tape of the early-morning phone call.

"You were so good," the eerie, electronic voice whispered, *"so beautiful. I can still hear your soft, sweet moan, that little sound you make when . . ."*

Disgust twisted Maggie's mouth. That someone could speak of love in one breath, and death the next, sickened her.

"I must kill you. I don't want to, but I must. Try to understand. . . ."

The call ended with a click, and Taylor Grant's swift, indrawn gasp.

"All right," Jake said, his mouth grim. "Let's go over these dossiers on the three suspects one more time. Intel is champing at the bit to start your political indoctrination."

The dossiers didn't give her any more insight into which of the three prominent men might want to assassinate the vice president, but Maggie studied their backgrounds in minute detail. Then she spent hours in briefings on the political personalities and issues the vice president dealt with daily.

Finally she closeted herself in a small room to study videotapes of Taylor Grant's speech patterns and gestures. Given her background in linguistics, Maggie soon had the vice president's voice down pat. Copying her gestures and facial expressions took a bit more work, but after hours in front of the mirror and a video camera, Maggie passed even Jake's and Adam's critical review.

At that point, the wizards of the wardrobe, as she termed OMEGA's field dress unit, whipped into action. A gel-like adhesive "bone" shaped her chin and nose to match Mrs. Grant's profile. A quick dye job and an expert cut resulted in the well-known stylish auburn shag. Tinted contacts duplicated the vice president's distinctive violet eyes.

Reducing Maggie's more generous figure to the vice president's exact proportions, however, required a bit more ingenuity. After taking some rather intimate measurements and stewing over the matter for a while, the pudgy, frizzy-haired genius who headed Field Dress produced a nineties version of a corset that also, he proclaimed proudly, doubled as protective body armor. The thin Kevlar wraparound vest flattened Maggie's bust and trimmed several inches off her waist. The vice president's well-known preference for pleated pants and long tunic-style jackets would disguise her slightly fuller hips.

"Suck it in, Chameleon," the chief wizard ordered sternly, yanking on the adjustable straps at the waist of the bodysuit-corset.

Maggie clutched at the edge of a table. "Hey! Go easy there," she said over one shoulder. "I've got to be able to breathe for the next few weeks, you know."

"Don't panic," he replied, grunting a little with effort. "This baby should fit more easily in a day or so."

"It should?" she gasped. "Why?"

He backed away, surveying his handiwork. "A couple of days on the VP's diet will shave a few pounds off you."

Maggie straightened and took a few shallow, experimental breaths. "The vice president is on a diet?"

"Uh-oh. You didn't know?"

"Intelligence is going to cover her personal habits as soon as we're through here. What kind of a diet?"

"You'd better let intel brief you," the chief replied evasively. Not meeting her eyes, he held out a cobalt blue St. John knit tunic with a double row of gold buttons.

Maggie poked her head through the square-cut neck of the tunic and eyed the pudgy chief suspiciously.

"What kind of diet?" she repeated. "Come on, spill it."

"She's, uh, a vegetarian."

"You've got to be kidding!"

"It's true, I swear. It's not public knowledge because Mrs. Grant doesn't want to get the beef and poultry lobby groups up in arms."

"Wonderful," Maggie muttered.

While she wouldn't exactly classify herself as a junk food junkie—after all, she did enjoy sampling Washington's wonderful diversity of restaurants—Maggie preferred hamburgers and pizzas to vegetables any day. In fact, she'd recently discovered that she was violently allergic to a distant relative of the carrot family.

"It's only for two weeks," the frizzy-haired wizard reminded her.

"Oh, sure. What's a mere two weeks without real food?"

Sucking in her tummy to ease the bite of the constrictive corset, Maggie headed for the laboratory in the basement of the town house to check out her equipment for this mission.

A spear of regret lanced through her when she surrendered her faithful Smith & Wesson .22 automatic. Although small, when loaded with hollow-point long-rifle stingers, the weapon could cause as much tissue damage as a .38 Police Special. But not even the high-tech masterminds in the Special Devices Lab could figure out how to shield her Smith & Wesson from the sophisticated security screens that surrounded the vice president. In its place, Maggie was issued a palm-size, .22-caliber derringer.

"This is the same model Mrs. Grant keeps in her California home," the chief of Special Devices told her. "It's single-action, with a spur trigger, and carries five rounds."

After a few practice rounds at the firing range, Maggie felt comfortable with the derringer. But she felt decidedly uncomfortable with the fact that she wouldn't have a weapon in her possession until she reached California. For the first time, she was going out on a mission naked. All she had to protect her from a potential assassin was her training, her instincts and her wits.

And Adam.

He joined her at the range a few moments later. The acrid scent of cordite filled the air as Maggie watched him test fire the small, rapid-fire Heckler & Koch 9 mm Special Devices had issued him. Legs spread, arms lifted, he pumped round after round into the targets. His tight expression underscored the grim reality of her mission.

Back in the lab, Special Devices fitted Maggie with the combination directional beeper and body bug they'd hurriedly devised for this mission. To her amazement, she discovered that they'd soldered a state-of-the-art miniaturized radio transmitter/receiver to the inside of a wide gold wedding band.

"It's identical to the one Mrs. Grant wears," the technician explained.

Maggie turned the heavy gold band over and over in the palm of her hand, but couldn't find any trace of the tiny embedded device. She did, however, see the inscription engraved on the inside. Her heart thumped painfully as she read the words *Now, and forever.*

How tragic, she thought. The woman who wore this ring, or one identical to it, hadn't had much of a forever with her husband. Some years older than his attractive young wife, Harold Grant had died while still in his mid-thirties. They'd had only a few good years together, yet his widow had never remarried, and still wore her wedding band.

"Because the bug is so small," the head of Special Devices explained, "its range is more limited than we'd like. You'll be able to communicate only with the chief, who'll relay the necessary information to OMEGA headquarters via his own, more powerful device."

"Which is why we won't be more than a few miles apart during this entire operation," Adam said, coming to stand beside her. He took the ring from her unresisting fingers to examine it himself.

Maggie frowned, not entirely sure she liked this turn of events. She was used to operating independently in the field. Very independently. The idea of passing all her communications through Adam was a little unsettling.

She slanted him a quick speculative look as he hefted the gold band in his palm. She'd worked for and with Adam Ridgeway for three years now. In the process, she'd learned to respect his sharp, incisive knowledge of field operations. Like the other OMEGA operatives, she trusted him with her life every time he sent her into the field.

Still, for all her personal and very private admiration of Adam, Maggie had to admit they sometimes clashed professionally. They'd had more than a few disagreements in the past over her occasionally unorthodox methods in the field. In fact, the only times any of the OMEGA agents had ever seen Adam come close to losing his legendary cool were during Maggie's mission debriefs.

Well, the next few weeks would no doubt provide a severe test of his restraint, she thought. She was the field operative on this mission, and she fully intended to follow her instincts, just as she always had. Her generous mouth curved in a private smile. She'd always hoped to be on the scene when the iron-spined Adam Ridgeway's control finally slipped its leash.

Maybe, just maybe, she would be.

He caught her sideways glance. "Let's see how well this works," he said, holding out his hand.

A funny little quiver darted through her stomach as she placed her left hand in Adam's right. His palm felt warm and smooth beneath her fingertips, like supple, well-tanned leather. Nibbling on her lower lip, she watched him slide the gold band over the knuckle of her ring finger. When it slipped into place, his hand closed over hers.

Startled by both the tensile strength of his hold and the intimacy of the gesture, Maggie glanced up at the face so close to her own. His blue eyes locked with hers.

A voice at her shoulder jerked her attention back to the hovering technicians. "How does it feel?"

Her hand slipped from Adam's hold. "Fine."

Actually, the heavy circle felt odd. Unfamiliar. Maggie rarely wore jewelry, and when she did, it was more the funky, fun kind. This solid ounce of precious metal weighting her hand was a new experience for her. Using her thumb, she twisted the ring around her finger. It fit perfectly. Not too tight, not too loose. Yet when she tried to remove it, the thing balked at her knuckle.

"The inside of the band is curved to slide on easily, but that sucker won't ever come off," the team chief told her with a smug grin.

Her newly dyed dark red brows snapped together. "What?"

"Not without a special lubricant."

"Wait a minute. This special lubricant isn't another one of your no-fail formulas, is it? Like the solvent that was supposed to instantly remove the tattoo you put on my chin? It took three months for the thing to fade completely."

The technician waved a hand to dismiss that minor inconvenience. "The lubricant will work, I'm sure."

"You're *sure?* You mean you haven't tested it yet?"

"As a matter of fact, we haven't quite developed it yet. But we will by the time this mission is over. Besides, the chief suggested we size the ring like that."

"Oh, he did?" She turned to the man at her side, her brows arching.

"So you won't have to worry about losing it," Adam said easily. "And I don't have to worry about losing you."

After another round with intelligence and a final mission prebrief with Jake and Adam, Maggie pulled on the cobalt blue pea jacket that matched her designer knit outfit and slid into the back seat of a limo. A slow, simmering excitement percolated through her veins during the ride to the target point. She locked her gloved hands in her lap to keep from beating a nervous tattoo on the leather armrest and stared out at a capital still blanketed by a layer of white, now more slush than snow.

They'd decided to make the switch at the vice president's official residence. The old executive office building, where the VP's office and staff were located, swarmed with people all day and far into the night. By contrast, the pillared, three-story residence tucked away on the wooded grounds of the naval observatory in northwest Washington had limited access and much less traffic.

Outside of OMEGA, only three people knew exactly when and how the switch would take place. The vice president, of course. Lillian Roth, Mrs. Grant's personal assistant and dresser. And the SAIC—the special agent in charge of her personal security detail—William "Buck" Evans.

Maggie, Adam and Jake had debated strenuously whether or not to read Buck Evans into the script. With the treasury secretary himself under suspicion, they hesitated to include anyone in his chain of command in this deep-cover operation. But Mrs. Grant had insisted, and the president himself had concurred.

Evans had been assigned to the vice president's detail since the early days of the campaign. At one whistle-stop, he'd thrown himself in front of a two-hundred-and-fifty-pound crazy who objected to her stand in favor of government subsidies for AIDS research and treatment. In the ensuing brawl, the protester had chewed off the tip of Buck's ear. The agent had declined cosmetic surgery, claiming that the mangled ear added to his character. From that day on, he'd been permanently assigned to Taylor Grant's detail, and she trusted him with her life.

Besides, the vice president had said tartly, without Buck's assistance, it would be impossible to pull off this masquerade. As SAIC, he screened the agents assigned to her protective detail, approved all security procedures and set the duty schedules. He could ensure that the people accompanying the VP on her long-planned vacation were the ones least familiar with the twists and turns of her personality. He would also provide the real Mrs. Grant with protection during her secret treaty negotiations at Camp David.

So when Maggie's limo drove around to the back of the turreted turn-of-the-century mansion that served as the vice president's official residence, it was Buck Evans who stepped out of the shadows and yanked open the rear door. Digging a hand into her arm, he half helped, half hauled her out of the back seat.

"I've diverted the surveillance cameras. Let's get you upstairs, fast."

He hustled her through a side door, past a darkened room and up a set of narrow stairs. After scanning the wide hallway that ran the length of the second floor, he tugged her after him, toward a door set halfway down the hall.

"Go on inside. I'll reset the cameras, then come back for Mrs. Grant when she calls."

Maggie had barely stepped into a small foyer before the door shut behind her. She stood still for a moment, trying to slow her pounding heart. From her breathless state, she guessed that the total elapsed time from the moment Buck Evans pulled open the limo's door until he shut this one behind her had been less than a minute.

"Harrumph!"

At the sudden sound, Maggie spun to the left and dropped into an instinctive crouch. Her hand reached for her weapon before she remembered she wasn't armed.

"So you're the one!"

A diminutive figure in a severely cut navy blue suit, thick-soled lace-up shoes, and an unruly mass of steel gray curls stood framed in a set of glass-paned French doors. She held herself ramrod straight, her chin tilted at a belligerent angle and her mouth thinned to a tight line as she surveyed the newcomer from the tip of her auburn head to the toes of her black leather boots.

Maggie straightened slowly. From her intelligence briefings, she recognized the other woman instantly. Lillian Roth, the vice president's personal confidante and assistant for almost twenty years. The sixty-three-year-old woman had appeared rather formidable in the few photographs intel had dug up of her. Maggie now discovered that the photos hadn't really captured the full force of Lillian's character. In person, she radiated all the warmth and charm of a Marine Corps drill sergeant on a bad hair day.

"Well, I must say you've achieved a startling resemblance," the dresser said with a small sniff. "But it takes more than mere physical presence to emulate someone of Mrs. Grant's stature."

"I agree completely."

Maggie's cool reply duplicated exactly the vice president's voice and intonation. Lillian's gray brows rose, but she obviously couldn't bring herself to unbend enough to praise what Maggie considered a rather impressive performance.

"I'll take your coat. The vice president is waiting for you in her sitting room."

Having memorized the floor plans of the residence, Maggie walked confidently through the double doors into a tall-ceilinged, airy room. She paused just past the threshold, visually cataloging the fixtures and furniture in her mind. Although an attack on the VP was unlikely in this secure environment, Maggie wasn't about to take any chances. She'd spend only one night here, but she wanted to be able to find her way around these rooms in total darkness if she had to.

The furnishings in the spacious sitting room were a tribute to Taylor Grant's exquisite taste and vibrant personality. A framed print of Monet's famous water lilies of Giverny hung in a lighted alcove between tall curtained windows. Accent pieces scattered throughout the room took their cue from this masterpiece of swirling blues and greens and purples. A magnificent green jade Chinese temple dog, one paw resting imperiously on a round ball, dominated the huge coffee table set between two facing sofas, which were covered in a shimmering blue-and-purple plaid. A collection of crystal candlesticks in varying shapes and sizes decorated the white-painted wood mantel, reflecting the light from the fire in a rainbow of glowing colors.

But it was the woman standing beside the fireplace who drew Maggie's attention. For an eerie moment, she felt as though she were looking at her own reflection through a large invisible mirror.

The vice president wore royal blue pleated slacks and tunic exactly like the one Field Dress had procured for Maggie. Overhead spots highlighted the subtle gold tints in her wine-colored hair, which was styled in the simple, elegant shag the OMEGA agent now sported. Her eyes, deepened to a dusky violet by the bold color of her outfit, stared at Maggie with the same unwavering scrutiny.

For a long moment, neither woman spoke. Then Mrs. Grant's full mouth twisted.

"It's kind of a shock, isn't it? Every woman wants to think she's unique. Special in her own way. Yet here we are, two identical clones."

"Not quite identical," Maggie replied, smiling. "Underneath this very flattering outfit, I'm trussed up like a Christmas turkey."

The vice president's lips quirked in response. Without thinking, Maggie duplicated the small smile.

Mrs. Grant's eyes widened. "Good grief, you *are* real, aren't you?"

"Yes, ma'am."

"Adam said you were good," the vice president murmured, "but I see now that was somewhat of an understatement."

Adam, Maggie noted. Not the special envoy. Not even Adam Ridgeway. Just that casual, familiar *Adam*. A little too familiar, in her opinion.

Taylor Grant gestured toward one of the sofas, then took the other. "You go by the code name Chameleon, don't you?"

Maggie nodded. No one, not even the president, knew the OMEGA operatives' real names or civilian covers. That simple but rigid policy protected the president in the event anything should go wrong on a mission. It protected the agents, as well. With OMEGA maintaining absolute control over such privileged information, they didn't have to worry about the inevitable leaks that plagued the CIA or FBI.

"Well, I can certainly understand how you earned that particular designation," the vice president said. She eyed Maggie for a moment, her expression uncompromising. "You understand that I'm not happy about this charade? At all?"

"So I was told."

"If my presence at these secret treaty negotiations wasn't so necessary, I wouldn't allow you to be used as a decoy like this. I've never backed away from a challenge . . . or a threat . . . in my life."

"I know that, Mrs. Grant."

For all her refined appearance and well-known sense of humor, this woman was as tough and as resilient as they came. She'd battled her way up through the political ranks on her own, without a prominent family name or fortune to ease her way. Obviously, she didn't like someone else taking the heat for her. Her deep brown eyes speared Maggie.

"I understand I have approximately twenty minutes to fill you in on the more intimate details of my life."

"Yes, ma'am."

The vice president's jaw tightened. "I'm not used to sharing this kind of information," she said after a moment. "With anyone. Politics doesn't encourage a person to reveal her innermost secrets."

"Whatever you tell me doesn't go beyond this room," Maggie said with quiet assurance.

She and Adam had agreed that this half hour with the vice president would be private, unrecorded. The little bug in her ring wouldn't activate until Mrs. Grant left the compound. Maggie's innate honesty compelled her to add a kicker, however.

"Unless you tell me something that will help identify the man who called you this morning."

An emotion that wasn't quite fear, but was something pretty close to it, rippled across the vice president's face as she glanced at the phone on a table beside the sofa. Maggie could only admire the vice president's courage as she mastered that brief, unguarded emotion and turned away from the telephone with a contemptuous look.

"I don't like being threatened any more than I like revealing the details of my private life."

Realizing that they weren't making much headway, Maggie sat up straight, tucked her hands into her sleeves and assumed a soulful expression.

"I once went underground in a convent. If it helps any, just think of me as a *religiosa,* a sort of female father confessor."

Some of the stiffness went out of Mrs. Grant's slender frame. "Somehow I can't see you as a nun," she drawled.

"It wasn't my favorite assignment," Maggie admitted with a grin, abandoning her postulant's pose. "Those wool habits itch like the dickens."

The vice president chuckled. "I believe you. All right, where do you want me to start?"

"Let's start with Stoncy Armstrong, since I'll be meeting him in L.A. tomorrow. You dated for almost six months, didn't you, Mrs. Grant?"

"Taylor."

At Maggie's surprised glance, she smiled. "I can't bring myself to share the most intimate details of my love life with someone who addresses me as 'ma'am' or 'Mrs. Grant.' Please, just call me Taylor."

No wonder Adam had developed such a close friendship with this woman, Maggie thought. The power of her office hadn't diminished her charm or charismatic personality.

"What do you want to know about Stoney?"

"For starters, what's behind his studio image of a muscle-bound, over-sexed, gorgeous hunk of beefcake?"

"A muscle-bound, oversexed, gorgeous hunk of beefcake," Taylor responded dryly.

"So it wasn't his, ah, intellectual prowess that attracted
you to him?"

Absently the vice president plucked at the fringe on one
of the sofa pillows. "No, it wasn't. But at that point in my
life, I didn't need the challenge of a rousing debate on do-
mestic politics or international affairs. I needed, or thought
I needed, Stoney Armstrong."

She stopped playing with the fringe and glanced across the
coffee table at Maggie. Her remarkable eyes filled with the
gleam of laughter that had made her the darling of the international press corps.

"Every woman should have a man like Stoney in her life
at some point or another, if only to remind her that great sex
is highly overrated as the foundation for a permanent relationship."

"True," Maggie replied with an answering laugh. "But
it's certainly not a bad place to start."

Twenty minutes later, Lillian Roth knocked on the sitting room door, then poked her head inside. She glanced
from Maggie to the vice president for a moment in startled
confusion.

"Yes, Lillian?" Maggie asked, testing her skills.

The dresser's birdlike black eyes narrowed. She studied
Maggie for long, silent moments, then switched her focus to
Taylor. Giving a little sniff, she spoke slowly, as if not quite
sure of herself.

"Buck just called on your private line. They're just start-
ing the shift change. You have to go, Mrs. Grant."

Pleased with the fact that she'd managed to fool the dresser, at least for a few seconds, Maggie rose.

The two auburn-haired women faced each other. Mrs. Grant—Taylor—held out her hand.

"Good luck, Chameleon."

"Thanks. I'll need it! I just hope I don't do something stupid and totally ruin your image in the next couple of weeks."

"You won't. Besides, I don't worry about my image when I'm in the Sierras. That cabin is the only place in the world where I go without makeup, don't bother with my hair, and bundle up in layers of flannel and wool. You just have to make it through a couple of brief public appearances, then you're home free."

"Right." Maggie laughed. "One huge benefit at the Kennedy Center tonight, and a dinner for two hundred of your closest friends in L.A. tomorrow."

"Don't worry. Stoney will make sure all the media focuses on him tomorrow. And tonight...well, tonight you'll have Adam at your side."

There it was again, that easy, familiar *Adam*. Maggie's grin slipped a bit.

As Taylor eased into her coat, her amethyst eyes took on a distant, almost dreamy expression. "I've been wanting to invite Adam up to the cabin for some time. If it weren't for these treaty negotiations..."

"Yes?"

The cool note in Maggie's voice drew the vice president's gaze.

"Well," she finished after a moment, "let's just say that Adam's the kind of man any woman would want to have around whenever she was in the mood for a stimulating intellectual debate...or anything else."

At that moment, the foyer door opened and Buck Evans slipped inside. His rusty brown hair, worn a little long on the sides, didn't quite cover his half-chewed ear.

"You ready to go, Mrs. Grant?"

"I'm ready."

He paused with one hand on the knob and gave Maggie a hard look. "Officially, I'm on leave while Mrs. Grant is in California."

"I know."

"I'll be with her every moment at Camp David. Have your people contact me there if you need me."

"Roger."

The Secret Service agent's eyes narrowed. "Just for the record, I think this subterfuge is ridiculous. Every man and woman on this detail has sworn to protect the vice president with their lives."

Maggie didn't answer. The decision to keep the switch secret from everyone but Buck Evans had been made by the president himself. She wasn't about to engage in a debate, public or private, about it. But she saw the total dedication in this man's fierce, protective stance toward Mrs. Grant, and understood the depth of his anger.

"Let's go, Buck," the vice president said quietly. "We've only got an hour before the others begin arriving at Camp David."

With a final nod to Maggie, she followed the agent out the door.

Lillian closed it behind them. Clearly unhappy at being left behind, she scowled at Maggie, then reluctantly assumed her duties.

"Have you had dinner?"

"No, there wasn't time."

Her small mouth pursed into a tight bud. "I'll call down to the kitchens for a tray, then run your bath."

"Fine. In the meantime, I'll look around the suite."

"Humph."

The dresser turned and marched out, her back rigid. Lillian Roth possessed not only the disposition of a drill sergeant, Maggie decided, but the carriage, as well.

A short time later, a scrubbed and powdered Maggie tightened the belt of a fluffy terry-cloth robe. Wandering into the sitting room, she sat down at a small table pulled up to an armchair. Her stomach rumbled in anticipation as she lifted a domed silver cover.

In some consternation, she stared at the four stalks of an unidentifiable yellow vegetable. They were arranged in solitary splendor on a gold-rimmed plate bearing the vice-presidential seal. Swallowing, Maggie poked at the stalks with the tip of her fork, then cut off an experimental bite.

At the taste, her face scrunched up in a disgusted grimace. Laying down the fork, she pushed the tray to one side. Maybe she could sneak a bag of peanuts or a candy bar at the Kennedy Center during intermission, she thought hopefully.

She soon discovered that the role of vice president of the United States didn't include any intermissions.

Chapter 3

"Lillian, have a heart! Not so tight!"

As Maggie's protest pierced the well-engineered quiet of his sleek black Porsche, Adam glanced down at the gold watch on his wrist. The faint pattern of her voice had grown stronger and stronger as he neared the naval observatory. Now, less than half a mile away, it came through the receiver built into his watch with startling clarity. As did Lillian Roth's tart reply.

"Suck it in. Mrs. Grant is a perfect size eight, you know."

"Well, I'm not a perfect anything. Loosen the straps a bit."

"Humph."

Adam smiled to himself as he swung the leather-wrapped steering wheel, following the curve of Massachusetts Avenue. He had to agree with Maggie on that one. She was far from perfect.

Of all the agents he directed, Maggie Sinclair, code name Chameleon, was the most independent and the least predictable. There was no denying her fierce dedication to her job. Yet she approached it with a breezy self-confidence and an irrepressible sparkle in her brown eyes that had alternately fascinated and irritated Adam greatly at various times in the past three years. What was more, she possessed her own inimitable style of operating in the field.

His hands clenched on the steering wheel as he remembered a few of the impossible situations Chameleon had extricated herself from. Adam knew he would never forget the way she'd blown her way out of a Soviet nuclear-missile silo with the aid of a terminally klutzy physicist. He'd noticed the first streaks of gray in his hair when Maggie returned from that particular mission.

She hadn't been any more repentant over that incident than any of the others he'd taken her to task for. Although respectful—most of the time—Maggie Sinclair was by turns cheeky, irrepressible and so damned irresistible, that Adam didn't know how he'd managed to keep his hands off her as long as he had.

If he wasn't OMEGA's director... If he didn't have to maintain the distance, the objectivity, necessary to send her into danger...

The thought of touching Maggie, of tasting her, of burying his hands in that sweep of glossy, shoulder-length brown hair and kissing her laughing, generous mouth, sent a spear of hot, heavy desire lancing through Adam.

"Lillian! For Pete's sake!"

Willing himself back under control, Adam pressed the stem on his watch, cutting off Maggie's indignant protest. His jaw tight, he turned off Massachusetts Avenue onto the approach to the U.S. naval observatory.

Sited on what had once been a hilly farm well outside the capital, the sprawling complex still functioned as an active military installation. A battery of scientists manned the round-domed observatory, which tracked celestial movements and produced navigational aids. More experts maintained the master clock of the United States, accurate to within thirty billionths of a second.

In addition to its military mission, however, the complex also served as home to the vice president. Since 1976, the occupant of that office had also occupied the fanciful Victorian mansion built at the turn of the century for the superintendent of the observatory.

The entire facility was guarded by an elite branch of the marine guard, one of whom stepped out of a white-painted guard post at Adam's approach. The granite-jawed gunnery sergeant bent to shine a high-powered beam into the Porsche's interior.

"Evening, sir. May I help you?"

"Good evening, Gunny. I'm Adam Ridgeway. Mrs. Grant is expecting me."

He handed over the pass issued by the vice president's office. The plastic card looked ordinary enough but concealed several lines of scrambled code. After running a handheld scanner over it, the marine squinted through the window to compare Adam's face to the digitized image on the scanner's small screen. He returned the pass, then punched a button on his belt. Heavy iron gates swung open.

"Go on up, Mr. Ridgeway."

"Thanks."

As he drove the tree-lined drive, Adam searched for signs of the highly sophisticated defensive security system that supplemented the military guards. He saw none, but knew that canine patrols roamed the area and electronic eyes swept the grounds continuously, particularly along the approach to the vice president's residence. The mansion itself was wired from attic to subbasement. Even the food, purchased from a list of carefully vetted suppliers, went through chemical and infrared screening before cooking. The security surrounding the woman who stood only a heartbeat away from the Oval Office was almost as heavy as that around the president himself.

For that reason, Adam believed that whoever had called Taylor Grant in the early hours of yesterday morning wouldn't try to make good on his threat here. The attack, when it came, would occur when she was most vulnerable. At a public appearance. Or on the road. Or in that isolated cabin of hers high in the Sierras.

Whenever and wherever it came, Adam intended to be there.

Another guard stopped him at the gate in the wrought-iron fence surrounding the residence. After scrutinizing his pass once again, the marine stood back.

Adam drove up a sloping drive toward the Victorian structure, complete with wraparound verandah and a distinctive round tower. White-painted and green-shuttered, the mansion rose majestically above a rolling blanket of snow, a picture postcard of white on white.

Adam pulled up under the pillared drive-through and shifted into park, but left the motor running. Having escorted Taylor to several functions in the past, he knew the drill. A valet would park his car around back, a safe distance from the house in the unlikely event it had been tampered with and now carried explosives. He and the vice president would ride to the Kennedy Center in her armor-plated limousine, preceded and followed by Secret Service vehicles. The agent in charge would sit beside the driver in the limo and remain a only few steps away after they arrived at their destination.

Adam and Maggie wouldn't have a private moment the entire evening. Theoretically.

He pulled his overcoat from the front seat, nodded to the valet and strolled up the wide front steps. A navy steward showed him into a paneled sitting room and offered a choice of drinks while he waited.

"Hello, Adam."

He turned at the low greeting. The heat that spiraled through his stomach had nothing to do with the swallow of Scotch he'd just downed. This was a Maggie he'd never seen before.

In the past three years, she'd gone undercover in everything from a nun's habit to a slinky gold mesh halter that barely covered the tips of her breasts. That particular article of clothing had cost Adam a number of hours of lost sleep. Yet it hadn't carried half as much kick as this elegant, deceptively demure black velvet gown.

On second observation, Adam decided it wasn't the floor-length skirt, slit to the knee, that caused his knuckles to whiten around the heavy crystal tumbler of Scotch. Or the tunic studded with jet beads that shimmered seductively with her every step. Or the feathery cut of her auburn hair, framing a face that bore an uncanny resemblence to Taylor Grant's.

It was the gleam in her violet-tinted eyes. That sparkling glint of excitement, of shared adventure. And the conspiratorial grin that vanished before the cameras in the downstairs rooms could record it—but not before Adam had felt its impact in every part of his body. Carefully, very carefully, he set the tumbler down.

Stepping forward, he brushed a light kiss across her lips. "Hello, Taylor. You look ravishing tonight."

She stared up at him, startled by the intimate greeting, but then her mouth quirked upward in the vice president's distinctive smile.

"Thank you. You look rather delectable yourself."

Actually, when she recovered from the surprise of that brief kiss, Maggie had to admit that Adam looked more than delectable. He looked delicious. Good enough to eat. Which was, she realized immediately, an unfortunate metaphor. The mere thought of digesting anything, Adam included, made her stomach growl. Loudly. Embarrassingly.

He lifted a dark brow.

"It's getting late," she said, her cheeks warming. "Shall we go?"

As if on cue, the woman designated to serve as agent in charge during Buck Evans's absence stepped into the reception room. Promoted only a week ago from her position as head of the Secret Service's Chicago field office, the sandy-haired Denise Kowalski was brisk, efficient and still very new to vice president's detail. Buck Evans had vouched for her personally.

In keeping with the occasion, she wore a chic red plaid evening jacket that disguised the weapon holstered at the small of her back. Her black satin skirt was full enough to allow her complete ease of movement if she had to throw her body across the vice president's. Which, Maggie sincerely hoped, she wouldn't have to do tonight. Or any other night.

"Your car is at the front entrance, Mrs. Grant."

"Thank you, Denise. We'll be right out."

The agent nodded and went to get the rest of the team into position. The heavy oak front door swung open behind her, its leaded glass panels refracting the light of the brass lanterns mounted on either side of the porte cochere. Golden light flooded the covered drive, but beyond that, blackness beckoned. Beyond that, a possible assassin waited.

Maggie stared at the open door, pysching herself for her first public appearance as Taylor Grant. She drew in a slow breath, and suddenly the Kevlar body shield didn't seem to bite into her flesh quite as much as it had before.

Moving to her side, Adam lifted the silk-lined black angora cloak she carried over one arm. He held it out, and when she'd wrapped herself in its sybaritic warmth, he rested his hands on her shoulders for a moment.

"I'm glad you invited me to join you tonight," he murmured.

Maggie gave him her best Taylor-made smile. "Me too."

"Ready to go?"

"As ready as I'll ever be."

Maggie had been to the Kennedy Center several times before. In fact, she'd taken her father to a performance of Andrew Lloyd Webber's *Phantom of the Opera* just last week. Red Sinclair had thoroughly enjoyed both the lavish production and the spectacle of jeans-clad students and camera-snapping tourists rubbing elbows with socialites dripping mink and diamonds.

But this was the first time Maggie had driven to a private performance in an armor-plated limousine. Or stepped out of the car into a barrage of TV cameras and bright lights.

Adam turned to help her alight, shielding her with his broad back while the Secret Service agents fanned out to open a corridor through the crowd. The smile he gave her caused a ripple of murmured comment among the onlookers and a shock of sensual pleasure in Maggie. Her fingers curled in his before she reminded herself that they were playing to the audience.

The elegantly dressed crowd parted before them like the Red Sea rolling back for Moses. With Agent Kowalski a few steps ahead, Maggie and Adam made their way toward the grand foyer at the rear of the marble-walled structure.

Since tonight's concert was a special benefit to raise funds for a flood-ravaged province in India, the guests had been invited by that country's ambassador. The Secret Service's

Office of Protective Research had run all two thousand names through its computerized list of "lookouts." Reportedly, none of the persons present tonight had triggered a flag that would identify a potential threat to the vice president. Nevertheless, by the time Maggie and Adam reached the short flight of stairs leading down to the red-carpeted grand foyer, her heart was thumping painfully against her body armor.

The ambassador and his wife awaited them beneath the striking seven-foot-high bronze bust of John F. Kennedy that dominated the wide hall. Brilliant light from eighteen massive chandeliers overhead made the colorful decorations pinned to the sash across the ambassador's chest sparkle like precious gems. The same glowing light illuminated the rich green and purple jewel tones of his wife's sari.

The diplomat bowed over Maggie's hand with polished charm. "Madam Vice President. We are most honored that you join us this evening."

"It's my pleasure, Ambassador Awani, Madam Awani. Do you know my escort, Special Envoy Adam Ridgeway?"

The tips of the ambassador's luxuriant mustache lifted in a wide smile. "But of course," he replied, pumping Adam's hand. "I have played both with and against this rogue on the polo field."

"Have you?"

Maggie arched an inquiring eyebrow at Adam, not really surprised that a man who sculled the Potomac in gray Harvard sweats to keep in shape also played a little polo on the side. Maggie herself was more the tag-football-and-long-lazy-walks type.

"Did he not tell you that he scored the winning goal for my team the last time he was in Bombay?"

"No, he didn't."

"It was a lucky shot," Adam said, with a small shrug of his black-clad shoulders. "I couldn't have done it without Sulim's fantastic pass."

The ambassador preened visibly at the compliment. With the fervor of a true enthusiast, he plunged into a recap of that memorable game. To Maggie's amusement, the ensuing conversation was soon peppered with terms like *chukker* and *grass penalty*. A spirited argument broke out over a controversial call in the last challenge for the Cup of the Americas. Even the ambassador's wife joined in, denouncing the officiating in a soft, melodic voice. Polo was a passion in India, she confided to Maggie in a smiling aside. It had been played in her country for over a thousand years.

As Maggie listened to the lively exchange, a sense of unreality gripped her. She'd been so keyed up for this first appearance as vice president. So intent on maintaining the fierce concentration necessary to stay in character. So determined to dodge any protocol gaffes—not to mention any stray bullets. Yet here she was, chuckling at the increasingly improbable tales of polo games won and lost, as though she moved in these sophisticated circles every day.

She gave most of the credit for her smooth insertion into this glittering world to Adam. This was his world, she thought, slanting him a quick glance. He moved comfortably among ambassadors and artists, Greek shipping magnates and the high-priced gunmen who guarded them. With his cool air of authority and commanding blue eyes, he appeared every bit as regal as any king or prince she could imagine. Although he wore no jewelry except the small gold studs in his white dress shirt and a thin gold watch, he didn't need to advertise either his background or his breeding. It showed in his understated, casual elegance and the ease with which he kept both the ambassador and his wife entertained.

And in the ways he displayed his interest in the woman at his side.

Adam Ridgeway didn't resort to any sort of this-is-my-woman caveman tactics to advertise his budding relationship with the vice president. The signals he sent out were subtle, but unmistakable. There was that small, private smile when Maggie laughingly asked if he'd *really* fallen off his pony in full view of India's prime minister. The glance that lingered on her face a few seconds longer than necessary. The relaxed stance at her side, not quite touching her, yet close enough for her to catch the clean scent of his after-shave with every small movement.

He was playing a role, Maggie reminded herself sternly. The same role he'd been playing when he kissed her earlier. When he'd taken her hand to help her out of the limo.

But then the foyer lights flashed, and Adam's hand moved to the small of her back to guide her toward the opera house. The gesture was at once courteous and possessive. Comforting and strangely disturbing. Maggie felt it right through her layers of Kevlar and velvet. Tiny ripples of awareness undulated through her middle.

Of course, she thought ruefully, those rippling sensations might well be hunger pangs. As their party mounted the wide, red-carpeted stairs to the opera house, she gave a silent prayer that her stomach wouldn't drown out the guest artist's performance.

Once they were inside the opera house, a black-suited usher escorted them up a short ramp to the box tier. Denise Kowalski halted the party just outside the entrance to the presidential box.

"If you'll wait here, please, I'll do a final visual."

Maggie knew that the Secret Service had swept the entire theater for hidden explosive devices earlier this afternoon. According to Denise, they'd done another sweep just prior to the vice president's arrival. Now the senior agent made personal eye contact with each of the other agents stationed around the three-tiered red-and-gold auditorium.

Watching Denise Kowalski in operation, Maggie felt a mounting respect for her cool professionalism. She also tried very hard to ignore the fact that President Lincoln had been assassinated as he sat in a theater box only a few miles from this one.

At Denise's nod, Maggie pasted a smile on her face and stepped into the box.

Heads twisted.

Necks craned.

Murmurs snaked through the opera house.

A seat cushion thumped against a chairback as a lone figure rose. As if in slow motion, he twisted around to face their box.

Adam stepped to her side, and Maggie felt her nails dig into her palms.

Then another man rose, and the woman beside him. Within moments, the entire audience was standing. The orchestra broke into "Ruffles and Flourishes," then played the Indian and American national anthems.

Unclenching her fist, Maggie placed her palm over her heart. She wasn't surprised to feel it drumming wildly against its velvet-covered shield. She'd had some interesting moments in her OMEGA career, but for sheer hair-raising, knee-knocking excitement, that second or so when she and the man in the center section had faced each other ranked right up there with the best—or worst—of them. By the time she sank into the plush red seat, her smile was so stiff, it could have been cut from cardboard.

Immediately, the lights dimmed. The featured artist, a slender, dark-haired flutist of Indian birth and growing international fame, walked out to center stage. Maggie was certain she wouldn't hear a note over the pounding in her ears, yet the haunting woodwind call gradually pierced the drumming in her ears. The music soothed. Soared. Evoked images of the flowing Ganges and the moonlit Taj Mahal. Beat by beat, her heart picked up the flute's rhythm. Her spine slowly relaxed. When the last notes of the first half of the program died away, she joined in the thunderous applause.

During the brief intermission, the ambassador relinquished his place at her side to circulate among his other guests and to allow them access to the vice president. Maggie cast a quick glance at the buffet table, loaded with platters of lobster pastries and succulent slices of smoked ham. Suppressing a sigh, she turned her back on the forbidden feast and forced herself to concentrate on the steady stream of people vying for her attention.

With Adam at her side, she got through the nerve-racking interval relatively unscathed.

She soon discovered that most of the politicians who elbowed their way into her circle were more interested in hearing themselves speak than in anything the VP might say. The only near-disaster occurred when the chairman of the senate fiduciary committee groused that the peso's steep nosedive was going to wreak havoc on international markets.

Maggie nodded in agreement.

"Given today's unrestrained markets, that's a real possibility," Adam interjected smoothly. "Of course, the president's Pan-American Monetary Stabilization Plan, which you helped draft, will help prevent future disasters like that."

Right. The president's Pan-American Monetary Stabilization Plan.

On behalf of Taylor Grant, Maggie smiled and accepted Adam's accolade. The senator immediately launched into a long and incredibly boring explanation of his own strategy to single-handedly save third-world economies. Thankfully, the grand foyer's lights dimmed before he wound down, saving Maggie from having to formulate a reply.

By this time, she was feeling the combined effects of her few sips of champagne and her taut nerves, not to mention the pressure of Lillian's determination to make her a perfect size eight.

"Do I have time to powder my nose?" she murmured to Adam.

His mouth lifted. "You have time to powder anything you want. They won't start the second half of the program until you're seated."

The belated realization that several thousand people would have to wait while she went to the bathroom effectively eliminated Maggie's need. Before she could tell Adam she'd changed her mind, however, he had steered her toward the ladies' room on the second-floor landing.

Denise Kowalski quickly grasped the situation and stepped ahead of them. Signaling to Maggie to wait, she threaded her way through the women standing patiently in line and checked out the facility.

Good grief, it hadn't occurred to Maggie that the vice president of the United States couldn't even tinkle without a security check. She was discovering that this job wasn't quite as glamorous and exciting as it appeared to the rest of the world.

Evidently no assassins lurked in the stalls. Denise returned in less than a minute to escort Maggie to the head of the line. The other women graciously yielded their places, but Maggie, now thoroughly embarrassed by the whole affair, paused with one hand on the stall door.

"This is ridiculous," she commented. "I'll bet there isn't a line like this in the men's room."

The other woman gaped at her for a moment, then broke into laughter.

"Maybe it's time the government took a look at the distribution of public toilets by gender," one of them suggested.

"Maybe it is," Maggie agreed. "I'll put it on the agenda as soon I get back from California."

To a chorus of cheers and applause, she sailed into a stall. One way or another, she'd convince Taylor Grant to follow through on her rash promise to look into public potties.

"What was that all about?" Adam asked when she and the grinning agent in charge emerged a few moments later.

Tucking her hand in his arm, Maggie smiled demurely. "It's a woman thing."

The presence of the driver and the Secret Service agent prevented Maggie discussing the evening's events with Adam during the drive back to the naval observatory. Still wired, and reluctant to see their time together end, Maggie forced herself not to fidget, but her fingers tapped an uneven beat on the leather armrest.

When Adam's hand closed over hers, she wasn't sure whether his intent was to still the nervous movement or to further their supposed relationship. Whatever the reason, she obligingly turned her palm up and entwined her fingers with his.

"Did you enjoy the concert?" he asked conversationally.

"Very much." She gave him a quick grin. "Although I enjoyed hearing about your exploits on the polo field even more. Especially the part where you fell off your horse."

"I hope that tale didn't totally destroy my credibility with you."

"Well," she murmured provocatively, "your romantic image is a bit tarnished around the edges. You'll have to apply some polish to restore it to its former state."

He lifted their entwined hands and brushed his mouth across the back of her hand. "I'll see what I can do."

Ruthlessly ignoring the streaks of fire that shot from her hand to her elbow to her heart, Maggie followed Adam's lead and fell into an easy bantering dialogue for the rest of the ride. All the while, she was blazingly conscious of the warm, strong fingers nesting hers.

A part of her thrilled to his touch.

To her considerable surprise, a small part of her also resented it.

She'd always kept her relationship with her boss strictly professional, which hadn't been difficult at first. Adam Ridgeway could be somewhat daunting when he chose to. If Maggie had been the dauntable kind, she might have wilted like a limp lettuce leaf the first time he turned that icy stare on her. Or rocked back on her heels the first time those chiseled features had relaxed into a genuine smile.

Adam's smile could cause a less sensible, less professional woman than Maggie to weave all kinds of ridiculous fantasies.

Okay, she admitted, so she'd done some weaving. And some fantasizing. So she'd imagined the feel of his hand in hers more and more often lately, and the memory of his after-shave would tease her at the most unexpected moments. In unguarded moments like this, she found herself wondering just when, or if, they'd tear down the barriers that kept them from acknowledging the attraction simmering between them.

Because it wasn't all one-sided. Despite the elegant, so-phisticated women Adam escorted to various diplomatic functions, despite the unshakable air of authority he al-ways displayed on the job, Maggie had sensed his growing awareness of her as a woman.

But being aware of her as a woman and doing something about it were two entirely different matters. Maggie had no idea if he'd felt the same leap of excitement she had at the thought of their spending two weeks together. If his pulse hammered from the feel of her hand in his. Or if he was simply playing his assigned role.

As they sped north along Rock Creek Parkway under a pale winter moon, she reminded herself that she, too, was playing a part. Still, she couldn't help wondering just how far they'd take their respective roles when the limo pulled up at the vice-presidential residence.

After her experience in the ladies' room, she was just be-ginning to realize just how little privacy the vice president enjoyed. Conducting a romance, even a fake one, under the watchful eyes of half a dozen agents and those all-pervasive cameras was going to take a bit more savoir faire than she'd realized.

So when they stepped out of the limo under the shelter-ing overhang of the porte cochere and Adam suggested a walk in the moonlight to stretch their legs, Maggie readily agreed. Unless she invited him up to the vice president's bedroom, which she couldn't quite bring herself to do, the only place they could talk privately was the open air.

"Are you sure you'll be warm enough?" he asked, lift-ing the collar of her angora cloak to frame her cheeks.

With her face cradled in his hands and his blue eyes gaz-ing down at her like that, Maggie discovered that warm was *not* a problem.

"I'm fine."

"Good."

He pulled on the black wool overcoat he hadn't bothered with in the limo and tucked her gloved hand in his arm. As he led the way toward the rose garden at the west side of the house, Maggie saw Denise Kowalski nod to another agent who'd stepped out of the chase car. The man bundled his collar up against his ears and trudged after them, staying far enough behind to remain out of earshot.

Wonderful. Just what she needed, the first time she was alone with Adam Ridgeway on a star-studded, moonlit night. A chaperon.

Chapter 4

With the Secret Service agent trudging some distance behind them, Maggie and Adam walked side by side through the dappled moonlight. Snow-laden trees shielded them from the distant murmur of traffic still moving along Massachusetts Avenue. Their footsteps echoed softly on the wet pavement, almost lost in the pounding of Maggie's pulse.

She was vividly, stunningly aware of Adam's nearness. Of the way he slowed his long stride to match hers. Of the warmth of his body where he kept her hand tucked against his side.

"You did well tonight," Adam said quietly. "Very well."

Her small laugh puffed out in a cloud of white vapor. "I almost blew it on the Pan-American Monetary Stabilization Plan. Thanks for rescuing me."

"My pleasure, Madam Vice President."

With a confidence that told Maggie he knew his way around, Adam led her to a brick path cutting through a winter white garden. Concentric rings of severely pruned rosebushes poked through the blanket of snow, like ghostly dwarfs standing sentinel around the small arched arbor at the center of the garden. Despite the bright moonlight streaming through the latticework, Maggie soon discovered that the airy bower provided an illusion of privacy. She ran a gloved finger along a wooden slat, causing a soft shower of white, and tried not to wonder just how many times Adam had escorted Taylor Grant to this same little arbor.

Their Secret Service escort halted at the perimeter of the garden. Hunching his shoulders against the cold, he stomped his feet once or twice and turned slowly to survey the surrounding area. As if to take advantage of their privacy, Adam's shadow merged with Maggie's from behind, and then his arms slid around her waist. He pulled her back against his chest, and she promptly forgot all about their escort.

They were playing a role, Maggie reminded herself once more. This intimate contact with Adam was integral to their mission. Despite her stern reminder, however, she was finding it more and more difficult to separate reality from this enactment of her secret, half-formed fantasies. With a little sigh, she laid her head against his shoulder.

"Did Taylor pass you any information we need to check out?" he asked, his warm breath fanning her ear.

Taylor, Maggie noted. Not the vice president, or even Mrs. Grant.

"She thinks Stoney Armstrong was motivated by something other than a desire to see an old friend when he asked to escort her to the fund-raiser in L.A. tomorrow night. He wasn't particularly pleased when she told him no."

Adam tightened his arms, drawing her closer into his warmth. "What does she think was behind his call?"

"She wasn't sure, but suggested we talk to his agent and his hairstylist."

"His hairstylist?"

Maggie turned in his arms. Mindful of the cameras that swept the grounds continuously, she flattened her palms against the fine wool worsted of his lapels. The steamy vapor of her breath mingled intimately with his as she tilted her head back to look up at him.

"Evidently Stoney's stylist has more input into his career than his agent."

Adam's hand tunneled under the collar of her cape to cradle her neck. "We'll check it out."

His caressing smile made Maggie's heart thump painfully against her bodysuit. When it came to role-playing, she thought, Adam Ridgeway could give Stoney Armstrong a run for his money at the box office.

"Anything else?"

Maggie stared up at the face just inches from her own. The bright moonlight reflecting off the snow cast his lean, aristocratic features into sharp relief. Cameras or no cameras, she felt the impact of his presence to the tips of her toes. Forcing herself to concentrate on her mission, she relayed what the vice president had told her about the other men who'd appeared so briefly in her personal life.

"Mrs. Grant hasn't seen Peter Donovan, her former campaign manager, in over three years. He and his new wife received invitations to the inaugural ball but didn't make it. Donovan had just had surgery, I think."

"An emergency appendectomy," Adam confirmed. "What about the treasury secretary?"

"Mrs. Grant meets frequently with James Elliot. Whenever the president calls a cabinet meeting. Or when Elliot needs to talk to her separately on Treasury business."

The hand cradling her head brought her mouth to within inches of his. Anyone watching would see two people in an intimate embrace, but only Maggie knew just how intimate it was. She'd never realized how well she and Adam would fit together.

"And?" he prompted, his warm breath feathering her cheeks.

She could do this. She could keep her voice calm and her mind focused on the mission with her hips nestled against his and his mouth a whisper from hers.

"She can't believe the secretary is behind this threat. Besides being one of the president's closest friends, he's a good man, according to Mrs. Grant. The crazy weekend they spent together was just that—a moment out of time that neither one expected to happen and neither wants to repeat. James reconciled with his wife shortly after that, and they seem—"

She broke off as his lips traced across her cheek.

"Keep talking," he murmured.

Right. Uh-huh. She was supposed to talk while Adam planted explosive little kisses on her face and her heart was jackhammering in her chest.

"You said my romantic image needed polishing, remember?" he said, angling her face up for a slow, sensual exploration. "I'll polish while you tell me what else Taylor had to say."

There it was again. That friendly little *Taylor*.

"That's about it," Maggie got out. "Anything new from your end?"

"Not much. Jake's checking out a classified program Donovan's company, Digicon, is trying to sell the Pentagon. He's heard rumors that the program is a last-ditch effort to keep the company from going under."

"Mmm?"

Carefully filing away that bit of information for future reference, Maggie focused on more immediate aspects of her mission. Like the heat that burned just under her skin when

Adam trailed a soft kiss toward the corner of her mouth. And the cold that was creeping up under the back hem of her cloak.

"Adam?"

He raised his head. "Yes?"

"Just how much polishing are you planning to do tonight?"

"Quite a bit."

"Then you'd better do it quickly." Her lips curved into a quicksilver grin. "My front is all toasty from snuggling up to you like this, but my backside is freezing."

His blue eyes glinted. "Let's see what we can do to warm you up."

Maggie had been kissed by a respectable number of men in her thirty-two years. Some had exhibited more enthusiasm than finesse. A few had demonstrated very skilled techniques. More than one had raised her body temperature by a number of degrees. But none had ignited the instantaneous combustion that Adam did.

At the crush of his mouth on hers, heat speared through Maggie's stomach. Tiny white-hot flickers of desire darted along her nerves, setting them on fire. In those first, explosive seconds, she decided that Adam's kiss was all she had dreamed it would be. Hard. Demanding. Consuming.

Then she stopped thinking altogether. Wrapping her arms around his neck, she did some polishing of her own.

When they finally broke contact, Adam's image had been restored to its full glory and Maggie could barely find the strength to drag air into her starved lungs.

His eyes raked her face, their blue depths gleaming with a fierce light that thrilled her for all of the two or three seconds he allowed it to show.

"Warm enough now?"

"Roasting," she answered truthfully.

He started to reply, but at that moment a loud, reverberating thump shattered the stillness of the night.

They sprang apart.

Adam whirled toward the sound, his hand diving under the flap of his overcoat.

Maggie jumped to one side to get an unobstructed view around him. She reached instinctively for her weapon, then grimaced when she remembered she wasn't armed. Muttering a rather un-vice-presidential oath under her breath, she peered across the moonlit rose garden.

Pinned by their combined glares, the Secret Service agent standing guard at the entrance to the rose garden paused, one foot lifted high in the air.

"Er, sorry..."

Shamefaced, he lowered his foot to the ground.

Guilt flooded through Maggie as she straightened. The poor man had obviously been trying to stomp some warmth into his chilled feet. While she and Adam were polishing away, he must have been freezing.

"We'd better go inside," she murmured.

"I'll take you back to the house, but I won't come in. Not tonight."

Try as she might, Maggie couldn't tell whether the reluctance in Adam's voice was real, or part of this charade of theirs. Her reluctance, on the other hand, was very real. "I'll see you at the airport tomorrow, then."

He brushed a thumb across her mouth, which was still tender from his kiss. Although his touch and his posture were those of an attentive lover, his message held a hint of grim reality.

"You'll see me before that, if you need me. We've rigged a communications center in the British embassy, right across the street. It's well within range of the transmitter in your

ring. I'll hear every sound, every breath you take throughout the night.''

Maggie swallowed as an unforeseen aspect of this tight
communications net suddenly occurred to her. Good Lord,
what if she snored in her sleep?

If the memory of Adam's searing kiss wasn't enough to
keep her tossing and turning, that daunting thought was.
Her own romantic image might need serious polishing come
morning, if she treated Adam to a chorus of snores and
snuffles.

Tucking her hand in his arm, they strolled back toward
the house. Just before they stepped into the pool of light cast
by the glowing brass lanterns, Adam pulled her to a halt.

''Here, you'd better take this.''

Keeping her body between his and the watchful eyes of
the Secret Service man, he slipped a small, handkerchief-
wrapped package into the pocket of her cloak.

''What is it? Something from Special Devices?''

Maybe they'd come up with some kind of a weapon for
her, after all.

''No,'' Adam replied, escorting her to the front door.
''Something from me.''

As she watched the taillights of his car disappear down the
long, winding driveway, Maggie felt strangely bereft. She
folded her right hand over her left, taking comfort from the
feel of the heavy band under her glove.

When the last crunch of tires on snowy pavement faded,
she said good-night to her foot-stomping watchdog, went
inside and climbed the curving staircase to the second floor.

The soft click of the bedroom door brought Lillian Roth
awake. Jerking upright in a chintz-covered armchair, the
dresser ran a hand through her fuzzy gray hair. Fatigue
etched her face before it settled into its habitual severe lines.

"You shouldn't have waited up," Maggie protested, shrugging out of the cape.

Lillian pushed herself to her feet. "I always wait up for Mrs. Grant. Well, how did it go?"

"It went..."

A kaleidoscope of colorful images flashed through Maggie's mind. The Kennedy Center's brilliant red-and-gold opera house. The huge ruby winking in the decoration pinned to the Indian ambassador's sash. A moonlit, winter white garden, and Adam's face hovering inches from hers.

"...very well," she finished softly.

"Humph." Lillian reached for the cape lying across the back of a chair.

"I'll take care of that," Maggie said. Whatever Adam had tucked in her pocket, she wanted to check it out herself. "Why don't you go to bed? I can undress myself."

"Mrs. Grant always—"

"Lillian."

The small woman squared her shoulders. In the quiet of the sitting room, two strong wills collided.

"Perhaps you intend to sleep in that corset you're strapped into?"

Maggie conceded defeat. "No, I don't."

"I'll get your gown and robe."

The expression in Lillian's black eyes as she sailed toward the huge walk-in closet wasn't exactly smug, but it was pretty darn close to it.

By the time she returned with a lemony silk nightdress and robe, Maggie had stashed Adam's package under her pillow and loosened as many of the back buttons on the velvet tunic as she could reach. Turning, she waited while Lillian undid the rest. When the Velcro fastening on the bodysuit gave way, she heaved a sigh of relief.

Only later, when the big house had settled down to an uneven, creaking slumber and Maggie was finally alone, did she pull the package from its hiding place under the pillow. With infinite care, she unwrapped the folds of Adam's crisp, starched handkerchief.

Two bags of cashews and a souvenir box of Godiva chocolates stamped with the seal of the Indian embassy tumbled onto the sheet.

Maggie gave a gasp of delight. Lifting her hand, she murmured into the ring, "Thunder, this is Chameleon. Do you read me?"

"Loud and clear."

"You doll! Thanks for the emergency rations. I owe you one."

After a pause so slight Maggie thought she might have imagined it, his reply drifted through the stillness. "I'll let you know when I'm ready to collect."

"Time to get up."

Maggie opened one eye. She peered at Lillian, then squinted past her at the curtained windows.

"It's still dark out," she protested, pulling the covers up around her ears.

"Mrs. Grant always runs early."

"This early?"

"This early," Lillian confirmed unsympathetically.

Intel had briefed Maggie about the vice president's morning jog, of course, but they'd left out one or two key points. Like the fact that it was apparently accomplished in cold, dank darkness.

"I've laid out some running clothes in the bathroom. Breakfast will be ready by the time you get back."

Breakfast!

The thought of food gave Maggie the impetus she needed to crawl out of her warm cocoon. Frigid air washed over her body, raising goose bumps on every patch of exposed skin. She shivered as the silk of her nightdress cooled and new bumps rose. Although she'd much admired this frothy confection of pale yellow silk and gossamer lace last night, Maggie now heartily wished the vice president's tastes ran to warm flannel pajamas. Pulling on the matching lemon robe, she glanced at the small gold carriage clock on the bedside table.

Five-twenty—a.m.

If she'd slept a full hour last night, she'd be surprised. The knot of tension caused by concentrating so fiercely on her role had taken forever to seep out of Maggie's system. The tension generated by a certain dark-haired special envoy had refused to seep, however. Instead, her inner agitation had coiled tighter and tighter every time she felt the weight of the ring on her finger. It was as though Adam were with her in the darkness. Which he was.

With every restless toss, she remembered the touch of his mouth on hers. Every turn brought back the scent of his expensive after-shave. And every time her stomach grumbled about its less-than-satisfied state, she snuck another chocolate from the foil-covered box.

As she hurried to the bathroom, Maggie smiled at the memory of those luscious vanilla creams and melt-in-your-mouth caramels. Somehow, that little box of candies symbolized more than anything else the subtle shift that had occurred last night in her relationship with Adam Ridgeway.

Over the past three years, they'd shared some desperate hours and days and weeks. They'd grown close, as only members of a small, tightly knit organization can. But until last night, they hadn't allowed themselves to step through the invisible wall that separated OMEGA's cool, authoritative director from his operatives. Maggie had always maintained her independence, and Adam had always kept his distance.

Right now, that wall didn't seem quite as high. Or as impenetrable. And after last night, the distance between them had shortened considerably. Twisting the gold ring around on her finger, she smiled and turned on the taps full blast.

She returned to the bedroom a short while later dressed in blue metallic spandex thermal leggings, a matching long-sleeved top, and comfortable Reeboks. Lillian eyed her critically, then held up an oversize gold-and-blue UCLA sweatshirt.

"I found this in the closet. It should be long enough to disguise your hips."

"Thanks," Maggie said dryly.

"Remember, Mrs. Grant usually does ten minutes of warm-up exercises before her run. Leg bends, calf stretches and twists. Then it's twice around Observatory Circle and back through the grounds."

As she tugged the sweatshirt over her head, Maggie did a rapid mental calculation of the circumference of the seventy-three acres that comprised the observatory grounds. She multiplied that by two, translated the distance into miles, and bit back a groan at the result.

Six miles. At least. Good grief!

Of necessity, OMEGA agents kept in top physical shape, but they had all developed their own individualized conditioning programs. Given a choice, Maggie would have far preferred her own regime of high-impact aerobics in a nice warm spa to slogging six miles in the icy, predawn air.

"By the way," Lillian let drop as she headed for the door, "the agent who usually jogs with Mrs. Grant won the Boston Marathon a couple of years ago."

This time Maggie didn't even try to hold back her groan.

Lillian's mouth softened into something suspiciously close to a smile.

"But that particular individual is in L.A.," she continued, "working the advance for her—for your trip. The other agents drew straws to see who has to run with you this morning. The loser's waiting downstairs. He's a few pounds overweight, and very slow."

Giving silent thanks for small blessings, Maggie made her way down the curving staircase. Okay, she told herself, it was only six miles. She could do this. She could run six miles in the service of her country.

Four and a half miles later, she was seriously questioning both her sanity and her dedication to her country.

Frigid air lanced into her lungs with every labored breath. Her heart slammed painfully against her ribs. Her legs felt like overcooked spaghetti and threatened to collapse with every step.

The slap of her sneakers against the wet pavement grew more and more erratic as Maggie struggled to pump her way up yet another damned incline. The rolling hills that had appeared so picturesque when she drove through the naval observatory complex yesterday afternoon now loomed in front of her like mountain peaks. Her only consolation was that the poor agent chugging along behind her couldn't hear the sound of her labored breath over his own heaving gasps.

At least the gloomy darkness had given way to a drizzly dawn. Headlights sliced through a soupy gray mist as military and civilian workers arrived for work at the various scientific facilities scattered around the extensive grounds. The civilians gave a cheerful wave, obviously used to seeing the vice president on her early-morning run. The military snapped to attention and saluted. Hoping her grimace would pass for a smile, Maggie returned their greetings.

When the two-story building that housed the nautical almanac office loomed out of the mist, Maggie sagged with relief. Thank God. Only a half circuit of the perimeter to go! Dragging in another lungful of cold air, she concentrated fiercely on placing one foot in front of the other once. Twice. Three times. Counting seemed to help, she discovered.

Sixty-two steps took her across the broad expanse of parking lot beside the almanac office.

Another thirty-seven brought her to the path that paralleled Massachusetts Avenue.

Five more paces, and she was shielded from the wind by the tall pines, thick on her right, thinner on her left, where the path edged almost to the wrought-iron fence. Her lungs on fire, her calves cramping, Maggie following the curving asphalt trail.

At one hundred and three steps past the west gate, the distinctive conical turret of the vice president's mansion poked into view above the tops of the snow-laden pines. She almost sobbed in relief.

At exactly one hundred and twenty-six paces, the shot rang out.

With a startled "Umph," Maggie hit the ground.

Chapter 5

In a small room on the fourth floor of the British embassy, less than a half block away, Adam froze.

He tore his gaze from the bank of flickering monitors and stared down at the face of his watch, as if expecting an instant replay of the single sharp report—and of Maggie's surprised grunt. Then he exploded into action.

Racing for the door, he snarled an order at the stunned communications technician. "Call Jaguar! Tell him Chameleon's down."

He ripped open the door and raced into the deserted hallway, cursing himself every step of the way. How could he have underestimated the threat? How could he have been so damned cold, so analytical, about the security on the grounds of the naval observatory? He shouldn't have trusted that abstract analysis. Not with Maggie.

His heart battering against his ribs, he crashed through the door to the stairs. The stairwell was empty, as Adam had known it would be. He'd pulled a few strings for this mission. Without a single question, the British ambassador had cleared the entire fourth floor of the embassy for OMEGA's use. It had proven an ideal site for an observation post. Only the broad expanse of Massachusetts Avenue, a screen of pines and a rolling lawn separated it from the vice-presidential mansion and the surrounding grounds.

Even more to the point, the embassy was close enough for OMEGA to tap into the Secret Service's own surveillance system. Adam had tracked Maggie from the moment she emerged from her bedroom this morning. Infrared cameras so sensitive that they picked up even the trickle of sweat rolling down her cheek had recorded her jog through the predawn gloom. With the aid of the concealed transmitter in her ring, Adam had heard her every gasp—and every increasingly acerbic comment she muttered under her breath as she jogged up yet another hill.

As he barreled down the stairs, Adam replayed over and over in his mind those moments when she'd entered the home stretch. There, in those few yards where the pines branched over the path and obscured the camera's angle, she'd disappeared from view for a few seconds. Christ! A few seconds, and he—

"Get . . . off . . . me! Puh-leez!"

Maggie's voice jerked Adam to a halt. His chest heaving, he stared down at his watch.

"Are you . . . all right?"

He didn't recognize the panting male voice, but guessed immediately it was the agent who'd trailed Maggie during her run.

"I'm . . . fine."

"Are . . . you . . . sure, ma'am?"

She sucked in a rasping breath. "I'm sure."

"But you...went down!" The man was still huffing. "That bus, when it backfired...I thought it was a shot. And you went down."

"I thought...it was a shot, too. That's why I went down." Chagrin, and the faintest trace of rueful laughter, crept into her voice. "I guess I'm a little jumpy this morning."

Alone in the empty stairwell, Adam closed his eyes. His throat was so damn tight he couldn't breathe, cold sweat was running down his back, and Maggie was laughing. Laughing! With great physical effort, Adam unclenched his jaw and headed back to the control room.

Joe Samuels, OMEGA's senior communications technician, stood with one big hand fisted around a radio mike.

"She okay?"

"She's okay. It wasn't a gunshot. A bus backfired."

The grim expression on Joe's face eased, and his brown eyes lost their fierce glitter. "A bus!"

"A bus."

The black man shook his head as tension drained visibly from his big body. "Well, with Chameleon, you never know."

"No, you don't," Adam replied, an edge to his voice that he couldn't quite suppress.

Joe's brows lifted in surprise at the director's acid tone, but he refrained from commenting.

"Get Jaguar on the net, would you? I'll give him a quick update before I go upstairs to the heliport."

Nodding, Joe reseated himself at the communications console. An acknowledged expert in satellite transmissions, he'd been actively recruited by half a dozen major corporations when he left military service a few years ago. He could have named his own salary, strolled into work wearing tailored suits and vests and jetted across continents in sleek corporate aircraft. Instead, he'd joined the OMEGA team at about the same time Maggie had.

Adam was well aware of the bond between them. During long, tense days and nights in the control center, the technician worked his electronic magic to keep her plugged into whichever field agent she was controlling at the time. When Chameleon was in the field, Joe always arranged the duty schedules so that he manned the control center himself.

Adam suspected that their friendship might have been tested a bit lately, however. To Joe's disgust, his twins had developed a passion for Maggie's repulsive house pet. The boys begged to keep the reptile whenever she left town. They delighted in Terence's unique repertoire of tricks, particularly his ability to take out a fly halfway across a room with his yard-long tongue. Joe had been visibly relieved when Maggie informed him she'd drafted her father for iguana duty this time.

While he waited for Jaguar to come on-line, Adam forced himself to relax his rigid muscles. Gradually the tension gripping his gut eased. In its place came a different and even more unsettling sensation.

For the first time in a long, long time, he'd reacted without thinking. Sheer animal instinct had sent him crashing out into the hallway. The last time he reacted like that had been in a dark alley outside a Hong Kong hotel. Eight years ago. Just before the night had erupted in a blinding explosion, and he'd dived for cover.

When he'd heard Maggie's surpised cry a few moments ago, Adam had felt the same as he had when the world blew up all around him.

With a wry grimace, he acknowledged that her cry had irrevocably, irretrievably shattered the detachment he'd forced himself to maintain all these years as OMEGA's director. The distance he'd kept between himself and Maggie

Sinclair had narrowed to a single heartbeat. To the sound of a bus backfiring.

Adam refused to deny the truth any longer. He wanted her. With a need so fierce, so raw, it consumed him.

Thirty minutes, he thought, dragging in a slow breath. Thirty minutes until he met her at Andrews Air Force Base for the flight to California. Thirty minutes, and Adam wouldn't have to watch her from a half block away over these damned monitors. When they met at the airport, he promised himself, the "relationship" between the vice president of the United States and the president's special envoy would enter a new and very intimate stage.

"Thirty minutes!"

Sweat-drenched, her lungs on fire and her legs wobbling like overstretched rubber bands, Maggie stared at Lillian in disbelief.

"I thought our plane wasn't scheduled to leave until nine!"

"The White House command post called a few moments ago. There's another snowstorm moving in. The pilot would like to get off before the front hits, if you can make it. I told them you could."

The dresser jerked her mop of frizzy gray curls toward the bathroom. "You have seven minutes to shower and do your makeup. Your breakfast tray and travel clothes will be waiting for you when you get out. We leave the house at exactly oh-seven-twenty."

"Were you ever in the Marines, by any chance?" Maggie tossed over her shoulder as she forced her vociferously protesting legs to carry her toward the bathroom.

Lillian snorted. "Before I came to work for Mrs. Grant, I ran a preschool. I'd like to see any platoon of Marines handle that. You'd better get it in gear."

Maggie got it in gear.

She sagged against the shower tiles for two precious minutes, letting the steaming-hot water soak into her aching muscles, then soaped and shampooed with record-breaking speed. Thankfully, the vice president's short, stylish shag took all of ninety seconds to blow-dry. A slather of concealing foundation, a quick application of mascara and mauve eye shadow, a slash of lipstick, and she was out of the bathroom.

The sight of the VP's breakfast tray, with its single granola bar on a gold-rimmed china plate and its crystal goblet filled with a greenish liquid, stopped Maggie in her tracks.

"What's in that glass?" she asked suspiciously.

"Guava juice," Lillian replied, bustling forward with a creamy wool pantsuit over one arm.

"*Guava* juice?" Maggie groaned. "Why couldn't your boss be a grease-loving biscuits-and-gravy Texan instead of a California health nut?"

Her mouth pursing, the older woman laid the pantsuit on the bed. She lifted the Kevlar bodysuit and dangled it in one hand.

"Maybe if you drank more guava juice and ate fewer biscuits," she said, with patently false sweetness, "you wouldn't need this."

Grinning, Maggie acknowledged the hit. That would teach her to criticize Mrs. Grant to Lillian Roth! Intelligence hadn't understated the bond of affection between the two women.

"Drink your juice," Lillian instructed. "We have exactly fifteen minutes to get you suited up and out of here."

Fourteen minutes later, Maggie and Lillian descended the curving central staircase. After a hurried last-minute update by a staffer on the short speech she was to give tonight in L.A., she said goodbye to the various members of the staff who drifted out to wish the vice president an enjoyable vacation.

A car waited under the portico to take her and her small party to the naval observatory helipad. Gray, drizzly mist closed around the vehicle, almost obscuring the grounds, as they drove the short distance. Like an impatient mosquito, a navy-and-white-painted helicopter squatted on its circular pad, its rotor blades whirring.

Maggie, Lillian and Denise Kowalski, who would accompany the vice president to California, had no sooner strapped themselves in than the chopper lifted off, banked sharply and headed east. Maggie had flown out of Andrews Air Force Base in Maryland, just across the Potomac from Washington, many times. She settled back against the padded seat to enjoy the short flight and grab the first few moments of relative calm since Lillian had rousted her out of bed two hours ago.

"Have you seen this morning's *Post?*" the sandy-haired agent asked, raising her voice to be heard over the thump of the rotor blades.

"No."

Denise held out a folded section of Washington's leading newspaper. "They did a whole center spread on your appearance at last night's benefit."

"Really?"

Just in time, Maggie bit back the observation that she'd never thought of herself as centerfold material.

"The special envoy looks rather distinguished in black and white, doesn't he?" the agent commented mildly.

He looked more than distinguished, Maggie thought. He looked devastating. Her stomach gave a little lurch when she saw the enlarged close-up shot of her and Adam. Or rather

Taylor Grant and Adam. The photographer had caught them just as she emerged from the limo. Adam was holding his out his hand to help her out. Her face was in profile, but his was captured in precise detail. If Maggie hadn't remembered just in time that he was playing a role, the expression in his eyes as he looked down at her, or at Taylor—whoever!—would have caused a total meltdown of her synthetic corset. She stared at the picture, mesmerized, for several long minutes before studying the accompanying article.

The reporter covering the glittering gala had evidently found the VP and her escort far more titillating than the event itself. The story included several more shots of Maggie/Taylor and Adam, as well as a gossipy little side note about the fact that the wealthy, sophisticated special envoy was accompanying the vice president to her private retreat for two weeks. Judging by the way his eyes devoured the lovely Mrs. Grant, the reporter oozed, it should be a most enjoyable vacation for all parties involved.

Maggie might have agreed with her, but for the fact that sometime during this supposed vacation she hoped to lure a killer into the open.

She spent the rest of the short trip leafing through the thick *Post,* although she couldn't help sneaking repeated glances at the folded section in her lap. As she studied the shot of them getting out of the limo, the curious niggle of resentment she'd felt when Adam first took her hand last night returned.

Her lips twisted as she identified the feeling for what it was. Jealousy. Weirdly enough, she was jealous of herself.

She'd wanted Adam to look at *her* like that, to touch *her,* for so long. Almost as much as she'd wanted to touch him. But he'd held himself back, just as she had. Neither of them had been ready to acknowledge the attraction that sizzled between them, as electric and charged as a sultry summer night just before a storm. Neither had wanted to upset the delicate balance between their professional responsibilities and their personal needs.

Now they hovered in some kind of in-between state. That shattering kiss in the snow-swept garden, not to mention those sinful chocolates, had destroyed that balance forever. When this mission was over, when they stopped playing these assigned roles, they'd have to find a new level, a new balance. What that balance would be, she had no idea, but for the first time since joining OMEGA she was more excited about concluding an operation than about conducting it.

Adam's helicopter landed at Andrews Air Force Base a few moments before the vice president's.

Home to the fleet of presidential aircraft and the crews who flew and maintained them, Andrews was well equipped to handle the entourages that normally traveled with their distinguished passengers. Although the various craft used by the chief executive and his deputy were always parked in a secure area a safe distance from the rest of the flight-line activity, a well-appointed VIP lounge was only a short drive away.

Yanking open the helo's door, a blue-suited crew chief gestured toward a waiting sedan. "There's hot coffee in the lounge, sir, if you'd like to wait there. The driver will take you over."

Ducking under the whirring rotor blades, Adam shook his head. "I'm fine. I'll wait by the plane." Turning up the collar of his tan camel-hair overcoat, he walked to the Gulfstream jet warming up on the parking apron.

When discharging the duties of her office, the vice president usually traveled aboard Air Force Two, a huge, specially equipped 747 crammed with communications gear and fitted with several compartments for the media and assorted staff members who traveled with their boss. For this trip—a combination of party business and personal pleasure that didn't require her normal entourage—she'd fly aboard a smaller, more economical plane.

Cold wind whipped Adam's hair as he waited beside the sleek white-painted Gulfstream. Around him, crew members performed a last-minute visual check of the aircraft while a portable power cart slowly revved up the twin Rolls-Royce turbofan engines. Having flown jet fighters during his long-ago stint in the navy, Adam had maintained his flight proficiency over the years. At any other time, he would have observed the takeoff preparations with a keen eye, and his hands would have itched to take the stick. Today, the fists he'd shoved into the pockets of his overcoat remained tightly clenched.

During the short flight to Andrews, reality had set in. The raw male need that had surged through him when he finally admitted that he wanted Maggie had given way to an even fiercer need. The need to protect her.

She was at risk, as she'd never been before. Like a sacrificial goat staked out at the end of a tether, she was offering herself as a target for an assassin. Adam couldn't believe he'd allowed himself to consider, even for a moment, unleashing his desire. He couldn't allow himself or her to be distracted from their deadly mission during the days ahead.

But when this mission was over...

By the time he heard the distant *whump* of rotor blades, he had himself well in control again. Narrowing his eyes against the drizzle, he searched the dense gray haze. A few seconds later, a blue-and-white chopper broke through the mist and hovered above the runway. It drifted down until its skids touched lightly. Then the copilot jumped out to open the passenger-compartment door.

Maggie climbed out first. She smiled her thanks at the helmeted copilot and darted out from under the turning rotor blades. The downwash from the blades ruffled her auburn hair and whirled the skirts of her cream-colored wool coat around her calves.

Although Adam was expecting it, her likeness to Taylor Grant still generated a small shock. The resemblance didn't have anything to do with the wine-colored hair or the jawline that Field Dress had molded so exactly, he decided as he watched her cross the wet tarmac. It was a matter of style. An inner vitality. A shimmering essence that the two women had in common.

But the mischievous gleam that filled Maggie's eyes as she returned the greetings of the crew members who snapped to attention was hers alone. She knew very well that her less-than-precise rendition of a military salute would make Adam grimace inwardly. Which it did. After this mission, he promised himself, he'd teach her just how to bend that elbow. Among other things.

"Good morning."

Taylor's voice carried over the whine of the Gulfstream's engines and the whir of the helo's blades. This was Chameleon at her finest, Adam thought in silent admiration. No one in OMEGA could come close to matching Maggie's skill at pulling a deep-cover identity around her like an invisible cloak.

"Good morning," he replied, taking her outstretched hands in both of his.

In the periphery of his vision, he saw the news team from the White House pool who'd braved the cold to cover the VP's departure recording their greeting.

So did Maggie. Suddenly ridiculously self-conscious, she smiled up at Adam. She felt like a teenager about to go out on a closely chaperoned date, for Pete's sake!

"Are you sure you want to exchange two weeks of Washington's cold, snowy weather for California's cold, snowy weather?" she asked, tilting her head in a coquettish gesture while the cameras whirred.

"I'm sure. Come on, let's get you aboard before your... nose freezes."

She bit back a grin as he passed her hand to the steward who was waiting to help her aboard.

Shrugging out of her wool coat, Maggie handed it to the hovering attendant. She could get used to this pampering, she thought, if not to the idea of being constantly under surveillance. The interior of the plane was like none she'd ever seen before, all gleaming oak, polished brass and plush blue upholstery.

She had no trouble identifying her seat. A slipcover embroidered with the vice president's seal draped a huge armchair, one of two in a private forward compartment. While she strapped herself in, Adam took the seat opposite her. She shifted her feet under the smooth oak table to make room for his long legs.

Lillian and Denise settled themselves in the rear compartment, along with several other Secret Service agents, who'd coordinated the final details of the L.A. visit. Even before the hatch had closed, Denise had bent over an outspread map and begun a review of the security along the route from the airport to the hotel.

Within moments, the pilot's voice came over the intercom, welcoming them aboard and detailing the flight times and refueling stop. After a smooth, swift roll down the runway, they were airborne. Immediately dense, impenetrable mist surrounded the plane and cut off any view of the capital. The aircraft climbed steeply, and eventually leveled out at twenty thousand feet.

"Would you care for juice, Mrs. Grant?"

Maggie repressed a shudder at the sight of the grayish liquid filling the decanter on the steward's tray. It wasn't guava juice, obviously, and that had been bad enough.

"No, thank you. I'm fine."

"And you, sir?"

"Coffee, please. Black."

Maggie's mouth watered as the aroma of fresh-brewed coffee filled the compartment.

"Mrs. Grant doesn't care for them, sir, but I have an assortment of rolls and Danish for the other passengers. Or I can prepare eggs and bacon in the galley, if you'd like."

Carefully avoiding Maggie's eyes, Adam shook his head. "No, in deference to Mrs. Grant, I'll skip the bacon and eggs. Just bring me a Danish."

Maggie kicked him under the table.

"And some rolls."

"Very good, sir."

As soon as the door closed behind the steward, Maggie fiddled with the intercom switch on the communications console beside her seat. The low hum of voices from the cockpit was cut off.

"Can we talk?" she asked, couching her question in a playful tone, in case the cabin contained listening systems she wasn't aware of.

"We can," he replied, relaxing. "Joe went over the communications wiring diagram of the plane last night, and our people did a sweep this morning. This cabin is secure."

Maggie sagged back against her seat. "Thank God. I never realized how nerve-racking it is to live in an electronic fishbowl every day of your life." She eyed the steaming mug in front of him. "Are you going to drink that coffee?"

"No, you are. Go ahead. I'll listen for the steward."

Cradling the cup in both hands, she inhaled the fragrant aroma before taking a hearty gulp. Her eyes closed in sheer delight as she savored the hot, rich brew.

"Ahh . . ."

"Better than guava juice?"

She opened one eye to find Adam watching her. "You heard that, did you?"

"I did."

Maggie refused to ask what else he'd heard. Sometime during her restless night, she'd decided that if she snored, she didn't want to know about it.

His voice took on an edge. "I also heard the bus backfire this morning."

She took another sip of coffee. "Talk about your basic motivational techniques! I wasn't sure I could get up that last hill, but after a near-miss by a killer bus, I didn't have any difficulty making it to cover."

"I'm glad you find the incident so amusing."

The acid in his words surprised her. "Didn't you?"

"Not particularly. It just demonstrated how vulnerable you are. How vulnerable the vice president is."

Maggie set the mug down carefully. "So do we have anything more on our list of potential assassins?"

"Nothing on the treasury secretary. Other than his one brief fling with Mrs. Grant during a rocky period in his marriage, Elliot's squeaky-clean. Before being confirmed by the Senate, he went through a background screening that revealed everything from his personal finances to his taste in food."

"Let's not talk about food! What about his finances?"

"He built a personal fortune speculating on the market, but over the years converted his riskier ventures to T-bonds."

She frowned. "T-bonds? Isn't it a conflict of interest for him to hold treasury bonds in his current position?"

"It would be, if he hadn't placed them in a blind trust, administered by his lawyers and the board of directors of First Bank."

"First Bank?" Something nagged at the back of Maggie's mind, but she couldn't quite place it. "Isn't that the one headquartered in Miami?"

"With branches all through Central and South America."

She frowned, searching her memory. "I've heard something about First Bank recently."

Adam waited for her to continue. When she didn't, a smile tugged at his mouth. "First Bank helped draft the president's Pan-American Monetary Stabilization Plan."

"Oh. Right."

She was going to have to read up on that darn plan, Maggie thought. Stretching out her legs, she leaned back in the buttery-soft leather armchair. Her feet bumped Adam's under the oak table, then found a nest between them.

"Well, so much for James Elliot. What about the others?"

"Jaguar's digging into the contract Digicon, Donovan's firm, is pressing on the Pentagon. He should have something today."

"That leaves the gorgeous hunk of muscle-bound beefcake," she murmured, then caught Adam's cool look. "According to Mrs. Grant. And just about every female over the age of thirty," she added under her breath.

"Evidently Stoney Armstrong's public doesn't consider him quite as gorgeous as it used to. His last five movies were box-office bombs. The word is that he's washed-up in the industry. The exact phrasing, I believe, was that his sex appeal has gone south.''

"Did we get that from his agent?"

"His agent's en route to Poland to consult with an international starlet he's just taken on as a client." Adam paused, his eyes gleaming. "This information came from Armstrong's hairstylist."

"Someone got to him already? That was quick work."

"It took a near act of God, but Doc managed a late-evening appointment with the man."

Maggie choked back a laugh. "Doc? Our Doc had his hair styled?"

Dr. David Jensen was one of OMEGA's most skilled agents. In his civilian cover, he headed the engineering department of a major L.A. defense firm. Brilliant, analytical and cool under fire, he was also as conservative as they came. Maggie would give anything to see him with his short brown locks dressed by an avant-garde Hollywood hair designer.

"The things we do in service to our country," she commented, shaking her head.

"In this case, Doc's sacrifice paid off. Armstrong's stylist also let drop that the star attributes the downward spiral in his career to the fact that Taylor dumped him. As long as he was in her orbit, they shared the limelight. When she moved on, the spotlight followed her, and left him standing in the shadows."

A knock on the door heralded the arrival of the steward with more coffee and a basket of sweet rolls.

Maggie eyed the basket greedily and could barely wait for the steward to pour Adam's coffee and leave. This bundle of yummies would have to hold her until the banquet this evening. She needed all the calories she could ingest to maintain the intense concentration necessary for her various roles as vice president, former lover of an over-the-hill sex symbol, and present companion to the special envoy.

When Stoney Armstrong stepped out of the crowd gathered in the hotel lobby to greet the vice president a few hours later, Maggie realized immediately that Doc had received some faulty information. Whatever else had gone south, it wasn't the star's sex appeal.

Tanned, tawny-haired, and in possession of an incredible assortment of bulging muscles under a red knit shirt that stretched across massive shoulders, he grinned at Maggie.

"Hiya, Taylor—uh, Madam Vice President."

Since he carried no weapon in his hands and there was no way he could conceal anything under his body-hugging knit shirt, she responded with a cautious smile.

"Hello, Stoney."

At which point he sidestepped the ever-present Denise, brushed past Adam and swept an astonished Maggie into a back-bending, bone-crushing embrace.

A barrage of flashes exploded throughout the lobby. Dimly Maggie heard waves of astonished titters sweep through the crowd. Cameras whirred, and news crews climbed over each other for a better shot.

When he set her upright some moments later, Maggie was breathless, flushed, and almost as shaken as when the bus had backfired this morning.

Chapter 6

A million-dollar smile beamed down at her. "You're looking great, Taylor. Really great."

"You too, Stoney," Maggie returned, easing out of his hold.

"I like you with a little flesh on your bones."

"Thanks."

At her dry response, Stoney flashed another one of his trademark grins, all white teeth and crinkly eyes.

"What say I sneak you away from all this political hoopla for a few hours tonight? Like I used to, when you were governor?"

"What say you don't?" Adam's cool voice cut through the babble of the crowd. "The lady will be with me tonight."

Another barrage of blinding flashes went off as the two men faced each other. Talk about your basic headline-grabber, Maggie thought wryly. The vice president's former and current romantic interests squaring off in the lobby of L.A.'s Century Plaza Hotel. The media were going to play this one for all it was worth. With a flash of insight, she realized that Adam had once more stepped into the breach and diverted attention from her.

Stoney's sun-bleached brows lifted. "Who are you?"

"Adam Ridgeway. Who are you?"

The onetime movie idol blinked, clearly taken aback at the question. "Me? Hey, I'm—"

He caught himself, then gave a bark of laughter. "You almost got me there, Ridgeway."

Grinning good-naturedly, he stuck out a paw the size of a catcher's mitt. Adam took it, a sardonic gleam in his blue eyes.

The media went wild.

The scene had all the drama of a daytime soap, and then some. Two men shook hands in a glare of flashing lights. When this shot hit the newspapers, Maggie thought, every woman in the country would envy Taylor Grant. Imagine being forced to choose between your basic sun-bronzed, superbly muscled Greek god and a dark-haired aristocrat whose eyes held a glint of danger.

When Stoney had milked the scene for all it was worth, Maggie knew it was time to move on.

"Will I see you at the banquet tonight?" she asked.

"Sure. But—" he glanced at Adam "—I kind of hoped we'd have a chance to talk. Privately."

"Maybe after the banquet," she suggested easily. "I'll be tied up until then."

"Yeah. Okay. After dinner."

Maggie spent a long afternoon listening to the California Council of Mayors present their list of grievances against the heavy-handed federal bureaucracy. Fortunately, all she was required to do was nod occasionally and, at the end of the session, promise that their complaints about programs mandated by Congress without accompanying funds to implement them would be looked into.

By the time she and Adam and the ever-vigilant Denise took the elevator to the penthouse suite, the long night, the transcontinental flight and the packed day had drained even Maggie's considerable store of energy. Or maybe it was the lack of sustenance, she thought, collapsing onto one of the sleek white leather couches scattered about the suite.

Sunlight streamed through the two-story wall of glass that overlooked the city, for once miraculously clear of smog, and bathed Maggie in a warm glow. After Washington's snowy cold, L.A.'s balmy, unseasonable seventy degrees felt heavenly. Feeling an uncharacteristic lassitude, she slipped off her shoes, propped her stockinged feet on a glass coffee table the size of a football field and heaved a huge sigh.

"We've got an hour until the banquet," Adam replied, his eyes on her face. "Why don't you relax for a while? I'll go next door to check in with my office, then shower and change. Shall I join you for a drink before we go downstairs?"

"That would be nice," Maggie replied.

"The hotel left a basket of delicacies in my suite. Shall I bring it with me, and we can explore it together?"

"By all means."

The hotel had left a basket in the vice president's suite, as well. To Maggie's infinite disappointment, it had contained only fruit and fancy glass jars of what looked and tasted like dry oats.

Buoyed by the thought of both food and time alone with Adam, Maggie pushed herself off the sofa and headed for the bedroom.

A half hour later, Lillian zipped up the back of a stunning flame-colored gown in floating layers of chiffon, then stood back to survey her charge. Her keen black eyes took in every detail, from the dramatic upsweep of her short hair to the tips of her strappy sandals, dyed to match the gown.

"You'll do."

Coming from Lillian, that was high praise indeed. Maggie smiled as she peered into the mirror to make sure her matte makeup fully covered the gel-like adhesive bone on her nose and chin.

"Thanks, Lillian. I couldn't pull this off without you."

"After twenty-four hours in your company, I'm beginning to suspect you could pull off this or any number of other improbable capers."

Maggie grinned. "Capers? We refer to them as missions."

"Whatever. I'll be right across the hall. Call me when you get back from the banquet."

"Don't wait up. I can manage. Besides," she added to forestall the inevitable protest, "I may have a visitor after the banquet, remember?"

If things got tense when Stoney Armstrong showed up, Maggie didn't want the older woman in the line of fire.

Lillian gave one of her patented sniffs. "You're going to have more than one visitor tonight, missy. I don't imagine the special envoy is going to leave you alone with Stoney."

Maggie lifted a brow. "We'll see how the situation develops. I'm used to operating independently on a mission, you know."

"Who's talking about your mission?"

Lillian gave the bedroom a final inspection, then left Maggie to mull that one over. She was still thinking about it when she walked into the huge, white-carpeted living room some time later.

Denise Kowalski rose at her entry. Attired in the full-length black satin skirt that Maggie recognized as her uniform for formal functions, the sandy-haired agent was all brisk efficiency as she ran through the security arrangements for the banquet. When Denise finished, she stood and moved to the door.

"I've got to go downstairs for the final walk-though. We're using locals to help screen the guests as they arrive. I want to make sure they know how to operate the hand scanners."

"Fine."

"This entire floor's secure," Denise stated earnestly, as if needing to justify her brief absence. "There are two post-standers at the elevators, and one at each of the stairwells. If you need them, just call." She nodded toward the hot line that linked the vice president's suite with the command post across the hall. "Or hit the panic button beside the bed."

"I know the routine," Maggie said, smiling.

The other woman grinned sheepishly. "Yes, ma'am, I guess you do."

Maggie studied the agent thoughtfully as she gathered her things and left. She was good. Darn good. From the moment their plane touched down at Los Angeles International, she'd been the vice president's second shadow. During the trip in from the airport, she'd directed the motorcade via the radio strapped to the inside of her wrist like a general marshaling his forces. What was more, she'd been prepared to take Stoney Armstrong down when he stepped out of the crowd in the lobby, and no doubt would have done so if Maggie hadn't acknowledged him.

According to the background brief OMEGA had prepared on Denise Kowalski, the woman had almost fifteen years with the Secret Service. She had joined the service at a time when female agents were a rarity, and had worked her way up the ranks. One divorce along the way. No children. Who could manage children and a career that demanded months on the road? Maggie wondered. Or the eighteen-hour days? Or a job that required instant willingness to take a bullet intended for someone else?

Denise would be one hell of an addition to the OMEGA team, Maggie decided. She made a mental note to speak to Adam about it when he joined her.

At the thought of their coming tête-à-tête, Maggie wrapped her arms across her chest. A shiver of anticipation whispered down her spine. They hadn't had a moment alone together since stepping off the plane. In his position as the president's special envoy, Adam commanded almost as much attention as the vice president had. Lobbyists and party hopefuls had clustered around him at every opportunity, bending his ear, asking his advice.

For the next thirty minutes, at least, Maggie would have his complete and undivided attention.

They needed to strategize, she reminded herself. To co-ordinate their plans for an evening that would include an intimate dinner with two hundred party faithful and a possible assassin in the person of a tanned, handsome movie star.

Although...

After her admittedly brief meeting with Stoney Armstrong this afternoon, Maggie found it difficult to believe he was the one who'd made that call. She'd met her share of desperate men, and a few whose utter lack of remorse for their assorted crimes chilled her. But when she looked up into Stoney's eyes after that mind-bending, back-bending kiss this afternoon, she hadn't seen a killer.

Then again, she reminded herself, Stoney Armstrong was an actor. A good one.

Her brow furrowed in thought, Maggie wandered through the living room toward the wide flagstone terrace outside the glass wall. A balmy breeze warmed by the offshore Japanese currents lifted her layers of chiffon and rustled the palms scattered around the terrace. Drawn by the glow of lights, she crossed to the waist-high stone balustrade that circled the terrace.

The sight that greeted her made her gasp in stunned delight. Far below her, adorned in glittering gold diamonds, was the city of angels. Los Angeles by day might consist of palm trees and smog, towering skyscrapers and crumbling, thirties-era stucco cottages. But by night, from the perspective of the fortieth floor, it was a dreamscape of sparkling, iridescent lights. Thoroughly enchanted, Maggie leaned her elbows on the wide stone railing and drank in the incredible sight.

The buzz of the telephone sent a rush of pleasure though her veins. That had to be Adam. With his basket of goodies. She went back inside and caught the phone on the third ring.

"Yes?"

"This is Special Agent Harrison, Mrs. Grant. A Mr. Stoney Armstrong just stepped off the elevator. He'd like to speak to you."

Maggie didn't hesitate. "Of course."

In the blink of an eye, her excitement sharpened, changed focus. The woman whose senses had tingled at the thought of a private tête-à-tête with Adam transitioned instantly into the skilled, highly trained agent. Her mind racing with various ways to handle this unexpected contact with a prime suspect, Maggie lifted her left hand.

"Thunder? Thunder, do you read me?"

When he didn't respond, Maggie guessed Adam was still in the shower. As soon as he got out, he'd pick up on her conversation with Stoney and join her—if the circumstances required it. Actually, she thought, it might be better if Adam didn't appear on the scene. She'd be able to draw Stoney out far more easily without another man present, especially one he might consider a rival.

Quickly she dimmed the lights and retrieved the small gold lipstick Special Devices had included in her bag of tricks for this mission. As she tucked the tiny stun gun in the bodice of her gown, she wondered briefly if it was powerful enough to take down a man of Stoney Armstrong's massive proportions, as Special Devices had claimed.

If not, and if necessary, she'd bring Stoney down herself. He'd be unarmed, she knew. He couldn't have passed through the highly sophisticated security screens with a weapon on his person. She'd handled bigger men than him in the past.

When a knock sounded on the door to her suite a few moments later, she was ready, both mentally and physically, to face a possible killer.

If Stoney Armstrong harbored any deadly intent toward Taylor Grant, he didn't show it. His tanned cheeks creased in his famous studio grin that, for all its beefcake quality, was guaranteed to stir any woman's hormones. Perfect white teeth gleamed, and his Armani tux gaped open to reveal a broad expanse of muscled, white-shirted chest as he leaned one arm negligently against the doorjamb.

"Hello, Taylor."

"Hello, Stoney."

"I'm a little early."

"So I noticed. Come in."

He strolled into the penthouse, looking around with unabashed interest. The glass wall drew him like a magnet. Shoving his hands in his pockets, he strolled out onto the terrace.

"It's something, isn't it?" he murmured, his eyes on the endless sweep of lights against a now-velvet sky.

"It is," Maggie agreed.

His mouth twisted. "Hard to believe a thin crust is all that separates the glitter and glamour from the tar pits underneath."

His subtle reference to the La Brea tar pit, the famous archaeological site in the center of the city, wasn't lost on Maggie.

"You sound as though a few saber-toothed tigers might have crawled out of the sludge," she commented softly.

If OMEGA's information was correct, those predators were circling Stoney Armstrong even now, about to close in for the kill.

His broad shoulders lifted. "Hey, this is Tinseltown. Saber-toothed tigers do power lunches every Tuesday and Friday at Campanile."

Turning his back on the dazzling vista, he leaned his hips against the rail.

"God, you look great, Taylor. Sort of sleek and well fed, like a cat or a horse or something."

Stoney did a lot better in a tender scene when he used a script, Maggie thought sardonically.

He leaned against the railing, ankles crossed, hands in his pockets. With the breeze ruffling his gold hair and his tux gaping open to reveal a couple of acres of broad chest, he looked pretty well fed himself.

He cocked his head, studying her face. "It can't be all those raisins and sunflower seeds you put away that gave you such a glow. Is it this guy Ridgeway?"

When Maggie didn't answer, his smile twisted a bit.

"I saw some pictures of you two in the afternoon edition of the *Times*. Christ, I wish I had your publicist. Those were great shots. Especially the one where you were getting out of the limo."

Maggie had rather liked that one herself.

"I thought maybe they were posed," he said, "like the ones you used to do for me, but..."

"But?"

"But after seeing you two together, I guess not." He paused, his eyes on her face. "You used to look at me like that, Taylor, and not just for the cameras. What happened to us? We used to be so good together."

Maggie gave silent thanks for Taylor Grant's frankness about her relationship with this man. "What we had was good, Stoney. Very good. But it wasn't enough for either one of us."

"I know, I know. But, hey, we've both changed a lot since then. Our needs have changed. I mean, when we were together, you were governor and I was being courted by all the big studios."

"It wasn't our professional life that got in the way."

He raked a hand through his hair, destroying its casual artistry. "Yeah, I know. You were still hurting from your husband's death, and I was paying alimony to two ex-wives. You didn't want emotional ties, any more than I did. But that was then."

"And now?"

The tanned skin at the corners of his eyes crinkled as he gave her a rueful grin. "And now you've got this guy Ridgeway prowling around you like a hungry panther, and I'm paying alimony to three ex-wives."

No wonder Taylor had enjoyed this man's company so much during their brief time together, Maggie thought. For all his absorption with himself, Stoney had a disarming charm when he chose to exert it.

"We could be good together again, Taylor."

"What we had was right for that moment, that time," Maggie said softly, echoing the vice president's own words. "But not for now. Not for the future."

"Why not? Just think about it. You might decide to go for top billing in the next election. You'd make a hell of a president. Together we'd make an unbeatable team. Just think of the publicity if I hit the campaign trail with you. Hey, look at the press Barbra Streisand got when she campaigned for Clinton."

Maggie bit the inside of her lower lip, not wanting to be the one to break it to Stoney that he possessed neither the star power nor the political acumen of a Barbra Streisand.

"Taylor..."

He closed the small distance between them. Maggie kept her smile in place as he leaned forward, planting both hands on the balustrade on either side of her, but her mind coldly registered his vulnerabilities. With his legs spread like that, he'd left himself wide open to a quick knee to the groin. His outstretched arms gave her room to swing her hand at the side of his neck or to shove a fisted thumb into the bridge of his nose.

When she looked up into his eyes, however, Maggie knew she wouldn't need to exploit those vulnerabilities. In three years of living on the knife-edge of danger, she'd learned to trust her instincts, and every one of those instincts told her this man was no killer.

"Stoney..." she began.

"I want you, Taylor."

Water dripped from Adam's hair and rolled down his back as he yanked a pair of black dress pants off the hanger on the back of the bathroom door.

"It won't work for us, Stoney. Not now."

Maggie's voice, soft and too damned sympathetic, drifted out of the watch on the marble counter. His jaw working, Adam tugged the slacks up over still-wet flanks.

"I need you."

Stoney delivered the line with a husky, melodramatic passion that set Adam's teeth on edge. Christ! No wonder the man couldn't get a part in anything except B-grade action flicks.

"Give me another chance. Give us a chance."

"It's too late."

"No. I don't believe that. I'll prove it!"

"Stoney, for Pete's sake!"

Maggie hadn't requested backup, Adam reminded himself. She obviously wanted to play this one alone. But her muffled exclamation propelled him out of the bathroom, bare chested and still dripping.

He was halfway to the door connecting their suites when a note of panic entered her voice.

"Stoney! You're too heavy! You're— Watch out!"

Her shrill yelp of terror sent Adam racing for the glass doors leading to the terrace. A knife blade of fear sliced through his gut when he saw Armstrong bent over the stone rail. A single sweep of the terrace showed no sign of Maggie anywhere.

"I . . . I can't . . . hold . . . you!"

Armstrong's agonized cry seared Adam's soul.

He didn't stop to think, didn't allow himself to feel. In a blinding burst of speed, he tore across the terrace and reached over the railing to grab the wrist Stoney held in one huge paw. The instant Adam's right hand clamped around Maggie's wrist, his left swung in a vicious arc. His fist smashed into Armstrong's jaw with the force of a pile driver.

The brawny movie star crumpled without a sound, but Adam didn't even flick him a glance. All his attention, every ounce of his concentration, was focused on the woman who dangled forty stories above the Avenue of the Stars, held only by his bruising lock on her wrist.

"I've got you," he grunted, his neck muscles cording.

Maggie twisted at the end of his arm, her bloodred gown billowing around her flailing legs.

"I . . . can't . . . get a foothold!" she gasped.

"You don't need one! Dammit, don't twist like that!" Bent double, Adam kept his left arm anchored around the railing. The rough stone took a strip of flesh off his bare chest as he leaned farther out. "Just grab my arm with your other hand. I'll pull you up."

Maggie's fingers clawed at his, then crept up to fasten around his forearm. With a surge of strength, Adam dragged her up and over the railing. Holding her upright with an iron grip, he raked her with a fierce, searching look.

"Are you all right?"

"I . . ." She sucked in a huge gulp of air. "I will be. As soon as you . . . stop crunching my bones."

His adrenaline raging, Adam ignored her attempt to shake loose of his hold. "What in hell happened? Didn't you anticipate his attack?"

"Attack? He didn't attack me."

"He pushed you off a rooftop!"

"Adam, he didn't push me! He was just trying to make love to me. We sort of . . . overbalanced."

She stopped tugging at his iron hold on her wrist and managed a shaky grin. "I guess you could say he swept me off my feet."

It was the grin that did it. That exasperating, infuriating lift of her lips. For the second time in less than twenty-four hours, Maggie was laughing while fear pumped through Adam's veins.

With a low sound that in anyone else might have been mistaken for a snarl, he wrapped her manacled wrist behind her back. A single flex of his muscles brought her body slamming against his. His other hand buried itself in her hair.

"You're forgetting your role. I'm the only man who's going to make love to you during this mission."

Maggie's eyes widened. She stared up at Adam, stunned as much by his unexpected force as by the way he held her banded against his chest. His black hair fell across his forehead, damp and tangled and untamed. His eyes glittered with a savage intensity. The muscles of his neck and shoulders gleamed wet and naked and powerful in the dim light.

He was close, so close, to unleashing the power she'd always sensed behind the steel curtain of his discipline. The realization sent a thrill through every fiber of Maggie's being. But at that moment, she wasn't quite sure whether the thrill she felt was one of triumph, or anticipation, or uncertainty.

"Adam . . ." she began, her voice husky.

She stopped, not knowing whether she wanted to soothe this potent, powerful, unfamiliar male or push him past his last restraint.

They hovered on the edge, each knowing that the next word, the next breath, could send them over.

To Maggie's intense disappointment, the next breath was Stoney's.

Groaning, the star pushed himself up on all fours, then lifted a hand to flex his jaw.

"Damn, Ridgeway," he muttered. "I hope to hell you didn't break my caps."

Chapter 7

Still banded against Adam's body, Maggie didn't see the look he sent the aggrieved star. But it was enough to keep the man on his knees.

"If you touch her again, Armstrong, I'll break more than your caps."

Stoney blinked, as startled by the controlled savagery in his voice as Maggie herself had been a moment ago.

"Hey, man, I get the picture."

"You'd better."

When Adam stepped away, Maggie felt the loss in every inch of her body. She also saw the blood smearing his bare chest for the first time.

"Adam, you're hurt!"

"It's just a scrape," he replied brusquely, yanking the star to his feet. "Go call Kowalski. I'll entertain your friend here until she arrives."

Denise and two other security agents came rushing into

the suite a few moments later. The senior agent turned ashen when she saw the front of Maggie's gown.

"Are you all right, Mrs. Grant?"

Glancing down, Maggie discovered that Adam's blood had darkened the flame red chiffon to a deep wine. "I'm fine. I just fell on the terrace. Well, off the terrace, but..."

Denise paled even more. "You fell off the terrace?"

"Stoney, er, got a little carried away. We overbalanced, and Adam came to the rescue." She gestured toward the glass wall, and the two figures on the terrace.

Denise turned, her eyes rounding at the sight of the president's special envoy, his naked chest streaked with blood, his slacks riding low on lean hips.

With a less-than-gentle shove, Adam propelled Stoney through the open sliding glass doors, into the suite. The two agents with Denise leaped forward to grab the star's arms.

Indignant, he tried to shake them off. "Hey, watch it!"

"Get him out of here," Adam ordered.

"Take Mr. Armstrong downstairs to interrogation," Denise instructed the others. "I want a full statement in my hands as soon as you get it out of him. And, Harrison—"

"Yes, ma'am?"

"Keep him away from the media."

"Yes, ma'am."

The senior agent pulled herself together as she swept the room. Her keen gaze took in the open connecting door between the suites before returning to Adam. Maggie caught a flicker of something that might have been feminine awareness or even admiration in Denise's eyes as they skimmed his lean torso, but it disappeared immediately when she caught the icy expression on his face.

"Where were you?"

Both women stiffened at the whipcrack in Adam's voice. Denise because she'd never heard it before, Maggie because she'd heard it several times. The furious man who'd slammed her up against his chest was gone. In his place was the Adam Ridgeway Maggie knew all too well.

"Downstairs," the agent responded tightly. "Conducting a final walk-through."

"Just what kind of security screens have you set up, Kowalski? How did Armstrong get past your men?"

Maggie stepped into the fray. "Hold it, Adam. Stoney didn't get past them. I told them to send him up."

Two equally accusing faces swung toward her. Adam's could have been chiseled from ice, but Denise's was folded into a frown.

"Was that wise, Mrs. Grant? After Armstrong's stunt in the lobby this afternoon?"

"I thought so," she replied coolly.

Adam didn't say a word, but Maggie could see he was *not* pleased. She fought back a small surge of irritation. She wasn't used to justifying or explaining her actions in the middle of an operation. To anyone.

As quickly as the irritation flared, Maggie suppressed it. Adam was her partner on this mission. She owed him an explanation of Stoney's presence in her suite, but she couldn't give it in front of Denise.

"We'll conduct a postmortem after the banquet," she told the agent with crisp authority. "Right now, I need you to go across the hall and get Lillian."

Denise firmed her lips, then reached for the phone. "I'll call her."

"I'd prefer you go get her. I don't want her hearing about this over the phone and becoming all upset. You know how overprotective she is."

It was a feeble excuse, and they all knew it, but Denise dropped the receiver back into its cradle.

"Fine. I'll go get Lillian. And we'll conduct a *thorough* postmortem after the banquet."

The door shut behind her, and a small, tense silence descended.

Adam was the first to break it, his tone frigid. "I think we need to review our mission parameters."

"I agree."

"This is supposed to be a team effort, remember?"

Maggie's jaw tightened, but she kept her voice level. "I tried to contact you after I told Security to send Stoney up."

"After? It didn't occur to you to contact me before you told them to send him up?"

"No, it didn't. I saw a target of opportunity, and I took it."

"Try coordinating your targets with me next time."

The stinging rejoinder lifted Maggie's chin. "I don't operate that way. I won't operate that way."

His eyes narrowed dangerously. Maggie had never seen that particular expression in them before—not directed at her, anyway. But she didn't back down. Her gaze locked with his, unwavering, determined. There was more at stake here than operating procedures, or even her job. Far more. She knew it. Adam knew it.

"You shouldn't have tried to handle this situation alone," he said, spacing his words. "It was too dangerous."

"I'm trained to handle dangerous situations. You trained me yourself. You and Jaguar."

A muscle ticked in the side of his jaw. "As best I recall, your training didn't include rappelling down a forty-story building without a rope."

"No," she tossed back, "but it included damn near everything else."

Which was true. As the first OMEGA operative recruited from outside the ranks of the government, Maggie had run the gamut of a battery of field tests and survival courses. She'd come through them all, disgruntled on occasion and cursing a blue streak after a memorable encounter with a snake Jaguar had slipped inside her boot, but she'd come through.

"Look, Adam, you know as well as I do, this job isn't just a matter of training. I follow my instincts in the field. I always have."

"I wondered when we were going to come around to that sixth sense of yours." He stepped toward her, his mouth hard. "I'll admit it's gotten you out of more tight spots than I care to think about, but—"

"But what?" she asked him challengingly.

"But even instincts can fail in certain situations."

He was so close, she could scent the tincture of blood and sweat that pearled his body. So still, she could see the pinpoints of blue steel in his eyes. So coiled, she could feel the tension escalating between them with every breath.

The heady, frightening feeling of hovering on the edge returned full force. Maggie had caught a brief glimpse of another Adam behind the all-but-impenetrable wall of his discipline. A part of her wanted to poke and probe and test that discipline further, to take him over the edge, and herself with him. Another part held her back. She knew this wasn't the time or the place. Denise would return with Lillian at any moment.

The time would come, though. Soon. She sensed it with everything that was female in her. With instincts more powerful, more primitive, than any she brought to her job.

Something of what she was thinking must have shown on her face. Adam took another step closer, his eyes locked with hers.

"What does your sixth sense tell you now, Maggie? About *this* situation?"

She hesitated a moment too long. The sound of a door slamming across the hall cut through the heavy stillness between them.

"It tells me we'll have to finish our discussion later," she said, torn between relief and regret.

"We'll finish it," Adam promised. "We'll definitely finish it."

The murmur of voices in the hall grew louder. With a last glance at her face, he started to turn away.

"Thunder?"

"Yes?"

She chewed on her lower lip for a second. "I'm sorry you were wounded in the line of duty."

Driven as much by the overwhelming need to touch him as by the urge to dull the hard edge of anger between them, Maggie reached out to brush her fingertips over the swirl of dark hair that arrowed his chest. Avoiding the raw, reddened patch of scraped flesh, she stroked his skin. Lightly. Soothingly.

He'd been wounded before, she discovered. Her fingers traced the ridge of an old, jagged scar that followed the line of his collarbone and passed over a puckered circle on his shoulder that could only have been caused by a bullet.

"Thank you," she said, dragging her gaze back to his face. "For hauling me back onto the terrace."

His hand closed over hers, capturing it against his heated skin. Under her flattened palm, Maggie felt the steady drumming of his heart.

"You're welcome." The sharp lines bracketing his mouth eased. "Just try to keep both feet on the ground from here on out."

It was too late for that, she thought. Far too late for that.

He'd almost lost her.

Adam stood unmoving while a shocked Lillian painted his

chest with iodine, then covered the scrape with a white bandage. She brushed aside his quiet thanks and left to hurry Maggie into a fresh gown, tut-tutting all the while, in her own inimitable fashion.

With a damp cloth, Adam removed the ravages the stone railing had done to his dress pants. His hands were steady as he slipped on his white shirt, but the damned gold studs just wouldn't seem to fit the tiny openings. Clenching his jaw, Adam forced the last stud into place. Throughout it all, his mind followed a single narrow track.

He'd almost lost her.

This morning he'd finally admitted to himself how much he wanted Maggie, and tonight he'd almost lost her.

Before he possessed her—as much as it would be possible to possess someone like Chameleon—he'd almost lost her.

The raw need he'd acknowledged less than ten hours ago didn't begin to compare with the ache that sliced through him now. Seeing Maggie half a breath away from death had effectively stripped him of any illusion that he could control his need for her.

Two weeks, and this mission would be complete, he reminded himself. Two weeks until he could satisfy the gnawing hunger he didn't, couldn't, deny any longer. For the first time, Adam doubted his own endurance.

Grimacing at the tug of the bandage on his chest hair, he pulled on his black dinner jacket and left the bathroom. He stopped short at the sight of the towering, beribboned basket resting majestically on a glass-topped sofa table.

He'd take it to Maggie after the banquet. At least one of them wouldn't go to bed hungry tonight.

He was halfway to the door when his watch began to vibrate gently against his wrist.

"Thunder here."

"This is Jaguar, Chief. Thought you might want to know we finally cornered Stoney Armstrong's agent."

"And?"

"And he passed on the interesting information that his client floated an eight-figure 'loan' just a week ago. Seems Armstrong decided to produce and star in his own film. The funds went through half a dozen holding companies, but we finally traced them to First Bank."

Adam went still. "First Bank?"

"Yeah. Ready for the kicker?"

"I'm ready."

"Armstrong refused the loan when he discovered that First Bank was putting up the cash. Seems he'd heard some rumors about the institution and didn't want his name connected to it."

"What kind of rumors?"

"Nothing specific, but the agent hinted strongly that it might be doing business with some questionable characters in Central America. Said Armstrong didn't want anything to do with it."

The fact that the brawny star had a few scruples buried under those bulging muscles didn't particularly impress Adam.

"Put a team on First Bank, Jaguar. I want to know the source of every dollar it takes in, and every possible connection between the bank and the vice president."

"I've already got it working. Will get back to you as soon as I have anything."

"Fine. Anything else?"

"No."

Adam flicked a glance at the dial of his watch. "I'd better sign off. The vice president is waiting."

Jaguar chuckled. "How's Chameleon holding up in this role?"

The memory of Maggie's shaky grin after her brush with oblivion filled Adam's mind.

"Better than I am," he replied grimly.

The banquet went off without a hitch.

Stoney Armstrong failed to make an appearance, which didn't surprise Adam. From the determined set to Denise Kowalski's chin, he guessed the agent wasn't about to release the star until she was fully satisfied with his statement.

Maggie, stunning in a two-piece turquoise silk sheath beaded in silver, charmed the men seated on either side of her. From his place across the round table, Adam watched as she picked at the elaborate chef's salad she'd been served. Every so often, her eyes strayed to the succulent rack of lamb on her neighbor's plate.

Remembering the cellophane-wrapped basket in his suite, Adam smiled. The thought of feeding Maggie, bite by bite, the various delicacies snaked through his mind. Sudden, erotic images of what could be done with red beluga caviar and soft Brie made his hand clench around the stem of his wineglass. He kept his smile easy and his conversation with the women seated on either side of him lively, but he couldn't keep his body from tightening whenever he looked at the woman separated from him by a wide expanse of white linen. Adam knew that each lingering glance he gave Maggie added more grist to the rumor mills about the vice president's latest romantic interest.

He also knew that he'd long since stopped playing a role.

When the banquet finally ended, they made their way slowly through the crowded ballroom. Denise and her squad cleared the way, and Adam followed a step or two behind Maggie as they both greeted various guests. As much as it was possible in this press, he kept her body between his and the agent in front of her.

She was incredible, he thought, watching her work the crowd. The people who caught her ear didn't notice that she listened far more than she spoke, or that she waited for them to drop clues about their personal agendas before she gave a noncommittal response.

His gaze traveled from the auburn curls feathering her neck, down the slender back now encased in turquoise silk, to the swell of her hips. The modest slit in the back of her long skirt parted with each step, revealing a tantalizing glimpse of shapely calf. Maintaining her role had to be a tremendous physical and emotional strain, but she didn't allow any sign of it to show in her demeanor or her carriage.

Until they reached the elevator.

When Denise turned to issue a last-minute instruction to the task force leader, Maggie slumped back against the brass rail for a second or two. Adam caught the way her shoulders sagged and her eyelids fluttered shut. With a wry inner smile, Adam abandoned his plans to feed her in erotic, exotic ways.

As it turned out, Denise Kowalski had her own plans for them for the rest of the evening. After a quick but thorough security check, she joined Maggie and Adam in the sitting room.

"We still have to do that postmortem, Mrs. Grant."

Maggie glanced at the clock on the white-painted mantel. "It's almost 3:00 a.m., Washington time. Why don't we get together in the morning, before we leave for the cabin?"

"It's best if we go over what happened while the details are still fresh in your mind," the agent insisted politely but firmly. "Mr. Armstrong's statement, and his subsequent polygraph, substantiate your belief that he didn't intend you bodily harm, but I need to hear exactly what happened. You could have been killed."

"I know," Maggie replied, with a gleam in her eyes that Adam recognized instantly. "I was the one about to add a new, indelible splash of color to the Avenue of the Stars, remember?"

She realized her mistake almost as soon as the words were out of her mouth. The flippant tone and gallows humor were far more characteristic of Maggie Sinclair than of Taylor Grant.

Denise frowned, and Maggie recovered without missing a beat. Curving her mouth into Taylor's distinctive smile, she tossed her beaded bag down on the sofa.

"Look, I know you're just trying to do your job. I guess I'm a little tired."

A touch of reserve entered the agent's voice. "I'm sorry to badger you this late, but I'm charged with protecting you. I can't do it without your cooperation."

With one hand tucked casually in his pants pocket, Adam eyed the two women. Denise Kowalski was every bit as strong willed and determined as Maggie when it came to her job. She wasn't about to back down, any more than Chameleon had earlier.

Maggie gave in with good grace, recognizing a pro when she saw one. "You're right, of course. Why don't we sit down?"

"Would you join us, please?" Denise asked Adam. "I'd like your input, as well."

"I didn't intend to leave. Mrs. Grant and I have a few matters of our own to discuss when you're though."

Ignoring Maggie's quick sideways glance, he joined her on the buttery-soft sofa.

The Secret Service officer was too well trained to allow any expression to cross her face. But as she moved forward to take the seat opposite them, she slanted a quick look at the open connecting door.

The brass carriage clock on the mantel had chimed twice by the time Agent Kowalski finally called a halt to the questions.

"Well, I guess that's it." She rubbed a hand across her forehead, then rose. "I'll tell the folks downstairs to release Armstrong. We'll keep someone on him for a while, with orders to get real nasty, real quick, if he tries to, uh, approach you again."

"He won't," Maggie asserted.

"No, he won't," Adam promised.

The agent glanced from Maggie's confident face to Adam's implacable one. "I guess not. I'll see you in the morning."

When the door closed behind her, Maggie heaved a sigh. Letting her head loll back against the leather, she plopped her stockinged feet on the brass-and-glass table.

"That's one tough woman."

"She reminds me of someone else I know," Adam commented dryly.

"She does, doesn't she?" Maggie's hair made a bright splash of color against the white leather as she turned to face him. "I think we should recruit her for OMEGA after this mission."

"I may have to consider it. If you pull any more stunts like you did with Armstrong, I'll have an opening for an agent."

A gleam of reluctant laughter entered her violet-tinted eyes. "Okay, so maybe dangling above the Avenue of the Stars was a bit extreme," she conceded.

"It was. Even for you."

"Even for me. But at least it convinced me that Armstrong's not our man. I don't have anything to base it on, except the fact that Stoney didn't let go—and the sixth sense you took me to task for earlier."

"As much as it pains me to admit it, your instincts were right. Again."

She sat up straight. "Really?"

"Jaguar called just before we went downstairs to the banquet."

With a succinct economy of detail, Adam filled her in on the details of Jake's call.

"First Bank, huh? Stoney turned down a loan from First Bank because he thinks they might be laundering dirty money?"

"Evidently he was afraid a connection with them might . . . tarnish his image."

She grinned. "There's a lot of that going around lately."

A small silence settled between them. Reluctant to break it, Maggie slumped back against the soft leather. She and Adam still had matters left to resolve, not the least of which was exactly how she would operate for the next two weeks. But she couldn't seem to summon up the energy or the intensity that had driven her earlier.

"If we eliminate Armstrong, that leaves only two names on the list of possible suspects," Adam said after a moment.

"Digicon's CEO, and the president's best buddy."

"Peter Donovan, and James Elliot."

"Jaguar hasn't dug up anything on either?"

He shook his head. "Not yet."

The clock on the mantel ticked off a few measures of companionable silence, broken only when Maggie gave a huge, hastily smothered yawn.

"Sorry," she murmured.

Adam's gaze rested on her face for a long moment, and then he pushed himself to his feet and held out one hand to pull her up beside him.

Maggie put her hand in his. Despite the weariness that had dragged over her like a net, a sensual awareness feathered along her nerves at the firmness of his hold. She'd felt Adam's strength twice tonight. Once when he'd hauled her up to the terrace. Once when he'd hauled her up against his chest.

"You'd better get some sleep," he told her.

She hesitated, knowing she was playing with fire. "We didn't finish what we started, out there on the terrace."

"We'll finish tomorrow," he said slowly. "When we get to the cabin."

Tomorrow, she told herself. Tomorrow, they'd be at Taylor's isolated mountain retreat. Tomorrow, Maggie would be rested, in control of herself once more. There wouldn't be as many people hovering around her. Only Denise and a small Secret Service team. Lillian. The caretaker who lived at the ranch. And Adam.

Tomorrow, she and Adam would sort through roles and missions. Tomorrow, they'd finish what they'd started tonight.

"Good night," she said softly.

"Good night, Chameleon."

Leaving the door open behind him, Adam walked through the sitting room of his own suite. With every step, his body issued a fierce, unrelenting protest. But as much as he wanted to, he wouldn't allow himself to turn around, walk back through the door and tumble Maggie down onto that soft white leather.

She needed sleep. That much was obvious from the faint shadows under her eyes. From the droop of her shoulders under the beaded silk. She needed rest. A few hours' relief from the strain of her role.

And Adam needed to keep the promise of tomorrow in proper perspective. If he could.

Halfway across the sitting room, the glint of cellophane caught his eye. He halted with one hand lifted to tug at the ends of his black tie, and surveyed the towering collection of champagne, caviar, imported biscuits and cheeses. Somehow he suspected that those damned cheeses were going to figure in his dreams tonight.

Scooping up the basket, he walked back into the adjoining suite. The thick white carpet muffled his footsteps as he approached the bedroom door.

"You'd better eat something before—"

He stopped short on the threshold, transfixed by the sight of Maggie twisted sideways, struggling with the straps of her body shield.

She'd shed the beaded gown, and she wore only the thin Kevlar corset, a lacy garter belt that held up sheer nylon stockings, and the skimpiest pair of panties Adam had ever seen. No more than a thin strip of aqua silk, they brushed the tops of her full, rounded bottom and narrowed to a thin strip between her legs. In the process, they exposed far more flesh than they covered.

When she glanced up, Adam saw that she'd removed her violet-tinted contacts. Those were Maggie's brown eyes, he saw with a rush of fierce satisfaction. That was her body that beckoned to him.

Another woman might have flushed or stammered or at least acknowledged the sudden, leaping tension of the moment. Maggie gave him a wry grin.

"Remind me to tell Field Dress what I think of this blasted contraption when we get back. It was supposedly designed for easy removal, but I'm stuck."

"So I see. Need some help?"

"Yes, I..."

She straightened, and the last Velcro fastening gave with a snicker of sound. The body shield slipped downward, exposing a half bra of aqua and lace. Maggie bit her lip.

"No, I guess I don't."

Across the broad expanse of white carpet, their eyes met. For a long moment, neither moved. Neither spoke. Then her gaze dropped to the cellophane-covered basket in his arms, and she gave a whoop of delight.

"Adam! Is that food? Real food?"

"It is."

Snatching up a robe, she threw it on. "Thank God! I'm starving! I didn't know how I was going to get any sleep with my stomach rumbling like this."

Her forehead furrowed as she crossed the room, yanking at the sash of the robe.

"I got sloppy with Denise tonight, and I know it's just because I'm tired. And hungry. What's in the basket?"

"Caviar."

"Yecch!"

"And Brie."

Her face brightened, and she reached for the bundle of goodies. "Great! I love Brie. Especially warm, when it's so soft and creamy, you can spread it on all kinds of stuff."

Adam's jaw clenched. He'd spent over a decade in service to his country. He'd done some things he might have been decorated for if they hadn't been cloaked in secrecy. Some things he might have been shot for if the wrong people had caught up with him. But handing that basket over to Maggie was the toughest act he'd ever had to perform in his personal or professional life.

"Eat up," he told her, "then get some sleep. You can't afford to get sloppy. With anyone."

"Mmm..." she mumbled, busy delving into the assorted treasures.

Tomorrow, Adam promised himself as he walked back to his suite. Tomorrow, this hard, pounding ache would ease. They'd be at the cabin. There'd be fewer people around. He could put a little distance between himself and Maggie, yet still keep her under close surveillance.

By tomorrow, he'd have himself under control.

Chapter 8

The vice-presidential party arrived at the white-painted twenties-era frame house tucked high in the Sierra Nevada late the next evening.

Too late for Maggie and Adam to finish the "discussion" they'd begun on the terrace of the Century Plaza's penthouse suite. Too late for more than a cursory look around the rustic hideaway. Too late for anything other than a quick cup of hot soup in front of a low, banked fire and a weary good-night. The trip that shouldn't have taken more than a few hours had spun out for more than twelve.

The short flight from L.A. to Sacramento had gone smoothly enough. They landed in the capital city in time for a late lunch at one of Taylor's favorite restaurants. Maggie basked in the reflection of the former governor's popularity with the restaurant staff and managed a cheerful smile when she was served a glutinous green mass in the shape of a crescent with unidentifiable objects jiggling inside it. She was still too stuffed from her late-night raid on Adam's treasure trove of goodies to give his ham and cheese on sourdough more than a passing glance.

It was only after they lifted off in the specially configured twin-engine Sikorsky helicopter for the final leg of their trip that the problems began. The pilot, a veteran of the Gulf War, countered most of the sudden up- and downdrafts over the foothills with unerring skill. But when the aircraft approached the higher peaks, the ride took on a roller-coaster character.

At one violent thrust to the right, Maggie grabbed the armrests with both hands. Behind her, Denise sucked in a quick breath. Even the redoubtable Lillian gasped.

"Feels like we've run into some convective air turbulence," Adam commented.

"We've certainly run into something," Maggie muttered.

He stretched his long legs out beside hers, unperturbed by the violent pitch and yaw of the craft. Having seen him at the controls of various aircraft a number of times, Maggie wasn't surprised at his calm. Adam could handle a stick with the best of them. He knew what to expect. She, on the other hand, was bitterly regretting even the few bites of green stuff she'd managed to swallow at lunch.

"This kind of turbulence is common when flying at low levels over mountains." He scanned the tilting horizon outside the window. "From the looks of those clouds up ahead, we're going to lose visibility soon."

"Great."

He smiled at her drawled comment. "I suspect we'll have to turn back."

Sure enough, a few moments later the pilot came back to inform her that regulations required him to return to base. He couldn't risk flying blind, with only instruments to guide him through the mountains, while ferrying a code-level VIP.

On the ground in Sacramento, they waited over an hour for the front to clear. When the weather reports grew increasingly grim, Maggie was given the choice between remaining overnight in the capital city and driving up to the cabin in a convoy of four-wheel-drive vehicles. In blessed ignorance of the state of the roads leading to Taylor Grant's mountain retreat, she chose the drive.

At first, she thoroughly enjoyed her first journey into the High Sierras. Despite the lowering clouds, the scenery consisted of spectacular displays of light and shadow. White snow and gray, misty lakes provided dramatic backdrops for dark green ponderosa pine and blue-tinted Douglas firs.

When the convoy of vehicles turned off the interstate onto a narrow two-lane state road, Maggie spied deer tracks in the snow. Chipmunks darted along the branches arching over the road and scattered showers of white on the passing vehicles. Every so often the woods thinned, and she'd catch a glimpse of an ice-covered waterfall hanging like a silvery tassel in the distance.

As they climbed to the higher elevations, however, the two-lane highway gave way to a corkscrew gravel road that twisted and turned back on itself repeatedly. Fog and swirling snow slowed their progress even more, until the four-vehicle convoy was creeping along at barely five miles per hour.

It occurred to Maggie that one of those blind curves would make an excellent spot for an ambush. With the vehicles slowed to a crawl, a sniper perched in a nearby tree would have no difficulty picking off his target. As a result, she spent most of the endless trip alternately searching the gray snowscape ahead and wondering why in hell Taylor Grant would choose such an inaccessible spot for her personal retreat.

As soon as she saw the cabin, she understood. The small white frame structure nestled on the side of a steep slope in a Christmas-card-perfect setting. Surrounded by snow-draped pines and a split-rail fence, its windows spilled golden, welcoming light into the night. The scent of a wood fire greeted Maggie as soon as she stepped out of the Land Rover. While Adam went back to help sort and unload the bags, she stood for a moment in the crisp air. The profound quiet of the night surrounded her. Deliberately she willed the knotted muscles in the back of her neck to relax.

Boots crunched the path behind her. Lillian appeared at her elbow, looking much like a pint-size snowman in a puffy down-filled coat, with a fuzzy beret pulled over her springy curls.

"Feels good to be home," she said, sniffing the air.

"Mmm..."

"Too bad it's too late for you to jog down to the lake."

"Yes, isn't it?"

Maggie was *not* looking forward to running anywhere in this thin mountain air, much less down a steep mountain path to the tiny lake she knew crouched in the valley below, then back up again. Running was bad enough at sea level. At an elevation of nine thousand feet, a jog like that would be sheer torture. She had several excuses in mind to justify a change in the vice president's routine, including a desire for long, *slow* walks with a certain special envoy.

Mindful of the agents milling around behind them, Lillian shot her a look heavy with significance.

"You'll just have to wait until morning to trek down to the lake, even though you say you never feel at home until you've seen your tree. The one with the initials."

Biting back a sigh, Maggie resigned herself to the inevitable. "I don't. If the snow doesn't obscure the path, I'll go down in the—"

"Grrr-oo-of!"

She broke off with a startled gasp as the mounded snow-bank on her left suddenly erupted. In a blur of white, a shaggy creature sprang out of the snow and planted itself in front of her. Its shaggy coat hung in thick, uncombed ropes, and only the upright stub of a tail told Maggie which end was which. The thing looked like a well-used floor mop, only this mop had to weigh at least a hundred pounds and was making very unfriendly noises.

"Radizwell! Get back, you idiot!" Lillian swatted the woolly head with her purse. "It's too late to play games tonight. Go on! Shoo!"

The creature stood its ground, growling deep in its throat at the woman garbed in its mistress's clothes.

Maggie had been briefed that the livestock kept on Taylor's small ranch included several horses, a flock of sheep that grazed the high alpine meadows in spring, and a breed of sheepdog she'd never heard of before. According to intelligence, the komondor had been introduced into Europe by the Magyars when they invaded Hungary in the ninth century. The animal was ideal for the rugged Hungarian mountains. Its huge size and thick, corded coat enabled it to withstand the harshest winter climates, and at the same time protected it from the fangs of the predators that preyed on the flocks.

Maggie could understand how the creature in front of her would intimidate a bear or a wolf or a fox. It certainly intimidated her. Unfortunately, intel had stressed that Taylor Grant never went anywhere around the ranch without this beast at her side. Maggie knew she had to win him over, and fast.

Dragging in a deep breath, she crouched down on one heel and held out a hand. "Come here, Radizwell. Come here, boy."

Another growl issued from deep under those layers of ropelike wool.

Maggie set her jaw. If she could convince a bug-eyed iguana to respond—occasionally—to her commands, she could win over this escapee from a mattress factory.

"Here, Radizwell. Come here."

A warning rumble sounded deep in its throat.

Despite the almost overpowering urge to draw her arm back, Maggie kept her hand extended. "Here, boy."

One huge paw inched forward. A black nose poked out of the shaggy layers. The creature sniffed, growled again, then edged closer.

From the corner of one eye, Maggie saw the front door open and a jacketed figure step out onto the porch. She guessed it was Hank McGowan, the caretaker. Of all the dossiers she'd studied for this mission, his had fascinated her the most. An ex-con who owed Taylor both his life and his livelihood, he'd made this isolated ranch his home.

Before Maggie could give her full attention to McGowan, however, the showdown between her and Radizwell had to be decided. One way or another.

"Come here, boy."

A cold nose nudged her palm. Understanding his confusion, she let the dog sniff her for a few moments. When he didn't amputate any of her fingers, she lifted her hand and gave his feltlike coat a cautious pat. That proved to be a mistake.

Radizwell instantly moved forward to make a closer inspection. His massive head butted into her chest with the force of a Mack truck. Maggie lost her precarious balance and toppled backward.

Adam and the caretaker arrived at the same moment from opposite directions to find her on her back in the snow, with a hundred pounds of dog straddling her body. Thankfully, its growls had given way to a low rumble as his wet nose moved over her cheeks and chin. She managed a laughing protest to cover what she knew was the dog's uncharacteristic behavior.

"Radizwell, you idiot. Get off me!"

Shaking his head in disgust, the caretaker burrowed a hand under layers of wool to find a collar.

"I penned him up when they radioed that you were on the last mile stretch. Guess I should have put a lock on the shed."

He bent forward to haul the dog back, and Maggie saw his face clearly for the first time. Although the dossier she'd studied had prepared her somewhat, his battered features shocked her nonetheless. They added grim emphasis to his checkered past.

Henry "Hank" McGowan. Forty-three. Divorced. Onetime foreman of a huge commercial sheep ranch outside Sacramento. Convicted murderer, whose death sentence had been commuted to life imprisonment by the then-governor, Taylor Grant.

His conviction had been overturned when new evidence proved he hadn't tracked down and shot the drunk who'd battered him senseless with a tire jack after an argument over a game of pool. McGowan had drifted after that, unable to find work despite his exoneration, until Taylor hired him to act as stockman and caretaker.

In his last security review, McGowan had stated flatly that he owed Taylor Grant his life. He'd give it willingly to shield the vice president from any hurt, any harm.

Right now, that consisted of hauling a hundred pounds of suspicious sheepdog off her prone body.

"For heaven's sake, lock him in the shearing shed tonight," Lillian said tartly. "You know how excited the idiot gets whenever we come home. The last time he just about stripped the paint off the porch, marking his territory for the new agents who came with Mrs. Grant.''

To Maggie's relief, the dog allowed himself to be led away before he felt compelled to mark anything for this stranger in Taylor's clothes.

"There's a pot of vegetable stew on the stove," Mc-Gowan tossed over one shoulder. "If anyone's hungry."

If anyone was hungry! At this point, even veggies simmering in a rich, hearty broth sounded good to Maggie. She grabbed the hand Adam extended and scrambled up. Dusting the snow from her bottom, she gave him a grin.

"I certainly seem to be taking more than my share of falls lately."

"So I've noticed. Do you think you can make it to the cabin upright, or shall I carry you?"

Now there was an intriguing invitation.

"I can make it," she said, regret and laughter threading her voice. "Come on, let me show you the homestead, such as it is."

The vice president's home had been featured in a five-page spread in *Western Living* magazine, but not even that glossy layout had prepared Maggie for the stunning interior. Only a woman of Taylor Grant's style and confidence could pull off this blend of rustic and antique, polished mahogany and shining oak, plank floors and scattered floral rugs.

Most of the cabin's downstairs interior walls had been demolished, leaving only an open living-dining area, a small kitchen, and the bedroom Lillian occupied. A huge stone fireplace in the living room was the focus of a collection of comfortable dude-ranch-style furniture. A magnificent Chippendale dining room table with eight chairs dominated the dining area. Interspersed throughout were bronze pieces sculpted by Taylor's deceased husband, Oriental vases filled with dried flowers, framed Western art, and the occasional mounted trophy, including a huge moose head beside the door that served as a hat rack.

While Maggie showed Adam around, using the impromptu tour as an excuse to familiarize herself with the downstairs, Lillian went upstairs to direct the placement of the luggage. Denise dragged off her gloves and conferred with the agent who'd been sent to the cabin several days ago as part of the advance team. After a thorough walk-through of the entire cabin, she joined Maggie and Adam at the stone fireplace. Politely declining a mug of the steaming stew, she gave a brief report.

"The cabin and the grounds are secure, Mrs. Grant. We've activated the command center in the barn."

According to intelligence, the Secret Service had converted the barn behind the cabin into a well-equipped bunkhouse and a high-tech command-and-control center—at a cost of several million dollars. Idly Maggie wondered whether the horses were going to enjoy the central heat and exercise room when the Secret Service finally vacated the premises.

"If you don't need me any more tonight, I'll get the team settled. Dunliff will stand the first shift."

"All right. It's been a long day. Get some rest, Denise."

"You too," the agent responded.

Although Denise kept her face carefully neutral when she wished Adam a courteous good-night, Maggie caught the quick speculative look the other woman gave him.

A few moments later, Lillian came downstairs. "You're all unpacked, Mrs. Grant."

"Thank you."

"I think I'll turn in, too. It takes me a while to reacclimate to the altitude."

"Don't you want some stew? It's delicious."

Surprisingly, it was. Maggie might have awarded the rich stew her own personal blue ribbon, if it had contained just a chunk or two of beef or lamb or even chicken.

"No, thank you."

When Lillian retired to her room, the agent on duty discreetly left Maggie and Adam alone. More or less. Hidden cameras swept the downstairs continuously, allowing the occupants only the illusion of privacy.

Upstairs, Maggie knew, was a different matter. Upstairs there were only two small rooms, each with its own bath. Upstairs, Mrs. Grant had insisted on privacy for herself and her guests. Which meant Maggie and Adam didn't have to take their assigned roles as lovers any farther than the first stair. At this moment, Maggie wasn't sure whether she was more relieved or disappointed.

This complex role they were playing had become so confused, so blurred, she'd stopped trying to sort out what was real and what wasn't. Since last night, when she'd felt Adam's arms locked around her and his naked chest beneath her splayed hands, she'd hungered for a repeat performance.

Not that she'd either experience it or allow it. The rational part of her mind told her they wouldn't, couldn't, complicate their mission further by setting a spark to the fire building between them. But when she thought of that small, private nest upstairs, her fingers itched for a match.

Not an hour later, she tiptoed across the darkened hall and ignited a flame that almost consumed them both.

The soft scratching on the wooden door to his room brought Adam instantly awake. He didn't move, didn't alter the rhythm of his breathing, but his every sense went on full alert.

The door creaked open.

"Adam? It's me. Taylor. Are you awake?"

Maggie's use of her assumed identity in this supposedly secure part of the house tripped warning alarms in every part of Adam's nervous system. He rolled over, the sheets rustling beneath him, and followed her lead.

"I'm awake."

She stepped out of the shadows and moved toward the wide double bed that took up most of the floor space. Bright moonlight streamed through the windows, illuminating the fluid lines of her body. She wore only a silky gown, and without the constraining Kevlar her breasts were lush and full. Nipples peaked from the cold pushed at the thin gown.

Adam felt his stomach muscles go washboard-stiff. Forcing himself to focus on the reason behind her unexpected visit, he rose up on one elbow. The old-fashioned hickory-rail bedstead bit into his bare back as he propped a shoulder against it.

"I couldn't sleep," she whispered, her feet gliding across the oak plank floor.

She stopped beside the bed, so near that Adam could see the tiny beads of moisture pearled on her shoulders. Her hair was spiked with water, as though she'd hurriedly passed a towel over it once or twice.

As if in answer to his unspoken question, she ran a hand through her damp waves. "I took a hot bath. To help me relax. It didn't work."

His mouth curved. "I tried a cold shower. It didn't work for me, either." He raised an arm, lifting the covers, not sure where this was going, but following her lead. "Maybe we can help each other relax."

She hesitated, shifting from one bare foot to the other. "I know we promised to take this slow and easy, to use these two weeks to get to know each other, but . . ."

"Come to bed, Taylor."

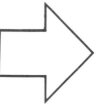

NO COST! NO OBLIGATION TO BUY!
NO PURCHASE NECESSARY!

PLAY "LUCKY 7"
AND GET FIVE FREE GIFTS!

HOW TO PLAY:

1. With a coin, carefully scratch off the silver box at the right. Then check the claim chart to see what we have for you—FREE BOOKS and a gift—ALL YOURS! ALL FREE!

2. Send back this card and you'll receive brand-new Silhouette Intimate Moments® novels. These books have a cover price of $3.99 each, but they are yours to keep absolutely free.

3. There's no catch. You're under no obligation to buy anything. We charge nothing—ZERO—for your first shipment. And you don't have to make any minimum number of purchases—not even one!

4. The fact is thousands of readers enjoy receiving books by mail from the Silhouette Reader Service™ months before they're available in stores. They like the convenience of home delivery and they love our discount prices!

5. We hope that after receiving your free books you'll want to remain a subscriber. But the choice is yours—to continue or cancel, anytime at all! So why not take us up on our invitation, with no risk of any kind. You'll be glad you did!

This beautiful porcelain box is topped with a lovely bouquet of porcelain flowers, perfect for holding rings, pins or other precious trinkets — and is yours absolutely free when you accept our no risk offer!

NOT ACTUAL SIZE

PLAY "LUCKY 7"

**Just scratch off the silver box with a coin.
Then check below to see the gifts you get.**

YES! I have scratched off the silver box. Please send me all the gifts for which I qualify. I understand I am under no obligation to purchase any books, as explained on the back and on the opposite page.

245 CIS AYLT
(U-SIL-IM-02/96)

NAME

ADDRESS   APT.

CITY   STATE   ZIP

 **WORTH FOUR FREE BOOKS PLUS A FREE PORCELAIN TRINKET BOX**

 **WORTH THREE FREE BOOKS**

 **WORTH TWO FREE BOOKS**

 WORTH ONE FREE BOOK

Offer limited to one per household and not valid to current Silhouette Intimate Moments® subscribers. All orders subject to approval.

© 1990 HARLEQUIN ENTERPRISES LIMITED   **PRINTED IN U.S.A.**

DETACH AND MAIL CARD TODAY

THE SILHOUETTE READER SERVICE™: HERE'S HOW IT WORKS

Accepting free books places you under no obligation to buy anything. You may keep the books and gift and return the shipping statement marked "cancel". If you do not cancel, about a month later we'll send you 6 additional novels, and bill you just $3.12 each plus 25¢ delivery and applicable sales tax, if any.* That's the complete price, and—compared to cover prices of $3.99 each—quite a bargain! You may cancel at any time, but if you choose to continue, every month we'll send you 6 more books, which you may either purchase at the discount price...or return at our expense and cancel your subscription.

*Terms and prices subject to change without notice. Sales tax applicable in N.Y.

"I need you to hold me, Adam. Please, just hold me for a little while."

She slid in beside him, her gown a slither of damp silk against his skin. He dragged the covers over them both.

Her body felt clammy through the gown where it touched his, which was just about everywhere. Wrapping an arm around her waist, Adam brought her closer into his heat. She burrowed against him and tucked her icy feet between his. Her head rested on his shoulder. Her mouth was only an inch from his.

They fit together as if cast from molds. Male and female. Man and woman. Adam and Maggie. Thunder and Chameleon, he amended immediately.

"I was thinking about what happened last night," she said softly, "and I started to shake."

That didn't help him much. A lot had happened last night. He didn't know if she was referring to Stoney's unexpected appearance, her near-fall, or the sharp difference of opinion they'd had over procedures. A difference that had yet to be resolved.

"I guess I experienced a delayed reaction to the fall," she murmured, her breath feathering his cheek. "It happened so fast, I didn't have time to be frightened last night. But now...now I shake every time I remember how...how..."

She shivered and pressed closer. Adam pulled the downy covers up higher around her shoulders, almost burying her head in their warmth.

"There's a bug in my room." The words were hardly more than a flutter of air against his ear. "I was so terrified, so helpless," she continued, a shade more loudly. "And then you reached for me and pulled me to safety."

The covers shook as she shuddered again.

"It's okay, Taylor. It's okay." His lips moved against her cheek. *"I thought you swept the room yourself."*

"I did. Either I missed this one, or someone planted it while I was downstairs scarfing up vegetable stew." She gave a tremulous sigh. "Oh, Adam, I could have pulled you over that railing with me. I could have killed us both."

"No way. I wasn't about to let go of either you or that stone rail. *Where did you find it?"*

"Above the bathtub." Her hand inched up to rest lightly on the bandage on his chest. "I'm so sorry you were hurt. You should have had a doctor take a look at this."

"It's only a scrape. *Where above the tub?"*

"Behind the wallpaper. When I ran hot water into the tub, steam dampened the paper. All but this one small patch. Are you sure you're all right?"

"I'm fine, darling. *Did you neutralize it?"*

"No. I didn't want to tip off whoever was listening. There's probably one in here, too." She nuzzled his neck. "I'm glad you're here, Adam. I'm glad you came with me."

"I'm glad, too. We both have too many pressures on us in Washington. *I'm sure there is."*

The knowledge that someone had planted devices in these supposedly secure rooms churned in Adam's mind, vying for precedence with the signals his skin was telegraphing to his brain at each touch of Maggie's body against his.

No one could have gotten into the cabin undetected. Despite its isolated location, the ranch bristled with the latest in security systems. Which meant that whoever had planted the bug had ready access to the grounds.

The caretaker, Hank McGowan? He certainly had access, although his loyalty and devotion to Taylor Grant supposedly went soul-deep.

Lillian Roth?

A member of the Secret Service advance team?

Denise Kowalski herself, when she'd done her walk-through of the cabin?

Which one of them, if any, was in league with the man who'd made that chilling call to Taylor? And why?

Suddenly the threat to Maggie became staggeringly immediate. Instead of narrowing, their short list of suspects had exploded. The sense of danger closing in rushed through Adam, and his arms tightened reflexively around her waist.

She took the gesture as a continuation of their roles, and snuggled into him. "Just think," she murmured. "Two weeks to learn about each other. Two weeks for each of us to discover what pleasures the other."

Her movement ground her hip against his groin. In spite of himself, Adam hardened. The dappled moonlight and soft shadows in the room blurred, merged into a swirling, red-tinted mist.

"I don't think it's going to take two weeks for us to get to know each other," he said, his voice low.

She tilted her head back to glance up at him from her nest of covers, a question in her shadowed eyes. "Why not?"

"Now that I have you in my arms, I don't think I can let you go."

He angled his body, allowing it to press hers deeper into the sheets. His hands tunneled into her still-damp hair. The muscles in his upper arms corded as he angled her face up to his.

He shouldn't do this. His mind posted a last, desperate caution. Deliberately Adam ignored the warning. Lowering his head, he covered her mouth with his. It was warm and full and made for his kiss.

After a moment of startled surprise, Maggie pushed her arms out of the enfolding covers and wrapped them around his neck, returning his kiss with a sensual explosion of passion. Her mouth opened under his, inviting, welcoming, discovering.

With an inarticulate sound, Adam plunged inside, tasting her, claiming her. Teeth and tongues and chins met. Exploration became exploitation.

Maggie couldn't be a passive player, in this or in any part of life. Her arms tightened around his neck, and she arched under him, lifting her body to his in a glory of need. She felt his rock hardness against her stomach, and a shaft of heat shot from her belly to her loins. Without conscious thought, she wiggled, rubbing her breasts against his chest. The tips stiffened to aching points. She shifted again, wanting friction. Wanting his touch.

As though he'd read her mind, Adam dragged a hand down and shaped her breast. His fingers kneaded her flesh. His thumb brushed over the taut nipple. Maggie gave a small, involuntary gasp.

"Adam!"

The breathless passion in her voice drew him back from the precipice. The very real possibility that someone else had heard her gasp his name acted on Adam like a sluice of cold water. He dragged his mouth from hers, his breath harsh and ragged. Resolve coiled like cold steel in his gut.

When he made love to Maggie, which he now intended to do as soon as he got her away from this cabin, it sure as hell wouldn't be with anyone listening or watching. There would be just the two of them, their bodies as tight with desire as they were now. But he'd be the only one to hear her groans of pleasure. No one else would see the splendor of her body. Would observe her responses to his kiss and his touch and his possession. Would watch while he drowned in the river of passion flowing in this vital woman.

He eased his lower body away from hers. "I'm sorry, Taylor."

The sound of another woman's name on Adam's lips slowly penetrated the haze of desire that heated Maggie's mind and body. Like a cold mist seeping under the door, reality crept back. It swirled around her feet and, inch by inch, worked its way along her raw, burning nerves, dousing their fires.

His body was heavy on hers. Hard and heavy. Yet when he looked down at her, she wondered who he saw—her, or Taylor Grant.

"I shouldn't have done that," he said softly. "I'm sorry. We both agreed to take this slow and easy."

Adam's withdrawal stunned Maggie...and shamed her. For the first time since joining OMEGA, she'd lost sight of her mission. In his arms, she'd forgotten her role. When it came to cool detachment in the performance of duty, she wasn't anywhere near Adam's league.

It took everything she had to slip back into Taylor's skin. "You don't have to take all the blame," she murmured throatily. "Or the credit. I was the one who asked to be held, remember?"

She pushed herself out of his arms. One bare foot hit the icy floor, and then the other.

"We've got time. Time to savor each other. Time to get to know each other." She struggled to pull herself together and grasped at the straw Lillian had offered earlier. "Why don't you come with me in the morning? We'll walk down to the lake, see the sunrise together."

"Taylor..."

"I want whatever it is that's between us to be right, Adam."

His eyes met hers. His seeming detachment was gone, and in its place was a blazing certainty that went a long way toward soothing Maggie's confused emotions.

"It's right," he growled. "Whatever it is, it's right."

Chapter 9

A distinctive aroma jerked Maggie out of a restless doze. She lifted her head, sniffing the cold air like a curious raccoon.

Bacon! Someone was cooking bacon!

She squinted at the dim light filtering through the closed shutters. Not even dawn yet, and someone was cooking bacon!

A crazy hope surged through her. Maybe Adam hadn't been able to sleep, any more than she had. Maybe he'd decided to take her up on her offer to see the sunrise, and was cooking himself breakfast while he waited for her. Maybe she could snatch a bite before the tantalizing scent lured everyone else out of bed, as well.

The thought of food, real food, galvanized Maggie into action. Throwing off the covers, she dashed into the bathroom and ran water into the old-fashioned porcelain sink. She washed quickly and, remembering Taylor's comment that she'd didn't bother with makeup in the mountains, slathered on only enough foundation needed to cover the artificial bone.

Returning to the bedroom, she tugged on a pair of thin thermal long johns. The lightweight silky fabric molded to her body like a second skin. Maggie wished she'd been issued subzero-tested undergarments like these for the hellish winter survival course OMEGA had put her through. They would have been far more comfortable for a trek over the Rockies than the bulky garments she'd had to wear.

Twisting and bending, she managed to strap the Kevlar bodysuit in place, then pulled on a white turtleneck and pleated brown flannel slacks. The palm-size derringer and spare ammunition clip Maggie had found in the bedside table fit nicely in the roomy pants pocket. Relieved to be armed again, if only with this small .22, she rummaged in the chest of drawers for an extra pair of wool socks. The thick socks warmed her toes and made the boots she found in the closet fit more comfortably.

The vice president might wear a smaller dress size, Maggie thought with a dart of satisfaction, but her feet were bigger. As ridiculous as it was, the realization that Taylor wasn't quite perfect helped restore Maggie's balance—a balance that had been badly shaken by those few moments in Adam's arms last night.

Grinning, she paused with her hand on the cut-glass doorknob. Okay, so she'd almost lost it for those breathless, endless, glorious moments. So she'd come within a hair of jumping the man's bones. So he'd been the one to pull back, not her.

It was right. He'd said it. She felt it. Whatever this was between them, it was right.

His parting words had lessened the shock of her loss of control, but they'd also kept her tossing all night. His words, and the utter conviction that she and Adam would make love. Soon. Maggie felt it in every bone in her body.

But they wouldn't do it in another woman's bed. What was more, she darn well wasn't going to be wearing another woman's skin. She wanted to hear Adam murmur *her* name in his deep, husky voice. She wanted to feel his hands in her hair. Dammit, she wanted him. Fiercely. Urgently. With a hunger that defied all logic, all caution, all concerns over their respective positions in OMEGA.

All she had to do was stay alive long enough to discover who among the various people at the cabin had planted that bug. Learn if that person was in league with a possible assassin. And track said assassin down. Then she could satisfy her hunger.

Another succulent aroma wafted through the thin wood, and Maggie twisted the doorknob. If she couldn't satisfy one hunger for a while longer, maybe, just maybe, she could satisfy another. Chasing the mouth-watering scent, she went downstairs.

A tired-eyed agent pushed himself out of an armchair beside the fire in the living room. In her rush to get to the kitchen, Maggie had forgotten all about the post-stander. No doubt the agent had heard her tiptoe across the hall to Adam's room last night. In spite of herself, heat crept up her neck. Good grief, she felt like a coed who'd been caught sneaking out of a boy's dorm room. No wonder Taylor's list of romantic liaisons had been so brief! The woman had no privacy at all. Bugs in her bathroom. Agents standing guard in her living room. Armed escorts on all her evenings out.

Summoning a smile, Maggie nodded to the man. "Good morning."

"Good morning, Mrs. Grant. You're up early."

"Yes, I wanted to catch the sunrise."

"Should be a gorgeous one." He lifted an arm to work at a kink in his neck. "The snow stopped around midnight, just after I came on shift."

"Mmm..."

Maggie was trying to think of some excuse to keep him from accompanying her into the kitchen when he supplied it himself.

"If you're going out, I'd better get suited up and let Agent Kowalski know."

"Fine."

He moved toward the front door, snagging a ski jacket from the convenient moose-antler rack. "Just buzz when you're ready to go."

Maggie hurried toward the kitchen, praying fervently that the person rattling pans on the top of the stove was Adam.

It wasn't.

Years of field experience enabled her to mask her intense disappointment when the figure at the stove turned. Resolutely Maggie ignored the thick slabs of bacon sizzling in a sea of grease and smiled a greeting.

"Good morning, Hank."

"Mornin', Taylor."

She barely kept herself from lifting a brow at his casual use of the vice president's first name. Either Mrs. Grant didn't bother any more with protocol than with makeup while in the mountains, or this was a test.

Maggie had nothing to fall back on in this moment but her instincts. And the memory of the charismatic smile Taylor had given her when she invited Maggie to call her by her first name. She guessed that the vice president didn't stand on ceremony with the man she'd rescued from death row. Nor was he likely to be intimidated by a position or a title.

In the well-lit kitchen, his rugged features appeared even more startling than they had when Maggie first glimpsed them last night. The drunk who'd wielded that tire jack had done so with a vengeance.

McGowan jerked his head toward a carafe sitting on the oak plank table that took up most of the small kitchen. "Coffee's on the warmer. Hotcakes are just about done."

He turned back to the stove, and Maggie pulled out one of the ridgepole chairs. Pouring the rich black brew into an enameled mug, she propped her elbows on the table and studied McGowan. He looked almost as formidable from the rear as he did from the front.

Brown hair, long and shaggy and obviously cut by his own hand, brushed the collar of his blue work shirt. The well-washed fabric stretched tight across wiry shoulders. Rolled-up sleeves revealed thick hair matting his forearms, one of which bore a tattoo of a snarling, upright bear. His scuffed boots had been scraped clean of all dirt, but looking at their stained surface, Maggie didn't doubt he wore them for every chore, including cleaning out the stables.

He walked over to the table and placed a heaping platter in front of her.

"Buckwheat hotcakes. Like you like them. No butter. No syrup."

"Thank you." She managed to infuse a creditable touch of enthusiasm into her tone. "They look wonderful."

"Figured your... friend might want something more substantial. Biscuits and bacon do for him?"

The hesitation was so slight, most people might have missed it, but Maggie's training as a linguist had sensitized her to the slightest nuances of speech.

"Biscuits and bacon will be fine," she replied casually.

McGowan nodded and returned to the stove. Her eyes thoughtful, Maggie forked a bite of the heavy pancake.

Did the caretaker resent Adam Ridgeway's presence in Taylor's cabin, not to mention her life? Had his supposed devotion ripened into something deeper? And darker? Had he been corrupted into planting that bug in her room, or had he done it for his own purposes? His closed face gave her no clue.

After a moment, he tossed the spatula into the sink and leaned his hips against it. Folding his arms, he raised a brow in query.

"You want the snowmobiles?"

Maggie chewed slowly to cover her sudden uncertainty. Did she want the snowmobiles? Would Taylor want them?

"You don't need them," he added on a gruff note, watching her. "I cleared the path down to the lake with the snowblower before I started breakfast. Knew you'd want to go down there first thing."

The lake. Evidently everyone was aware of Taylor's little ritual of walking down to the lake to find her tree, whatever and wherever that was.

Before Maggie could reply, the kitchen door opened. The lump of buckwheat lodged halfway down her throat.

After last night, she should have anticipated Adam's impact on her traitorous body. She should have expected her empty stomach to do a close approximation of a triple flip. Her thighs to clench under the table. Her palms to dampen. But she darn well hadn't expected her throat to close around a clump of dough and almost choke her to death. She took a hasty swallow of coffee to ease its passage.

Damn! Adam Ridgeway in black tie and tails was enough to make any woman whip around for a second, or even third, look. But Adam in well-worn jeans and a green plaid shirt that hugged his broad shoulders was something else again.

He wore the clothes with a casual familiarity that said they were old friends and not just trotted out for a weekend in the woods. He hadn't shaved, and a dark stubble shadowed his chin and cheeks. Seeing him like this, Maggie felt her mental image of this man alter subtly, like a house shifting on its foundations—until she caught the expression in his blue eyes as he returned the caretaker's look. That was vintage Thunder. Cool. Assessing. In control.

"We didn't get a chance to meet last night," he said, crossing the small kitchen. "I'm Adam Ridgeway."

A scarred hand took his. "Hank McGowan."

Their hands dropped, and the two men measured each other.

"I understand from Taylor you run the place."

A wiry shoulder lifted. "She runs it. I keep it together while she's away."

"It's a big place for one man to handle."

"A crew comes up in the spring. To help with lambing, then later with the shearing. The rest of the time, we manage." He flicked Maggie a sideways glance. "Me and the hound."

"You met him last night," Maggie interjected, although she knew Adam wouldn't need a reminder. Even if they hadn't been briefed on what to expect at the cabin, the first encounter with that strange-looking creature would have stayed in anyone's mind.

"So I did. Radizwell, isn't it?"

"Actually," she replied, dredging through her memory for details, "his registered name is Radizwell, Marioffski's Silver Stand."

McGowan's lips twisted. "Damnedest name for a sheepdog I ever heard. You going to take him down to the lake with you?"

"Of course. You know very well that I couldn't get away without him, even if I wanted to."

His battered features relaxed into what was probably meant as a smile. "True. Biscuits and bacon are on the stove, Ridgeway."

Politeness demanded that Taylor share the table with her guest while he ate. Adam, bless him, took pity on Maggie.

"I'm not hungry right now. I'll just have a cup of coffee and tuck a couple of those biscuits in my pocket for later. A walk down to the lake should help me work up an appetite."

"Suit yourself."

"You'd better take more than a couple," Maggie suggested blandly. "It's a long walk."

When the huge, shaggy sheepdog bounded through the snow toward her, Maggie saw at once that he was still suspicious of her. Her hands froze on the zipper of her hot-pink ski jacket as he circled her a few times, sniffing warily.

Before he issued any of the rumbling growls that had raised the hairs on the back of her neck last night, however, Adam dug into the pocket of his blue ski jacket and offered the dog a bacon-stuffed biscuit.

"Here, boy."

Maggie bit back her instinctive protest as she watched, and the delicacy disappeared in a single gulp. The animal, now Adam's friend for life, cavorted like an animated overgrown dust mop, then took off for the trees.

Muttering under her breath, Maggie zipped up her jacket, tugged a matching knit band over her ears and trudged after him. Adam followed her, and the ever-present Secret Service agent trailed behind.

The path to the lake was steep, snow-covered in spots, and treacherous. It pitched downward from the side of the cabin, wound around tall oaks and silver-barked poplars, then twisted through a stand of Douglas fir. On her own, Maggie would have been lost within minutes. Luckily, the komondor knew exactly where they were headed. Every so often he stopped and looked back, his massive head tilted. At least Maggie assumed it was his head. With that impenetrable, shaggy coat, he could very well have been treating her to a calculated display of doggy disdain. Or waiting for Adam to offer another biscuit as an incentive. Ha! There was no way the creature was getting any more of those biscuits, Maggie vowed.

Although cold, the air was dry and incredibly sharp. The snow, a foot or more deep along the slopes, thinned as they descended to the tiny lake set in its nest of trees. Maggie was huffing from the strenuous walk by the time they left the path to circle the shoreline. Her silky thermal undershirt stuck to her shoulder blades, and the Kevlar shield trapped a nasty little trickle of perspiration in the small of her back.

Well aware that wet clothes led to hypothermia, which could kill far more swiftly than exposure or starvation, she slowed her pace and strolled along the shore beside Adam as though they were, in fact, just out to enjoy the spectacular sight of the sun burnishing the surrounding peaks. In the process, she searched the trees ringing the lake.

Maggie had no idea which was Taylor's special tree—until a lone twisted oak on a narrow spit of land snared her gaze. Lightning had split its trunk nearly in half, but the tree had defied the elements. Alone and proud, it lifted its bare branches to the golden light now spilling over the snow-capped peaks. Sure enough, Radizwell raced out onto the narrow strip and bounded around the twisted oak. His ear-splitting barks echoed in the early-morning stillness like booming cannon fire.

"He probably thinks he's going to get another treat," Maggie muttered.

"Isn't he?"

"If you give away another one of those biscuits, that shaggy Hungarian won't be the only one howling."

He sent her an amused look. "You get a little testy when you're hungry, don't you?"

"Very!" she warned. "Remember that."

"I will," he promised, his eyes glinting.

The agent patrolled the shore while Maggie and Adam walked out onto the spit for a few moments of much-needed privacy. They had to contact headquarters. Relay the latest developments to Jaguar. Formulate a game plan for communicating in an insecure environment. None of which could be done in a house wired from rooftop to wood-plank floor.

Despite the urgency of their mission, however, the initials carved into the weathered trunk tugged at Maggie's concentration. Pulling off a glove, she traced the deep grooves.

"*T* and *H*. Taylor and Harold."

"Hal," Adam reminded her, leaning a forearm against the tree. His breath mingled with hers, soft clouds of white vapor in the sharp mountain air. "She called him Hal."

Maggie nodded. "Hal."

With the tip of one finger, she followed the smooth cut. It had been blunted a bit over the years, but had withstood the test of time.

"Did you know him?" she asked.

"I met him once, just before he died. He was a good man, and a gifted sculptor. I have a bronze of his at home."

The glint of gold on Maggie's finger caught her gaze. "They must have loved each other very much," she said softly. "The words inside this ring make me want to cry. *Now, and forever.*"

When Adam didn't reply, she squinted up at him, her eyes narrowed against the now-dazzling sunlight reflected off the lake's frozen surface.

"Don't you believe in forever?"

Unaware that she was doing so, Maggie held her breath as she waited for his answer. There was so much she didn't know about this man, she acknowledged with a stab of uncertainty. He kept his thoughts to himself. His past was shrouded in mystery. Their only contact was through OMEGA and their work together.

Only recently had she finally acknowledged how much she wanted him. Yet now, staring into eyes deepened to midnight by the dark blue of his ski jacket, she realized with shattering clarity that wanting wasn't enough. Physical gratification wouldn't begin to satisfy the need this man generated in her.

In that moment, with the sun cutting through the distant peaks and their breath entwined on the cold, clear air, Maggie knew she wanted more. She wanted the forever Taylor had never had. With this man. With Adam.

"I believe in a lot of things, Maggie, my own," he said softly, in answer to her question. "Several of which I intend to discuss with you very soon."

My own.

She liked the sound of that. A lot. Suddenly very soon couldn't come fast enough for Maggie.

"It seems as though the list of things we have to discuss with each other is getting longer by the hour," she replied, her smile answering the promise in his eyes. "Right now, though, I guess we'd better contact Jaguar."

They moved to a boulder at the end of the spit. While Maggie brushed the snow off its flat surface, Adam punched the necessary codes into the transceiver built into his watch.

To the agent on the shore behind them, it must have appeared as though they were enjoying the panoramic vista of an ice-crusted lake skirted by towering dark green firs. Shoulder to shoulder, Maggie and Adam shared the rock and waited for headquarters to acknowledge the signal. He kept his arm tucked against her body to muffle the sound of Jake's voice.

"Jaguar here. Been wondering where you were."

"I couldn't check in this morning. Chameleon discovered a hidden device in her room. We had to assume there was one in mine, as well."

Through the crystal-clear transmission, Maggie could hear the frown in Jaguar's voice. "What kind of device?"

"One that our scanners didn't pick up when we swept the rooms last night. Or someone planted while we were downstairs."

"Can you describe it?"

Maggie bent her elbows across her knees and leaned forward. Keeping her voice low, she spoke into the transmitter. "About an inch square. Wafer-thin. Blue-gray in color, made of a composite material I've never seen before. It looks like plastic, but it's a lot more porous, almost like a honeycomb."

"That doesn't fit any of the designs I know. I'll have the lab check it out."

"Tell them to dig deep. This might be the first break we've had on this mission."

A hint of excitement had crept into her voice. She'd had plenty of time to think through this unexpected turn of events during the long hours of the night . . . after she'd left Adam's bed.

"Tell the lab to talk to the Secret Service's technical division. Those guys have access to the latest materials."

"You think the Secret Service planted a bug in the vice president's bedroom without her knowledge or approval?"

"I don't know," Maggie confessed. "But if they did, the order had to come from high up in their chain."

"Like from the secretary of the treasury himself," Jaguar drawled.

"Exactly."

"Slip someone into Digicon's labs, as well," Adam instructed. "I'm willing to bet they're using this composite material in the work they're doing for NASA."

"I'd say that's a pretty good bet," Jaguar commented. "By the way, you might want to know that we've confirmed Stoney Armstrong's suspicions about First Bank."

"First Bank is laundering drug money?"

"Laundering it, dry-cleaning it, and serving it up starched and folded. It took our auditors some time, but they finally uncovered a blind account that traced back to a dummy corporation fronted by a major cartel."

"Tell them they did good work."

"They didn't do it all on their own. We got some inside information. From a source tracking it from the other end."

"Is the source reliable?"

"Ask Chameleon," Jake drawled. "She had dinner with him when he was in Washington a few weeks ago."

"Luis!" Maggie exclaimed. "*That's* where I heard about First Bank! I knew it was in connection with something other than the president's inter-monetary whatever."

Adam's black brows snapped together. The idea of Maggie having dinner with the smooth, oversexed Colonel Luis Esteban, chief of Cartozan security, didn't sit particularly well with him.

"What's Esteban's interest in First Bank?"

"His government's trying to unfreeze the assets of the drug lord Jaguar and I helped take down last year. Evidently First was holding some."

"And?"

Maggie shrugged. "Cartoza's a small country. They were getting the runaround from some bureaucrat or another. I made a few calls to one or two of my contacts and hinted at high-level government interest on our side."

"How high?"

Her eyes gleamed. "I more or less left it to their imagination."

Adam frowned. There were too many references to First Bank cropping up for simple coincidence. First, there was the president's plan for stabilizing the Latin-American economies, which the bank had helped draft. Then Stoney Armstrong. Now Maggie and her smarmy Latin colonel. There was a connection. There had to be.

"Is that team of auditors still in place?" he asked Jaguar sharply.

"I was going to pull them out today."

"Keep them there. Have them examine every transaction, every wire transfer, for the last two years. See if Digicon does any business with them."

"Roger."

"And have them look into any blind trusts that may have been set up to handle accounts for persons currently in public office."

"Like the secretary of the treasury?"

"Like the secretary of the treasury. Get back to me immediately if they turn anything up. Anything at all. There's a link here that we're missing. Something that ties it all together."

"Will do."

Adam signed off. Rising, he shoved his hands into his back pockets and frowned at the lake.

"What do you think it could be?" Maggie asked. "This link?"

"I don't know. But it's there. I'm sure of it."

She regarded him with a solemn air. "Careful, Thunder. Your sixth sense is showing."

Adam turned, and felt his heart twist.

Maggie shone through the facade of her disguise. His Maggie. Irrepressible. Irresistible. Her eyes alight with the mischievous glow that snared his soul.

Surrendering to the inevitable, he reached for her. At that moment, he didn't care who was watching. Who was listening. He had to kiss her.

"Mmm..." she murmured a few moments later. "Nice. See what happens when you let yourself go and operate solely on instinct?"

"I've been operating on instincts where you're concerned for a long time," he said dryly. "You defy all logic or rational approach."

Laughter filled her eyes. "I'll take that as a compliment."

Adam caught her chin in his hand. Tilting her face to his, he warmed himself in her vibrant glow. "It was intended as one."

"Hmm... I think this is something else we have to add to our list of topics to discuss. Soon."

"*Very* soon."

Her breath caught. "Adam..."

He would always remember that moment beside the lake and wonder what she might have said—if the distant throb of an engine hadn't snagged her attention. If the agent on the shore hadn't turned, his head cocked toward the humming sound. If the dog hadn't risen up off its haunches and swung its massive body around.

Adam lifted his head and searched the tree line.

"It sounds like a snowmobile," Maggie murmured, a frown sketching her forehead. She listened for a moment, then stiffened in his arms. "It's not coming from the direction of the cabin."

"No, it's not. Come on, let's get off this unprotected spit."

Tension, sudden and electric, arced between them. The dog picked up on it immediately, or perhaps sensed the danger on his own. He growled, deep in his throat, and pushed ahead of them onto the pebbled shore. His huge paws had just hit the snow when the first snowmobile burst out of the screen of trees.

It darted forward, a blue beetle whizzing across the snow on short skis. A second followed, then a third. The white-suited driver in the lead vehicle lifted his arm, and a burst of automatic gunfire cut the Secret Service agent down where he stood.

Maggie and Adam dived for cover. In a movement so ingrained, so instinctive, that they could have been synchronized swimmers, they rolled across the snow. On the first roll, Maggie had freed Taylor's puny little weapon from her pants pocket. On the second, Adam's far heavier and more powerful gun was blazing.

The first attacker came at them, spewing bullets and snow as he swerved to avoid the counterfire. Maggie left him to Adam and concentrated on the second, who was circling behind them. She got off one shot, and then a shaggy white shape hurtled through the air.

An agonized scream rose over the sound of gunfire and roaring engines, only to be cut off by a savage snarl.

Chapter 10

Adam saw at once that they were outgunned and outmaneuvered.

Their Secret Service escort lay writhing in the snow, blood pumping from a hit to the stomach. They couldn't reach him without running along a stretch of open, exposed shoreline. The downed man's only hope of survival was for them to keep the attackers focused on their primary target. And her only hope was escape.

Obviously Maggie reached the same conclusion at exactly the same moment. She thrust herself upward, leaving the shelter of the shallow depression her body had made in the snow.

"Cover me!"

"No! Get down! Dammit, Maggie—"

Since she was already plowing across the snow, Adam had no choice. Cursing viciously, he rose on one knee. His blue steel Heckler & Koch spit a stream of fire at a white-suited figure zigzagging through the trees on a gleaming blue snowmobile. The driver jerked, and a sudden blotch of red blossomed on his shoulder. The hit was too high, only a flesh wound, but the assailant fell back, out of range, before Adam could get another clear shot.

Cursing again, he swung around.

Radizwell had knocked the second figure sideways, out of his seat. The riderless vehicle had skidded forward for another fifty or so yards before running up a high drift at an angle and tilting over. Screaming and thrashing, the driver flailed his arms in an effort to protect his face from the dog's savage assault. Adam didn't dare risk a shot from where he knelt. The sheepdog's massive body all but covered the downed man.

The third attacker circled through the Douglas firs, spraying automatic rifle fire in wild arcs as he tried to handle both his vehicle and his weapon. Adam couldn't get a clear line of fire through the screen of trees. In frustration, he raised his arm and squeezed off a shot. An overhanging branch snapped, dumping a shower of white just as the figure passed under it. For a few precious seconds, the automatic went silent.

Those seconds were all Maggie needed. Plunging through the knee-high snow, she reached the overturned snowmobile. At that point, she had to choose between charging forward another fifty yards to retrieve the Uzi the driver had lost when Radizwell hit him and snatching at their only chance of escape. The sound of rifle fire behind her decided the matter. She couldn't hope to reach the weapon before the other two attackers cut her—or Adam—down.

Grunting with effort, she heaved the sputtering snowmobile upright. Bullets stitched a line in the snowbank just above her head as she threw herself onto the seat and grappled frantically with the controls. The vehicle jerked forward, almost tumbling her backward. She grabbed at the handles for balance, then leaned low and gunned the engine.

The few moments it took her to reach Adam would repeat themselves in her nightmares for the rest of her life. He knelt on one knee, arm extended, pistol sited at a target darting through the trees. His black hair and blue ski jacket stood out against the dazzling whiteness of the snow and made him a perfect target. He was trying to draw the attackers' fire, Maggie knew. Away from her.

At the sound of the snowmobile coming at him from an angle, Adam swung around. For a heart-stopping moment, his weapon was trained directly on Maggie. It jerked in his hand. A sharp crack split the air.

Glancing over her shoulder, she saw that the figure struggling to escape Radizwell had made it to his knees. Adam's shot sent him diving facedown in the snow for cover. The dog promptly landed on his back.

Maggie reached Adam half a heartbeat later. Throttling back on the controls, she slowed a fraction. As soon as she felt his weight hit the seat behind her, she rammed the machine into full power. His arm wrapped around her waist like an iron band, cutting off her air. She barely noticed. She hadn't drawn a full breath since the first shot. Opening the throttle all the way, she aimed for the tree line.

The chase that followed could have come right out of a movie. A horror movie. Using every evasive tactic she'd been taught, and a few she invented along the way, Maggie dodged under low-hanging boughs, swerved around granite outcroppings and sailed over snowbanks. At one point, she took a turn too close. Prickly pine needles lashed her face, momentarily blinding her. The snowmobile swerved, tilted, righted itself.

"There!" Adam shouted in her ear, pointing over her shoulder.

She squinted through the involuntary tears caused by the sting of the needles. Following the line of his arm, she saw a wall of serrated granite slabs thrusting out of the snow to their left. To her blurred eyes, the gray-blue mass looked impenetrable.

"Take it hard and fast! Right through the notch!"

"What notch? I can't see!"

He twisted on the seat behind her, shoving his weapon into his jacket. Then he reached forward, an arm on either side of her, and took the controls. Maggie felt a craven urge to close her streaming eyes completely as the sheet of granite loomed in front of their hurtling vehicle.

Just when it seemed they were about to hit the wall, Adam threw his weight to one side and took her with him. The vehicle tilted at an impossible angle. Its left ski lifted, scraped stone. The engine revved louder and louder as the right ski dug into the snow. The vehicle hung suspended for what seemed like two or three lifetimes, then shot through the narrow opening.

Maggie would have shouted in joyous relief, if her blurred vision hadn't cleared just enough to see what lay on the other side of the wall. A ravine. A big ravine. About the size of the Grand Canyon. At its widest point.

Adam's hands froze on the controls for half an instant, then twisted violently. The engine screamed into full power.

"Hang on!"

As if she had any choice!

Maggie didn't hesitate at all this time. She scrunched her eyes shut and didn't open them until a bone-jarring jolt told her they'd landed on the far side. When she saw the steep, tree-covered slope ahead, she was sorry she'd opened them at all.

Branches slashed at their faces, tore at their bodies, as they whipped down the incline in a series of snaking turns.

Her heart jackhammered against her ribs with each zig. Her kidneys slammed sideways on every zag. All the while she strained to hear behind her, listening for sounds of pursuit over the scream of their engine and the roar of her blood in her ears.

At the bottom of the slope, Adam yanked on the controls and slewed the machine to a halt. He shoved himself off, backward, and immediately sank to his knees in the snow.

"You take it from here."

"No way!"

"Get moving."

"No!"

Above his whiskered chin and cold-reddened cheeks, Adam's eyes flashed icy blue fire. "That's an order, Chameleon. Move!"

"I'm the field agent on this mission. I'm not dividing my forces, or what little firepower I have!"

"Dammit—"

"I'm not leaving you. Get on the vehicle!"

Every second wasted in argument could be their last. She knew it. He knew it.

His jaw working, Adam threw a leg over the rear of the snowmobile.

They finally slowed to a stop at the crest of a wooded rise. Maggie kept the snowmobile idling, afraid to shut it off completely, in case they had to make a quick getaway. Eyes narrowed against the sun's glare, bodies tense, they listened and searched the woods below for signs of pursuit. Maggie was the first to pick up the rise and fall of engines in the distance.

"There's at least . . . two of them," she panted. "Maybe three . . . if . . . Radizwell didn't have the S.O.B. for lunch."

Adam angled his head, listening intently. "They're following the ravine. Looking for a place to cross."

He shoved back his sleeve. The flat gold watch nestled among the dark hairs of his wrist glinted in the morning sun.

"Jaguar, this is Thunder. Do you read me?"

Their breath puffed out in white clouds, rapid and ragged, while they waited for a response.

"I read you. Go ahead, Thunder."

"We've run into a little unfriendly fire. How close is the backup team?"

"Twenty minutes by helicopter," Jake snapped instantly. "Give me your coordinates."

Anticipating the need, Adam had already dug a small rectangular case out of his pocket. Not much bigger than a package of chewing gum, the digital compass received signals from the Navstar Global Positioning System. Navstar had proved its capabilities during the Gulf War by guiding tank commanders across the vast, featureless Saudi deserts. Its current constellation of twenty-four orbiting satellites could pinpoint time to within one-millionth of a second, velocity to within a fraction of a mile per hour, and location to within a few feet.

"Latitude, three-nine degrees, six—"

He broke off as the distant sounds died. Maggie inched the throttles back as far as she dared to quiet the noise of their own engine and concentrated all her energies on listening.

"Six minutes," Adam continued. "Longitude, one-two-oh degrees—"

A sudden burst of horsepower cut him off once more. He stiffened, the tendons in his neck standing out like cords as he swiveled in the direction of the sounds.

"They got across!"

Engines revved. Grew louder.

"They're coming straight at us!" he snarled. "How the hell did they double back and find our tracks so quickly?"

Maggie turned a startled face to his, as stunned as he. Then her eyes dropped to the gold watch.

"Maybe they didn't find our tracks! Maybe they're homing in on the satellite signal!"

Adam didn't waste time in further speculation. The satellite signals were supposed to be secure. Scrambled. They'd never been broken or intercepted before. But an individual who knew how to bypass the sophisticated electronic filters in the White House switchboard might well have broken into a supposedly secure satellite system.

"Six-one, Jaguar! Six-one!"

With that emergency signal telling Jake to stand by until further contact, Adam abruptly terminated the transmission.

They managed to shake their pursuers once again.

The sounds of the distant motors fell away as Maggie steered an erratic course, up one slope, down another. Dodging fallen trees and low-hanging branches, she headed for a line of low, ragged peaks to her right. From the angle of the sun, she calculated they were headed due east, away from the cabin. Given the topography, however, she couldn't circle back. She had to follow where the mountains led.

Her face was stinging with cold and her numbed fingers were locked on the throttles when the machine under her began to sputter and miss. Maggie glanced down at the dash, trying to find the fuel gauge. She tore one gloved hand loose and rubbed it across the snow-covered indicator. Sure enough, the red bar danced at the bottom of the frost-encrusted gauge, almost out of sight.

Not two minutes later, the engine died. The snowmobile skidded a few feet farther up the slope, slowed to a crawl, stopped, then began a backward slide. Adam dug his boots in and brought them to a halt.

For a few seconds, neither of them moved. They remained silent. Listening. Searching the trees behind them.

Somewhere below them, their attackers were equally silent. Listening. Searching the trees above them.

"They're waiting," Adam said, his voice low. "For us to signal again."

"Bastards."

"They won't have used as much fuel as we did riding double. They'll catch us easily."

"Who?" Maggie muttered angrily. Her mission had just exploded in her face, and she was furious with herself for not having anticipated it. "Who are 'they'? How did we go from a narrow list of suspects to a whole damned strike team?"

"Whoever knew you were going to be at the lake this morning," Adam tossed back.

From the rigid set to his jaw, Maggie saw that he was no happier about this unexpected turn of events than she.

"Everyone knew," she snapped. "It was some kind of a ritual with Taylor."

"And if they didn't know, we told them," Adam added, disgust lacing his voice. "Last night, in my bedroom."

Maggie struggled to rein in her anger. "We're no longer dealing with a lone assassin here. This individual has a whole organization behind him. Obviously we need to reassess our mission parameters."

"Obviously." Adam pushed himself off the snowmobile and drew in a steadying breath. "Right now, though, our first priority has to be cover. If they don't pick us up soon, they'll call in air support and continue the search from the air."

"Denise and her people will have heard the shots and found their downed man by now. They'll be searching, too—assuming one of them wasn't behind the attack in the first place," Maggie finished heavily.

"I don't think we can assume anything at this point. I suggest we burrow in until dark. The chances of them picking us up at night after we signal Jaguar will be slimmer. Marginally slimmer, admittedly, but slimmer."

Nodding, she clambered off the snowmobile and surveyed the now-useless vehicle.

"I guess we'd better see what we can salvage from this hummer."

While Adam used the butt of his pistol to break off pieces of one of the small mirrors mounted on the handles, Maggie pried open the storage compartment. Inside, she found a pitiful cache of survival equipment—one metallic solar blanket, so thin it folded into a plastic pouch the size of a candy bar, a small tool kit, and a spare pair of goggles. Evidently their attackers hadn't planned on a prolonged stay in the wilderness.

Adam knelt on one knee to bundle their small cache of equipment in a piece of fender he'd broken off. "You'd better take that off," he said, nodding to indicate her bright pink jacket. "I'll wrap it up with the rest of this gear."

Maggie didn't need to be told that the vivid color made too visible a target. Her shiver when she tugged off the thick layer of down wasn't due to the chill air.

Adam removed his own jacket, as well, but didn't offer it to her out of any misguided sense of male gallantry. He knew as well as she that the exertion of walking through the snow would work up a sweat, which had to be allowed to evaporate, or it would freeze their clothes to their bodies.

They left the vehicle buried under a nest of branches. As she trudged up the slope, trailing a screen of branches to cover their tracks, Maggie repeated to herself over and over the principle her instructors had drilled into her during survival training. Stay dry. In the jungle. In the Arctic. Stay dry. Foot rot from wet boots while slogging through swamps was as dangerous as frostbite from sweat-dampened undergarments in cold climates.

With that in mind, she tugged the hem of her turtleneck out of her waistband to let air circulate. Adam did the same with his plaid flannel shirt. Maggie saw that he wore the same style of high-tech long johns she did—under his shirt, at least. She didn't see how anything would fit under those snug jeans.

As they neared the crest, the trees thinned, as did the snow. Bare, windswept slabs of granite made the going easier, but also made Maggie feel far too vulnerable. The skin between her shoulder blades just above the bulletproof corset itched as though a big round circle had been painted on it.

Once over the top of the ridge, they scouted for a spot that would protect them from both the elements and searching eyes while they decided on their game plan.

"There," she panted, out of breath from the steep climb. "Under that tree."

The conifer she pointed to was at least sixty feet tall and shaped much like a pointed stake. Its branches grew wide at the bottom to catch the sun and narrowed dramatically toward the top. Laden with snow, the lower limbs drooped to the ground. They'd provide both concealment and natural insulation.

Maggie and Adam scrambled down the slope, brushing away their tracks as best they could. Squatting, he peered under the sagging branches.

"Perfect. I'll tunnel us in. You gather some branches."

She smiled wryly at his ingrained habit of assuming command, but decided not to take issue with it. In this instance, it didn't matter who dug and who gathered, as long as the tasks got done, and fast. Besides, she didn't have enough breath right now to argue.

Using the fender from the snowmobile, Adam knelt on one knee and set to work scooping a shallow trench in the snow under the drooping limbs. He worked quickly, but took great care not to disturb the thick layer of white coating the branches.

When Maggie came back with the first armload of pine branches, she stopped abruptly a few feet away. Adam had shed his plaid shirt to keep it dry. His thermal undershirt showed damp patches, attesting to the strenuous effort physical labor required at this elevation. It also attested to his superb physical condition. The silky white fabric clung to his body with a loving attention to detail that made Maggie's mouth go dry.

His upper torso might have been sculpted by Michelangelo. Broad and well toned at the shoulders, narrow and lean at the waist, he was basic, elemental male. When he bent forward, his jeans rode low on narrow hips. A curl of dark hair at the small of his back drew Maggie's fascinated gaze. With each scoop, his muscles rippled with a primitive, utterly beautiful poetry.

At the sight, something wrenched inside her, and she knew she'd never view Adam the same way again. The image of the cool aristocrat that she'd carried for so long in her mind and her heart shattered.

"Want me to dig the rest?" she asked, dumping the prickly pine branches beside the entrance.

"No, I'm all right. We'll need more branches to line the interior walls, though."

She nodded, stooping to check his progress. "Better not make the opening too narrow," she advised him with a wry smile. "As Lillian is so fond of pointing out, I'm not quite a perfect size eight."

Adam rested an arm on the bent fender and watched her retrace her footsteps in the snow. A tantalizing snatch of conversation he'd overheard between her and Lillian the night of the Kennedy Center benefit came back to him. Maggie had protested then that she wasn't a perfect anything, and he'd silently agreed. He hadn't changed his opinion. If anything, the past few days had reinforced it.

Fiercely independent didn't begin to describe this woman. Her adamant refusal to follow his orders today came as close to insubordination as he'd ever allowed an OMEGA operative. Only her acid reminder that she was the field commander on this mission had stopped him from shredding her to pieces on the spot. That, and the fact that Maggie Sinclair wasn't particularly shreddable.

But Adam knew he'd never erase from his mind his stunned fury when she'd sprung up out of the snow and dashed for the snowmobile. Or his sudden, swamping fear. He'd expected a bullet to slam into her body at any second. To see her thrown back by the force of a hit. He'd kept his mind focused and his hand steady as he provided covering fire, but a silent litany had reverberated through him with every step she took.

No more talk.

No more waiting.

No more denying the raw need that gripped him. And her.

That same refrain echoed in his mind now as he bent to scoop fenderful after fenderful of snow out of the shallow trench.

No more talk.

No more waiting.

If they lived through this day, neither of them would ever be the same. Soon had become now.

While he dug, Maggie rounded up enough pine branches to construct a thick, springy mat that would keep them off the snow. More feathery branches provided insulation for the walls Adam built up around the depression. Above these walls the sagging tree limbs formed a natural sloping ceiling.

Within a remarkably short time, their hidden lair was complete. While Adam crawled inside to spread the light-weight solar blanket over the springy mat, Maggie gathered their meager gear.

She handed him the items one by one, still panting a little from her foraging trips. Pine needles stuck to her white turtleneck, which in turn stuck to her back and shoulders.

Adam got to his feet and dusted the snow from his knees, frowning as he took in the damp hair curling around her face.

"You crawl inside. I'll brush the rest of the tracks and seal the entrance."

Maggie nodded and dropped to her knees.

"Strip off as much as you can. I'll help you with the body shield when I'm done here, so you can get out of those damp long johns."

She paused halfway through the narrow tunnel. Bottom wiggling, she backed out again.

"Let's just review the situation here. We're in the middle of nowhere. Two, possibly three stalkers are searching for us as we speak. We don't know who sent them, we can't contact headquarters for help, and we have no idea at this moment how long we're going to be stranded here."

"That about sums it up."

"Not quite."

She eyed his chest, which was damp from exertion. Her fingers dug into her thighs with the need to stroke its broad planes. Dry them. Curl into their warmth.

Lifting her gaze to his face, she grinned. It wasn't much of a grin, more a grimace than an expression of mirth, but it was the best Maggie could do at the moment.

"If we crawl into that hole and get naked together, I'm not going to be held responsible for my actions."

He smiled at her then. Not the smooth, easy smile he'd given "Taylor" the past few days. Not the cool half smile he allowed himself on occasion at OMEGA headquarters. This was a slow, satisfied, devastatingly predatory twist of his lips.

"Maggie, my darling, when we get naked together, responsibility is the last thing I want from you."

At her start of surprise, his smile lost its razor's edge. "Go on, get inside. You know as well as I do that the next few minutes could make the difference between life and death."

Chapter 11

Mind racing, heart pumping, Maggie crawled through the narrow tunnel.

Okay. All right. It was a matter of survival. Hers and his. They had to strip off. They had to stay dry. In the Arctic. In the jungle.

She was a professional. She'd been trained for situations like this. It was a matter of survival.

Yet when she entered the chamber Adam had carved for them under the spreading boughs of the majestic fir, her chaotic thoughts centered on a different kind of survival. The kind that had to do with the continuation of the species.

Her blood rushed through her veins, bringing with it a heat that added to the moisture dewing her neck. Breathing hard, she made herself sit back on her heels. While she waited for her pulse to slow, she admired the fruits of their labors.

Both the size and the warmth of this subterranean nest surprised her. The tree's massive trunk formed a solid, rounded back wall. Mounded snow defined the rest of the area. Overhead, drooping, snow-laden branches slanted down at an angle from the base of the tree to the outer walls. The fragrant pine boughs Maggie had gathered lined the interior walls and made a thick mat for the floor, adding an extra layer of insulation.

Amazing. They'd constructed a tight, neat lean-to using nature's own materials, with no tools or modern implements except a fiberglass fender scoop. Adam had spread the thin Mylar blanket over the mat, but Maggie knew they could have survived without it.

Survival.

The pulse that had slowed a fraction leaped into action again.

It was a matter of survival.

And, as Adam had said, the next few minutes could make the difference between life and death.

Settling cross-legged on the shifting mat, she pulled off her gloves. Carefully she placed her weapon atop her folded pink ski jacket to keep it both dry and close at hand, then went to work on her bootlaces. Within moments, her brown pants hung from one of the overhead branches. She was just reaching for the hem of her white turtleneck when Adam backed into the chamber.

Suddenly the pine-scented nest didn't seem nearly as spacious as it had a moment ago.

Maggie edged over to make room for him. The springy mat shifted under her and tipped her sideways. Her elbow dug into his thigh. His shoulder thumped her chest. It took a bit of doing, but they finally maneuvered themselves back into sitting positions. He laid his weapon next to hers and glanced around the interior. A half smile curved his lips as he surveyed his work.

"The hole seemed a lot bigger when I was digging it. It's kind of tight in here."

"At least it'll be warm."

He nodded, eyeing the mounded walls. "When the snow sets, this cave will be as well insulated as any house. Better than most."

Maggie believed him. She already felt the extra heat his presence generated in the small chamber. He'd brought a musky warmth into the dim interior, which combined with hers to drive off the chill. The trapped air warmed perceptibly around them while he unlaced his boots. And when his hand went to the zipper of his jeans, Maggie could have sworn the temperature shot up another dozen degrees or so.

It was a matter of survival. It was...

Hastily she dragged her turtleneck over her head.

Matter-of-factly he shoved the well-worn denim down over his hips. He rose up on one knee to drape his pants over the limb beside her top.

To Maggie's intense relief and equally intense disappointment, he did wear high-tech long johns under those snug jeans. But where her bottoms covered her from waist to ankle, his came only to midthigh, like running or biking shorts. They might have been meant for his warmth, but they contributed greatly to hers.

If his upper torso had been sculpted by Michelangelo, his lower body was by the same unknown Greek artist who'd created the statue of Hercules she'd once seen in a museum in Athens. All long lines and corded sinews. Sleek. Powerful. Well muscled. And bulging in places that sent a shaft of heat spearing straight through Maggie.

"Are your socks wet?"

She dragged her gaze up to his face. "My socks?"

"Your socks. Are they wet?"

"No."

"Good. You'd better keep them on, along with the thermal underwear. But the body shield needs to come off. Bend over."

Maggie bit her lip.

"You're damp under the Kevlar. You need to dry off. It's a matter of—"

"I know. A matter of survival."

Pushing herself to her knees, she twisted to one side. The rasp of Velcro echoed through the nest. Once. Twice. When the corset fell away, she felt strangely naked. Without the constraining shield, her breasts regained their fuller, firmer shape. Beneath the thin covering of her undershirt, her nipples puckered with the cold. Or the heat. At this point, she couldn't have said which.

The damp, silky underwear molded to every line of her chest as faithfully as it did to Adam's. Maggie felt an instinctive urge, as old as woman herself, to hunch her shoulders and hide herself.

Immediately, another, even older urge flowed through her. The need to claim her man. Her mate. Her forever.

They might have only this hour together. Only these few moments. Yet Maggie knew they would last her a lifetime. Slowly she straightened her shoulders. Sitting back on her heels, she met Adam's eyes. The blue fire in them ignited the flames licking at her blood.

His gaze drifted from her face to her throat. Her breasts. Her stomach. Involuntarily her thighs clenched.

A muscle ticked in the side of his jaw, shadowed with the night's growth.

"Do you have any idea how beautiful you are?"

A momentary doubt shivered through her as she remembered the artificial bone that shaped her nose and chin. The violet contacts. The auburn hair. Who did he see? Who did he find beautiful? She had to know.

"Who, Adam? Me, or Taylor? Who do you see?"

In answer, he smiled and lifted a hand to curve her cheek. "I see you, Maggie. A woman of incredible courage and vibrant, glowing life."

That pretty well satisfied her doubts, but she had no objection when Adam expanded a bit.

"I see the same woman who sailed out of my office swathed from head to foot in a black nun's habit. I see the high-class hooker who took off for France in a slithery shoestring halter that kept me awake for a solid week."

She tilted her head into his hand. "A week, huh?"

"At least."

"Who else? Who else do you see?"

His thumb brushed her lower lip. "I see the woman who infuriates me on occasion, and intrigues me at all times. Who makes me want to lock my office door and throw her down on that damned conference table she always perches on."

Maggie's brows shot up. "Really?"

"Really."

"Hmm..."

The idea that he'd harbored a few fantasies about her thrilled Maggie to her core. Almost as much as the thumb rubbing across her lip. Incredible, what a single touch could do.

"Adam?"

"Yes?"

"Do you have any idea how many times I've imagined...us? Together? Alone?"

His hand curled around the back of her neck, urging her closer. Branches shifted. Mylar crinkled. They were chest to chest. Mouth to mouth.

"No. Tell me."

"A few."

"Only a few?" He kissed her right eyelid.

"Okay, more than a few. A dozen."

"Only a dozen?" He kissed her left eyelid.

She smiled up at him. "A hundred or two."

"And?"

"And never, ever, in any one of those thousands of times, did I picture us making love underground. In a nest of pine needles. Fully clothed. Well, one of us fully clothed."

"Maggie, my darling, I've pictured us underground and aboveground and on the ground."

Laughter welled inside her. "All that was going on behind your Mr. In Control, always-so-cool exterior?"

"All that, and more."

"Well, well . . ."

He kissed her mouth then, and brought her down with him. Legs entangled, she sprawled across his chest. Hungrily she explored his mouth with her tongue and teeth. His unshaven chin rasped against hers. The tiny, stinging sensation sent a rush of liquid warmth to Maggie's belly. Her hand slithered down his chest, and she discovered that clothes were no impediment to a determined woman. He filled her fist, rock-hard, ridged, sheathed in satiny softness.

His hand tugged up the hem of her shirt and found her breast. It swelled in his hold, the nipple throbbing with an ache that matched the one between her legs. An ache that grew with every kiss, every thrust of his thigh between hers.

Time and space dissolved. Merged. Melted into two bodies and one need. When she couldn't bear their separateness any longer, she lifted slightly and arched her pelvis against his hardness.

His hands stilled her hips. "Wait, Maggie. Wait."

"No. No more waiting."

"Not this way."

"Why not?"

His eyes glinted with regret. "Because, sweetheart, even my vivid fantasies didn't include making love to you in the snow beside a frozen lake. I didn't bring any protection when I walked out to view the sunrise with you."

Nonplussed, Maggie stared at him helplessly.

With a surge of his powerful body, he rolled her over. "Let me love you in a way that's safe. In a way that will still give us pleasure."

His hand found the convenient opening in the bottoms of her long johns. The wayward thought shot through Maggie that the manufacturers of winter survival wear knew what they were doing. A person didn't have to undress to perform any vital function. And taking Adam into her body was becoming more vital by the second.

He slid a finger inside her welcoming wetness, then another. His thumb pressed the hard core at her center. Gasping, she arched under him.

The scent of crushed pine needles, sharp and pungent, rose around her. Maggie knew she would never again walk through a forest or touch a Christmas wreath or open a bottle of kitchen cleaner without thinking of this man and this moment. Then his mouth came down on hers, and Maggie forgot about kitchen cleaners and walks and everything else.

Their breathing grew more labored. Their bodies hardened. As his hands and his mouth worked their magic, wave after wave of sensation washed through Maggie, drawing her closer to the edge.

With infinite skill, he primed her.

With infinite need, she caught his face between her hands. Panting, breathless, she could only gasp her desperate desire.

"Adam. Listen to me. We're in the middle of nowhere. On our own. We may never make it out of here alive. This could be the only moment we ever have."

"Maggie . . ."

"This could be our once. Our forever. I don't want protection. Not from you. I want you."

They fit together the way she'd always known they would. Female and male. Woman and man. Maggie and Adam.

He rose up and thrust into her. She lifted her hips and thrust against him.

He filled her, full and powerful and hard and urgent. She took him into her, wrapping her body and heart and soul around him.

Mylar twisted around their legs. Branches poked at backs and knees and elbows and bottoms. Maggie didn't feel any of it. Her entire being was focused on Adam.

When he reached down between their bodies and rubbed her tight, aching core, she climaxed in an explosion of white light and red, searing pleasure. She arched under him, groaning, flexing her muscles in an instinctive need to take him with her.

The violent movement dislodged a clump of snow from the branch overhead. It landed on Adam's shoulder, slid down to Maggie's chest.

Her eyes opened in shock, and she laughed.

Adam groaned at the sound and surged into her a final time.

Afterward, long afterward, they exchanged the clothes that clung to their slick bodies for the dry ones hanging over their heads. With a rustle of boughs, Adam propped his back against the tree trunk, stretched out his legs and brought Maggie into his lap. She laid her head against his shoulder, sighing.

"How much time do we have?"

Adam smiled at the reluctant question. He wasn't in any more of a hurry than Maggie to leave this small den. Resting his chin on the top of her head, he drew her closer into his warmth. The scaly bark of the tree trunk bit into his back through the flannel shirt, but he barely noticed. With one hand, he reached out to check his gold watch.

"It's not even ten. We have a long time to wait before we contact Jaguar and call in an extraction team."

She shifted a little. "Let's talk about that."

"What is there to talk about? As soon as the sun goes down, we go up on the net. We evade any searchers until the team arrives. They can have you—can have us out in fifteen minutes."

Adam cursed his slip, and Maggie didn't miss it. She twisted around in his arms.

"You're not going, are you?"

"No."

"Neither am I."

"The hell you're not."

One wine-colored brow arched, and Adam moderated his tone. "As you said yourself, our mission parameters have changed. Drastically. We're not trying to lure a lone assassin out in the open any longer. We're facing a strike team."

"And I'm their target."

Her words triggered a staggering suspicion in Adam. With great effort, he kept his face impassive. Before he said anything to Maggie, he needed to think this through.

She mistook his sudden silence for disagreement. Pushing herself out of his arms, she got to her knees. "I'm the only one who can bring them into the open, Adam. I'm the only one who can—"

A long, rolling growl filled the air, cutting Maggie off in midsentence. She clamped a hand across her stomach.

"Good grief. Sorry 'bout that."

Adam forced a smile. "Sounds like the natives are getting restless."

She sent him a sheepish grin. "Well, hungry, anyway."

Deliberately Adam decided to take advantage of the diversion her growling stomach offered. They had a few more hours. He needed the time to think. To absorb the gut-wrenching implications of her blithe comment. Maggie was right. He knew it with a cold, chilling certainty. She was the bait. She was the one they were after. Not Taylor Grant. Her.

Whoever had targeted the vice president could have hit without warning. Yet the assassin had signaled his intent with that anonymous phone call. He'd issued a threat he must have known would activate an elaborate screen of defenses.

Somehow, some way, that call had led to the attack on Maggie. Not Taylor. Maggie.

Adam didn't know why or who or how, and at this moment he didn't care. His only concern was to keep Maggie alive until they could unravel this increasingly bizarre situation.

They had a few more hours. A few precious hours. He needed to think.

"Maybe it's time to break out the emergency rations," he suggested evenly.

"Rations?" She swept their small pile of supplies with a quick glance. "What rations?"

He reached for his blue ski jacket.

"Adam!" She scrambled up on her knees, her face alight. "I forgot all about your stash of biscuits! And bacon!"

He fished around in the deep pocket, then withdrew his hand and flipped the jacket over to reach the other.

The eager anticipation in her eyes gave way to a look of comic dismay. "Oh, God, I hope they didn't fall out of your pocket when we did that wheelie through the pass. We were standing on our heads."

"No, here they are."

He drew out a napkin-wrapped bundle, and Maggie scuttled closer while he unwrapped the edges of the cloth. When the treasure was uncovered, it turned out to be little more than a handful of crumbled dough and bits of bacon, gray with cold, congealed grease.

The unappetizing sight didn't deter Maggie at all. She pinched a bite between thumb and forefinger and popped it into her mouth. Closing her eyes, she savored the tiny morsel.

He had to smile at her beatific expression. "Good?"

"Mmm...wonderful!"

Eyes closed, head back, she wiped her tongue around her lips in search of stray crumbs.

Adam's fist clenched on the napkin. Their small nest wasn't quite a penthouse suite, and the pile of crumbs in his hand hadn't come from a beribboned basket of imported delicacies. Yet the same primitive urge that had swept him in L.A. crashed through him once again. Now, as then, he wanted to feed her. Bit by bit. Bite by bite.

But here, in this tiny snow cave, with danger all around them, the swamping, driving urge intensified a hundredfold. Subtly, swiftly, it shifted from erotic to primordial.

It was a matter of survival. Of responding to the basic instincts that drove all species. This woman was his mate. Adam wanted to feed her, and protect her, and love her. The realization that he might be able to accomplish only two out of the three made his stomach twist. That, and the knowledge that Maggie didn't want protection.

Of any sort.

His gaze roamed her upturned face, and Adam knew he'd love her differently if she did. He'd still want her with a need so raw it consumed him. He'd still lose himself in her laughing eyes. Without the fierce independence that made her Maggie, however, he'd love her with a different need.

Somehow he suspected that need wouldn't be anywhere near as powerful as the one that drove him now.

Uncurling his fingers, he found a fair-size sliver of cold bacon.

"Open your mouth."

Her eyes opened instead.

She glanced from his face to the morsel in his fingers, then back to his face.

"Aren't you going to have any?"

"No."

"You didn't have any breakfast. Aren't you hungry?"

"Yes. Very. But not for bacon. Let's feed you, and then we'll feed me."

The small stash of food and their clothes disappeared at approximately the same time.

With the passing hours, the light filtering through the snow-laden branches overhead grew brighter, then gradually dimmed.

They took turns dozing, and risked one trip outside the cave for a quick surveillance and an even quicker trip behind some bushes. After the warmth of the air trapped in the small cave, the outside seemed twice as cold. Maggie eyed the shadows drifting across the slopes as the sun played hide-

and-seek among the tall peaks. They'd have to leave their small nest soon.

Her teeth were chattering by the time they'd blocked the entrance up again. She sat cross-legged on the Mylar mat and tucked her hands into her armpits to warm her fingertips.

"What time is it?"

Adam shoved back his sleeve. "Almost four. It should be dark in an hour."

"We'll have to leave then."

"We will."

She was silent for a moment, marshaling her thoughts. The muted growl that filled the small cavern took them both by surprise.

Maggie's red brows snapped together as she frowned down at her stomach.

"We cleaned out our entire supply of emergency rations," Adam reminded her. "You'll have to wait until we get back to—"

Another low growl rumbled through the air.

Maggie shook her head. "It's not me this time," she whispered.

Nodding, Adam reached for his pistol.

Maggie had hers in hand, as well, when they heard the scratching in the snow at the entrance to the tunnel.

Adam's jaw hardened. "Get dressed," he hissed. "Fast. Put on as many layers as you can."

As quickly and quietly as possible, Maggie scrambled into her clothes. Not for warmth. If a wild animal was digging at the entrance to their lair, she'd need the layers for protection against fangs and claws. And if the predator was of the two-legged variety, she didn't want to face him in her underwear.

Zipping her jacket up to her chin, she handed Adam his. While he pulled it on, she kept her pistol leveled at the entrance. Automatically they positioned themselves at either side of the tunnel entrance, out of the line of fire.

Another low, hair-raising growl convinced her their uninvited guest was close to gaining entry. Her finger tightened on the trigger.

The snow shifted. A black nose poked through the white. Sniffed. Pushed farther. More snow crumbled, and a muzzle covered in thick ropes of snowy fur appeared.

Radizwell!

Maggie sagged against the wall in relief, but had the presence of mind not to speak. The animal might not be alone out there. He might well have led a strike team right to them. Or a rescue team.

When he finally gained entrance, they discovered he hadn't led anyone to them at all. Apparently he'd come in search of Adam. And more bacon. The reproachful look the dog turned on Maggie when he discovered the empty, grease-stained napkin filled her with instant guilt.

Chapter 12

With the komondor's arrival, the air in the small cave became suffocatingly warm and decidedly aromatic. Crushed pine needles couldn't begin to compete with the aroma drifting from his ropes of uncombed fur, or his doggy breath. Nor could Maggie or Adam move without crawling over or under or around the animal.

She nodded when Adam suggested that the dog's arrival necessitated a change in plans. With less than an hour of daylight left, they couldn't take the chance that someone might pick up the dog's tracks and follow them here. They should scout out a better defensive position until they could call in the extraction team.

Maggie crawled out of the snow cave with mixed emotions. As much as she hated to leave their private nest, she needed air. Adam followed a moment later. Keeping to the shelter of the towering conifer, they breathed in the sharp, clean scent of snow and pines. Radizwell hunkered down on Adam's other side, pointedly ignoring her. Maggie suspected that he still hadn't quite accepted this stranger in Taylor's clothes. Or forgiven her for the empty, bacon-scented napkin.

They stood still and silent for long moments, searching the slopes above and below. Nothing moved. No sounds disturbed the quiet except the distant, raucous call of a hawk wheeling overhead and Radizwell's steady panting. The sun slowly slipped toward the high peaks, deepening the shadows cast by the towering trees and bathing the snow in a soft purple light.

"We'll have to head farther east," Adam murmured after a few moments. "Just in case they picked up Radizwell's tracks and are heading this way."

He pointed toward a jagged ridge a short distance away. "Let's try for those rocks. Even if the wrong people lock on to our signal, it will be harder to see us up there at night. We can hold them off until the extraction team gets here."

Maggie drew in a deep breath. "I don't think we should hold them off. We should try to pull them in."

He swung around to face her. "We've already talked about this."

"We started to," she said evenly, "but my growling stomach interrupted us. As I recall, we got sidetracked by a few cold biscuits and bacon bits."

A small smile tugged at his mouth. "So we did."

As much as she wanted to, Maggie didn't let herself be drawn in by the softening in his face or the glint in his eyes. She'd known this confrontation with Adam would come, and she was ready for it.

Keeping her tone brisk and businesslike, she reiterated the conclusions they'd reached in the cave.

"Look, we both agree the scope of the mission has changed somewhat."

"Somewhat?"

"Okay, a lot. But my basic role in the operation hasn't changed at all. I'm still the bait."

"You were the bait when we thought we were dealing with a single assassin. Now we know that individual has a whole team backing him up."

"That's just it, Adam. I'm still the one they want. I'm still—"

She stopped abruptly, frowning.

"I'm still the one they want," she said slowly. "The one *he* wants."

Adam stiffened, and in his eyes Maggie saw an echo of the same suspicion that was forming in the pit of her stomach like a cold, heavy weight.

"He wants me." She articulated each word with careful precision, not wanting to believe them, even as she said them. "He wants me. Not Taylor Grant. Me."

He didn't answer. Didn't say a word, and his silence hammered at Maggie like a crowbar striking against a metal wall.

"You think so, too, don't you? Don't you?"

"I admit the idea occurred to me. But—"

"But nothing! This unknown assassin knew how to bypass the White House phone system. Which meant he probably could have circumvented the personal security system and gotten to the vice president any time he wanted. But he didn't really want her, did he? He wanted me. I've been the target all along."

She stared at Adam, stunned. "That's it, isn't it, Adam? You know it as well as I do. He wants me."

A muscle ticked in his jaw. "All right, Maggie. Let's say you're right. Let's say he wants you. Who is *he?*"

She shook her head. "I don't know. Whoever made that call."

"Who? Who made it?"

"I don't know."

Snow crunched under his boot as he took a step toward her. "Think! Who wants you dead?"

"I don't know!"

Radizwell picked up on the tension arcing through the air between them. He whined far back in his throat and padded forward to nudge a jeans-clad hip. Adam ignored him, his attention focused on the woman before him.

"Who, Maggie? Who wants to get to you?"

She flung out a gloved hand. "Any one of a dozen men, and a few women, all of whom are behind bars now!"

"Why?" The single syllable had the force of a whip, sharp and stinging.

"Because they're behind bars!"

Adam's eyes were blue ice behind his black lashes. His breath came fast and hard on the cold air. "Not good enough. Try again. Think! Why would any of those people want you dead?"

"Because..." She wet her lips. "Because I know something I'm not supposed to know. Or I saw something I wasn't supposed to see. Or heard something I wasn't supposed to hear."

The shadows obscured his face now. Maggie couldn't see his eyes, but she felt them. Narrowed. Intent. Searing.

"What? What did you see or hear? What could you know that you're not supposed to?"

"I don't know, dammit! I don't know!"

The sharp frustration in her voice sliced through the tension-filled air like a blade. Radizwell gave a low growl, unsure of the source of their conflict, but obviously unhappy about it. He edged closer to Adam. If it came to choosing teams, Maggie thought in a wild aside, the dog had already chosen his.

"What I don't understand is, why here?" she said, bringing herself under control. "Why not in D.C.? Or anywhere else? Why set this trap, using me as bait? Luring me in like this. Or—" She stopped, her eyes widening. "Or out!"

"Out, how?"

"Out of my civilian cover. My God, Adam. Maybe that's it. Maybe someone staged this elaborate charade to draw me out, because he couldn't get to me any other way. He couldn't get to Chameleon."

The flat, hard expression on Adam's face might have signaled disbelief, or denial, or a combination of both.

"It's possible," she insisted. "No one outside OMEGA knows our real identities. Hell, only a handful within the agency have access to that information."

"You're saying someone set this whole thing up? Just on the chance you'd be tagged to double for the vice president?"

"It's possible," she repeated stubbornly.

"For God's sake, do you have any idea how remote that possibility is?"

"Not that remote," she snapped. "I'm here, aren't I?"

That stopped him. He went completely still, his arms at his sides, his hands curled into fists. His face could have been carved out of ice.

"If that's the case," he said finally, "this all boils down to a question of who knew you might double for the vice president. Who, Maggie?"

"No one," she protested. "No one knew, except the president, and the vice president. Lillian. Jaguar. The OMEGA team. And—"

She stopped, swallowing hard.

"And the director of OMEGA," Adam said slowly.

She didn't breathe, didn't blink. It seemed to Maggie that her body had lost all capacity to move. Her brain had certainly lost all ability to function. It had gone numb and completely blank. The white, silent woods seemed to close in, until her world became a single, shadowed face.

"Why, Maggie?" he asked softly, bringing them full circle. "Why would any of those people want you dead?"

She struggled for an answer. Any answer. One that would satisfy him, and her. The silence spun out, second by cold, crystalline second.

A hundred chaotic thoughts tumbled through Maggie's numbed mind. A thousand shattering emotions fought for preeminence in her heart. Could Adam have brought her to this isolated spot for some desperate reason of his own? What did she know of him? What did any of the OMEGA agents know of him? His past was shrouded in secrecy. Even now, he led a double life that few knew about. He'd always kept himself so remote. His feelings so shuttered.

Until today. Until he'd held her in his arms and she'd taken him into her body. When he'd looked down into her eyes. There had been no shutters on his soul then.

Her riotous emotions stilled. The confusion dulling her mind faded. She didn't need to know the secrets in Adam's past. She didn't care about his present double life. If she was ever going to trust her instincts, it had to be now.

Adam didn't, couldn't, want her dead.

She'd stake her life on it.

Drawing on everything that was in her heart, she summoned a valiant grin. "Well, I think it's safe to cross the OMEGA team off our ever-expanding list of suspects. I put my life in their hands every time I walk out the door. And I know the director of OMEGA wouldn't set me up like this."

He didn't respond for long, agonizing moments. "Do you?" he said at last.

The cool, even tone was so quintessentially Adam that Maggie didn't know whether to laugh or to cry. She did neither. Instead, she folded her arms across her chest and nodded.

"I do. Although he's tried to take my head off on several memorable occasions in the past three years, he's in love with me. He hasn't admitted it yet. He may not even realize it yet. But he is. What's more, I love him. With all my heart and soul."

If anyone had told Maggie that she'd finally articulate her feelings to Adam while standing knee-deep in snow, with cold nipping at her nose and a team of killers searching for her, she would've checked their medication levels. Of all the times and all the places to have the "discussion" she and Adam had delayed for so long!

Not that it was much of a discussion, she realized belatedly. So far, the exchange had been entirely too one-sided.

"You can jump in here anytime," she invited sweetly.

With a sound that was half laugh, half groan, Adam swept her into his arms. He locked his fists behind her back, holding her against his chest. The deepening shadows didn't obscure his eyes now. Now they blazed down at her with a fierce emotion that warmed Maggie's nose and toes and all parts in between.

"I am. I do. I know."

"Come again?" she asked, breathless.

"I am in love with you. I do realize it. I know you love me, too."

"Well, well, well . . ."

Her smug, satisfied grin made Adam want to pick her up and carry her back to the snow cave. Hell, it made him want to throw her down in the snow right here, rip off her various layers and lose himself in her fire. He had to satisfy himself with a shattering kiss.

They were both breathing fast and hard when he pulled back. It took some effort, but Adam put her out of his arms.

"We'll finish this interesting discussion when we get out of here."

Her mischievous smile almost shattered the remnants of his control. "It's finished. At least as far as I'm concerned. You are. You do. You know. What more is there to say?"

"Maggie..."

"All we have to decide now is what to do about it."

"Correction. Right now we have to get you out of here. We can decide about it—about us—after we get you to a safe haven."

Her teasing smile faded a bit. "I can't operate out of a safe haven. I'm a field operative."

He bent to pick up their small store of supplies. "It's too dangerous in the field. I'm calling you in."

She winced at his use of the euphemism every OMEGA agent dreaded hearing. He was calling her in. Out of the cold. Ordering her to abandon her cover and her mission.

Maggie shook her head. "Not yet, Adam. You can't terminate this mission yet. We won't find the answer in a safe haven. The answer's here, in the field."

He didn't reply. He didn't have to. They both knew she was right. Maggie saw his jaw work. He wanted to find whoever was behind this scheme as much as, or more than, she.

"I can't go in," she said softly, firmly. "Not yet. You wouldn't have any respect for me if I did. You wouldn't..." She circled a hand in the air. "You wouldn't see me the same way, ever again. As an agent, or as a woman. You wouldn't love me the same way."

Her uncanny echo of his earlier thoughts pierced Adam's wall of resistance. He would love her. He would always love her. But he would love her differently if she wasn't the Maggie who stood nose to nose with him, in the middle of nowhere, with no food, little firepower, and a killer on her trail, yet refused point-blank to run for cover.

Still, he made one last effort. "Do you think I'll ever see you the same way again after those hours in the snow cave? As a woman, or as an agent?"

"Good Lord, I hope not!"

Her startled exclamation wrung a smile out of him. Maggie pounced on it like a cat after a ball of catnip.

"Whatever else happens," she said softly, "we'll always have those hours in the snow cave."

"Maggie..."

"And the memory of those bits of bacon."

She cocked her head, inviting him to capitulate, giving him the means to.

"And don't forget the feel of pine needles," she murmured wickedly. "Prickling us in places few people have ever felt pine needles prickle before. And the interesting way we found to melt that handful of snow. And..."

"All right, Maggie. All right." His jaw clenched. "Suppose you tell me how you think we should handle this situation."

She wasn't the type to crow. "We keep it simple," she said briskly. "I'm the lure. We use me to bait a trap, then spring it."

"We stake you out like a skinned rabbit and wait for the hungry predators to arrive, is that it?"

"That's not quite what I had in mind," she drawled.

"So tell me."

"We have to assume they'll lock on to our signal when we contact Jaguar, right?"

"Right."

"So instead of trying to evade them while we wait for the extraction team to arrive, we let them find us. Or think they have. We draw them in and pin them down until the team gets here."

Thankfully, Adam didn't point out the obvious. He knew as well as Maggie that they didn't have enough firepower to keep attackers armed with automatic weapons and night-vision equipment pinned down. Which meant they had to use the terrain to their maximum advantage. And use their wits.

"We can do it, Adam."

"We can try it," he said slowly, reluctantly.

Yes! Maggie wanted to shout her relief, but one look at his face warned her he was not happy about this. At all. Wisely she kept silent while he scanned the darkening horizon.

"That ridge won't work. We'd lose them in the rocks and boulders."

"We'd better head down to lower ground." Shoving her hands in her pockets, she turned to scan the steep slope. "What we need is a canyon or crevice of some kind."

What they found was a shack.

Or rather Radizwell found it.

Maggie and Adam had only gone a few yards down the slope, angling through the trees to avoid detection and make the descent easier, when the komondor decided they were heading in the wrong direction. He stopped, and a low whine alerted Adam to the fact that the animal wasn't following.

"Come on, boy. Come on."

The dog backed up a few steps, rumbling a low sound deep in his throat.

"Heel!"

Even Radizwell recognized the voice of authority. Belly to the ground, he slunk across the snow, whining pitifully all the way.

Adam's dark brows slashed together. "What? What are you trying to tell us?"

Taking courage from the more moderate tone, the shaggy beast leaped up and bounded down the slope a few feet in the opposite direction. He skidded to a halt in the snow, turned back to face them, then let loose with a deep, rolling thunderclap bark.

"Good grief!" Maggie exclaimed. "Who needs a satellite transmission? Anyone within a five-mile radius can lock on to that."

It was an exaggeration, but only a slight one.

Adam quieted the animal with a slicing gesture of command. Radizwell snapped his jaws shut and plopped back on his massive haunches, as if sitting at attention.

"Obviously he wants us to follow him," Adam commented. "Since he appears to know these mountains better than we do, I suggest we see where he leads us."

He led them on what Maggie suspected was a merry chase. The moment he saw them start in his direction, Radizwell whirled and raced down the slope at a steep angle. He dodged around trees and over snow-covered fallen logs with surprising agility. Just before they lost sight of him completely, he skidded to a halt and waited for them to catch up.

When they were almost up with him, he jumped up and took off again. After the third or fourth relay, Maggie was huffing from the exertion and Adam's breath was coming in short, sharp pants. The sun had slipped behind the peaks now, and the shadows had deepened to long purple streaks across the tree-covered hillside. Overhead, a few early stars glowed in an indigo sky. Maggie caught a glimpse of a pale moon floating between the tips of the pines.

Although it was difficult to judge distance with their visibility obscured by the towering trees, an occasional clearing gave them some idea of progress. Maggie guessed they were three-quarters of the way down the slope when she had to stop to catch her breath. The dog padded back, not even winded.

She eyed him with mounting suspicion. "You don't suppose... this is his way... of getting back at me, do you?"

Adam propped a foot up on a half-submerged boulder. Leaning an elbow across his knee, he drew in several long breaths. "For what?"

"For scarfing... up all the biscuits... and bacon."

"Could be."

Maggie groaned. "I knew it!"

"Come on. Let's keep moving. We're almost at the bottom of the slope."

The ground began to level out a little while later. To Maggie's relief, the trees thinned, then ended abruptly. A few more steps brought them to the edge of a flat expanse of snow, about the width of a football field and twice as long. A narrow, ice-encrusted stream cut a crooked path across the field, dividing it almost in half. On the far side of the field, tree-studded slopes rose to touch the dark sky.

As soon as he saw the open space, Radizwell charged forward. Just in time, Adam grabbed a fistful of his ropy fur and hauled him back. The dog growled a low protest, but stood beside Adam while he and Maggie surveyed the still, flat area.

"It's an alpine meadow," Adam murmured after a moment. "I would imagine some of Taylor's sheep graze here in the summer. Which means..."

He glanced down at the sheepdog at his side.

"Is there a shelter here, boy? A shepherd's hut? Is that where you're taking us?"

Maggie hunched her shoulders and huddled closer to Adam. Excitement shot through her.

"That would work. A hut would work. It would make a perfect trap."

"I'm only guessing there's anything here at all, Maggie."

"It's a good guess. Radizwell brought us here for a reason. Besides, my feet are freezing and we're both sweating. Before we set our trap, we should dry off and thaw out. Or thaw out and dry off."

She jerked her chin toward the eager animal. "Let him go. Let's see where he heads."

He headed straight across the meadow toward the trees on the other side. His white coat made him difficult to follow against the sea of snow. Maggie squinted, watching carefully to track the shadow flying with astounding speed across the open space. For a big, klutzy-looking guy, the Hungarian could sure move.

Weapon drawn, she crouched beside Adam in the shelter of a dead pine and watched the dog's unerring progress. On the far side of the open space, Radizwell skidded to a stop, just short of the tree line. Lining up on a dark patch among the trees, he gave a deep, basso profundo bark.

The sound echoed from the surrounding peaks and rolled back at them. Maggie stayed absolutely still beside Adam's rigid form. Nothing moved on the other side of the meadow. No one answered Radizwell's call.

"Do you see anything?" she hissed.

"No."

They waited a while longer. The komondor padded back and forth in front of the dark tree line, then stretched out in the snow. He laid his head down on his paws, waiting.

A snicker of metal brought her head jerking around. Moonlight gleamed on the blue steel of the weapon in Adam's hand.

"Here, take my weapon."

"Why? What are you—?"

He grabbed her derringer and slapped the heavier, more powerful pistol into her hand.

"Cover me!"

"No! Adam, wait!"

It was Maggie's nightmare scene from this morning in reverse. This time it was Adam who plowed across an open, unprotected space and Maggie who dropped to one knee, weapon raised.

Her heart crashed against her ribs as she watched his progress, and the acrid taste of fear rose in her throat. At any moment, she expected to hear gunfire shatter the stillness. To see Adam's body jackknife through the air.

When he made it to the tree line on the far side, she almost sobbed in relief. Then reaction set in. By the time he returned, Radizwell plunging in circles at his side, she was so furious she was ready to shoot him herself.

Chapter 13

Maggie stormed through the ankle-high snow, the P7 gripped in her gloved hand.

"Don't ever do that to me again!"

Her vehemence sent Adam's brows winging. "Do what?"

"Go charging off like that! Without coordinating with me first!"

"The way you did this morning at the lake, you mean?"

In the face of that piece of calm logic, Maggie fell back on an age-old, irrefutable argument. "That was different!"

"Of course."

She stomped up to him, still furious. "Listen to me, Thunder. I love you. I do *not* want you dead. I do *not* want to see your body splattered across a snowy field. I have *plans* for that body!"

Evidently the dog did *not* like the threatening tone she directed toward Adam. With a deep warning growl, he placed himself between Maggie and his good buddy.

She glared at the huge lump of uncombed wool, then at the man surveying her with a cool glint in his eyes. The intensity of her fury surprised Maggie herself. In a back corner of her mind, she realized she'd just had a taste of what Adam must have gone through all these years as OMEGA's director. It was a hell of a lot harder to stand back and watch someone you loved run headlong toward danger and possible death than to make the charge yourself. For the first time, she understood his icy anger during the debriefs after some of her more…adventurous missions. Still, she wasn't quite ready to forgive him for the fear that had twisted through her body like barbed wire.

Adam handed her the derringer and took the P7 in exchange. "Remind me to ask about these plans of yours when we get out of here."

"They'll probably change—several times—before then," she muttered.

"I wouldn't be surprised. Mine are changing by the minute. Would you like to know what I found under the trees?"

She checked the safety on the .22 and shoved it into her pants pocket. "Yes."

"A small shack, just as we guessed."

"Good."

"Well stocked with blankets and fuel."

Maggie stomped over to pick up their small bundle of gear. "Good."

"And food," he added with a small smile.

She swung around. "Food?"

"I thought that might get your attention."

"What kind of food?"

"There's a whole metal locker full of canned goods. Pork and beans. Beef stew. Chicken and dumplings."

"Chicken and dumplings, huh?"

Adam's smile edged into one of his rare grins. It lifted his fine, chiseled mouth and crinkled the skin at the corners of his eyes. The last of Maggie's uncharacteristic anger melted as he stepped forward and brushed a knuckle down her cheek.

"I can see that one of my main tasks in the future will be keeping your stomach full."

"Among other things."

"First things first. Come on. Let's get you fed."

Hunching her shoulders, Maggie plowed through the snow beside him.

The shack was small and airless and dark. While Adam kept watch outside, Maggie explored its single room cautiously. She didn't dare use the matches she found in a waterproof tin container to light the oil lamp left on the single table, but then, she didn't really need to.

Adam left the door cracked just enough to let in a sliver of moonlight and allow him a clear view of the open meadow.

"The food and other supplies are in the metal locker in the corner," he told her.

When she opened the locker, the first items Maggie reached for were musty, folded blankets. Passing one to Adam, she pulled another one out for her own use and tossed it on the narrow cot built into one wall. Then she stacked half a dozen cans on the table and rooted for a can opener. She could open the cans without one, but she'd rather not trudge out in the snow to find a sharpened stick if she didn't have to. Luckily, the middle shelf yielded an old-fashioned, rusted opener and several large spoons.

As hungry as she was, Maggie was too well trained to attack the food without taking care of other, more urgent needs first. Perching on the narrow cot, she tugged off her boots. Her lightweight waterproof footgear had keep most of the moisture out, but her toes were numb with cold, and she didn't want to risk frostbite.

While she massaged warmth into her stockinged feet, Radizwell made himself right at home. He took a couple of circuits of the small room, sniffing out scents left by various visitors since the last time he'd been there. When he poked his nose into a stack of long-handled tools in one corner, sudden mayhem erupted. His stub of a tail shot straight up, he let loose with a woof that made Maggie jump clear off the cot, and a half-dozen tiny furry creatures darted out from among the tools. Squeaking and squealing, they scattered in all directions, with Radizwell pouncing joyfully after them. His resounding barks bounced off the hut's walls.

"For God's sake, shut him up!" Adam ordered from his post at the door.

"Right. Shut him up."

Maggie planted herself in the middle of the shack to wait for the dog's next pass and jumped half out of her skin when one of the tiny squeaking creatures ran across her foot. Praying it hadn't taken a detour up her pant leg, she braced herself as the dog skidded to a halt. Or tried to. His momentum carried him smack into her. Once again, Maggie found herself flat on her back, with a hundred or more pounds of belligerent komondor straddling her. Doggy breath bathed her face as he growled his displeasure.

"Look, pal," she growled back, "I don't like you any more than you appear to like me. But let's declare a truce, okay? I don't want to waste what little ammunition I have on you."

Adam deserted his post long enough to drag the dog off her. "Maybe if you offered to share the chicken and dump-

lings with him, you two might just strike up a friendship,"
he suggested dryly.

Maggie scrambled up. "Ha! What makes you think I
want to be friends with an ugly, overgrown floor mop?"

"This from the woman who keeps a bug-eyed reptile for
a pet?" Adam shook his head and resumed his post.

Holding out her pant leg, Maggie gave her foot a vigor-
ous shake. When nothing more than a small clump of snow
hit the floor, she sighed in relief.

Despite the glare she sent the unrepentant dog, she could
no more let him go hungry than she could the frantic mama
wood mouse who'd scurried back into the stack of tools after rounding up her tiny charges. Opening the different cans,
Maggie dumped the contents of three of them into a metal
bowl she'd scavenged from the locker.

"Come on, hound. You can eat this outside and pull
guard duty at the same time."

Radizwell didn't move. Sitting on his haunches like an
upright bale of unprocessed cotton, he looked from the bowl
in her hand to Adam for guidance. Maggie shook her head.
When males bonded, they bonded.

At Adam's signal, the dog graciously condescended to
allow Maggie to feed him. Padding to the door, he stepped
outside. She set the bowl down in the snow, took a quick
glance around the serene moonscape, then ducked back inside. The knowledge that the moonscape wouldn't stay serene for long added impetus to her actions.

In short order, she handed Adam an open can and a
spoon, dropped a cold, soggy dumpling behind the stack of
tools and wrapped the blanket around her legs and feet to
warm them. Shuffling across the hut, open can in hand, she
joined Adam at the door.

"I'll stand watch. You go dry off."

"I'm not wet."

They shared a few moments of silent companionship while they ate, both wrapped in thought. Maggie tried to ignore the insidious, creeping realization that these quiet moments with Adam might be their last, but the cold reality of their situation intruded.

In a few minutes, they'd lure an unknown number of killers to this isolated spot and try to hold them off until the Jaguar's extraction team arrived. With a total of eight rounds of ammunition between them. Adam had expended all but two of the rounds in his nine-round Heckler & Koch during the firefight at the lake. Maggie had exactly six left for Taylor's .22, including the one in the chamber and five in the spare clip she'd tucked in her pocket this morning.

God, had it only been this morning? She tipped her head against the doorframe, thinking how much her life had changed since then. Her gaze slid to Adam's lean, shadowed face. Whatever happened, she'd have those hours in the snow cave. Whatever happened, she'd have the memory of his blue eyes smiling down at her when he'd taken her in his arms and said he was, he did, he knew.

"Adam?"

"Yes?"

"How long do you think we have?"

His eyes lingered on her lips, then lifted. In their depths, Maggie caught a glimpse of raw, masculine need, overlaid with regret.

"Not long enough."

She sighed. "That's what I thought you'd say."

"They could be following the dog's tracks and be heading this way right now. We have to contact Jaguar."

"I know."

He curled a hand under her chin, lifting her face. "Tomorrow, Maggie. We'll have tomorrow. And forever."

"If we don't . . . thank you for today."

His cheeks creased. "You're welcome."

Maggie dipped her chin to kiss the warm skin of his palm. Closing her eyes, she savored his taste and his touch and his scent. Then she sighed again and moved away. With the blanket swaddled around her lower body, she began to pace the small hut.

"Okay, let's review the situation here. We need to contact headquarters to let Jaguar know our coordinates. As soon as we do, there's a distinct possibility the unfriendlies, whoever they are, will glom on to the signal."

"If they haven't already picked up our tracks," Adam reminded her.

"When they arrive on the scene, it's up to us to make sure they don't leave until the counterstrike team can get here."

Maggie felt adrenaline begin to pump through her veins in anticipation of the action ahead. She'd been in tight situations before. Not quite as snug as this one, perhaps, but pretty darn close.

Blanket swishing at her ankles, she strode across the small room and yanked open the metal locker. The rectangular red container she pulled out was heavy and full.

"All right. We have eight rounds of ammunition and one gallon of gasoline to hold off a possible army of bad guys armed with automatic weapons, high-powered night scopes, and every destructive device known to man." She grinned at Adam. "I've done more with less. How about you?"

He shoved his shoulders off the doorframe. "A lot more with a lot less. Let's get to work."

Pillaging the metal locker, they found the makings for crude flash bombs. While Maggie poured the gasoline into the bottles, Adam tore strips from his blanket to stuff in the neck as wicks. Carefully dividing the matches, he gave half to Maggie and tucked the other half in his pocket, along with the jagged pieces of mirror he'd smashed from the snowmobile.

Leaving Radizwell to stand sentry at the hut, they disappeared into the surrounding woods. Working silently, quickly, they gathered fallen limbs and dry timber. Within moments, they'd scattered the debris in a seemingly random pattern around the hut. After placing a few of the gasoline-filled bottles for maximium detonation, they doused the wood with the remaining fuel. A single careful shot could detonate the ring of fire.

After that they separated, Maggie going left, Adam right, searching for just the right tree to climb to put the hut in a cross fire and make the best use of their remaining flash bombs. The temperature had dropped significantly, but Maggie didn't notice. Her heart thumped with the realization that their time was running out. She zigzagged through the trees to find exactly the one she wanted.

Its thick trunk provided excellent cover and a full complement of stair-stepping branches. An easy climb took her a good thirty feet up. Using both hands and her body for leverage, she bent back a couple of obscuring limbs to give her a clear line of fire to the hut. With so few rounds of ammunition, she'd need it.

Her breath was coming in short, puffy gasps by the time she got back to the shack.

"You set?" Adam asked tersely.

"As set as I'll ever be. Let's get Jaguar on the net."

Maggie gave a small puff of surprise when he gripped her upper arms, his hands like steel cuffs.

"Listen to me, Chameleon. It's not too late. You can climb the ridge behind the hut. Take cover in the rocks until the extraction team arrives."

"And just what do you plan to do while I'm taking cover?"

He gave her a small shake. "You're the one they're after, not me. I can stay here. Talk to them. Delay them."

"After that scene beside the lake, do you think they're going to stop for a friendly chat? You took at least one of them down, remember?"

"Dammit, Maggie . . ."

"Chameleon."

"What?"

"You called me Chameleon a moment ago. That's who I am, Thunder. That's who I have to be. I am not running for cover, and I'm sure as hell not leaving you to face the fire alone. Any more than you'd leave me."

His fingers bit into her arms. Maggie could feel their tensile strength through the thick down of her ski jacket. Under its day's growth of dark beard, his jaw worked.

"Thunder," she said softly, "kiss me. Hard. Then get Jaguar up on the net."

He kissed her. Hard.

Then he dug in his pocket for the handheld navigational device. While waiting for the readings to display on the liquid crystal screen, he shoved his sleeve back and activated the satellite transceiver.

"Jaguar, this is Thun—"

Jake's voice jumped out of the gold watch. "I read you! You okay?"

"We are."

"Both of you?"

"Both of us."

"Give me your coordinates."

Adam rapped out the reading from his GPS unit.

Jake was silent a moment, then came back on the net. "The extraction team's in the air. Twenty minutes away. Cowboy's leading them in."

"Cowboy?"

Maggie felt a rush of wild relief. She and the lanky Wyoming rancher had worked together before. The last time, they'd repelled an attack similar to this one, led by a scar-faced Soviet major. After Adam, Nate Sloan was Maggie's number one pick for a partner in a firefight. The knowledge that he was leading the counterstrike team gave her a surge of hope.

"Tell Cowboy to hover behind the ridge line due east of us," she instructed Jaguar. "I don't want him to scare away our game. We'll call him in when we've sprung the trap."

"Roger. You two sure took your time getting back to me. I've been having to hold off the entire Secret Service single-handedly."

"What do you mean?"

"Special Agent Kowalski's demanded half the federal government and most of the state of California to search the Sierras for you two. I convinced the president to hold her off until I heard from you, but she's mad. Hopping mad. Someone's attacked her charge, and she's taking it real personal. She doesn't understand why we've kept word of the attack quiet, and she doesn't like it." He paused. "Either that, or she's putting on one hell of an act."

"What do you mean?" Adam asked sharply.

"The lab confirmed that the listening device Chameleon found in the VP's bedroom is manufactured by Digicon— for the Secret Service. The Presidential Protective Unit personnel are the only ones using it."

Adam muttered a vicious curse. "Digicon and the Secret Service. Peter Donovan and James Elliot. Even if Kowalski planted the bug, we still don't know who the hell's behind this."

"We will soon," Maggie promised, her mouth grim.

Adam nodded. "Look, Jaguar, we've got to get into position. Tell Cowboy to wait for my signal. I'll bring him in."

"Roger. Good hunting, Chief."

"Thanks.

"And, Chameleon?"

"Yes?"

"When you catch that polecat you're baiting the trap for, I'll skin him and tan the hide for you. I remember how much you disliked gutting your catch during survival training."

"I don't think I'll have a problem with this one," Maggie replied, grinning crookedly.

Adam dropped his sleeve down over the gold watch. For a few moments, the only sounds in the small shack were their rapid breathing and the faint thump of the sheepdog's paw on the snow as he scratched himself.

"You ready, Chameleon?"

"I'm ready."

His gaze, blue and piercing, raked her face a final time. Maggie ached to touch him once more, to carry the feel of his bristly cheek with her into the night, but she didn't lift her hand. The time for touching was past.

He nodded, as if acknowledging her unspoken resolve. "Let's get moving before our company arrives."

"Too late. It's already here."

Maggie and Adam spun around as a bulky figure in a sheepskin coat kicked the door back on its hinges.

"Don't!" McGowan shouted. "Don't reach for it! I'll shoot her, Ridgeway, I swear!"

Adam froze in a low crouch, his hand halfway to the weapon holstered at the small of his back.

For long seconds, no one moved. No one breathed. McGowan kept his rifle leveled squarely on the center of Maggie's chest. She didn't dare go for her gun, and she knew Adam wouldn't go for his. Not with the caretaker's weapon pointed at her.

"There's an oil lamp on the table, Ridgeway. Matches beside it. Light it. And keep your hands where I can see them, or she's dead."

Adam straightened slowly. As though she were inside his head, Maggie could hear the thoughts that raced through his mind. With light, they could see McGowan's eyes. A person's eyes always signaled his intent before his body did. With light, they could anticipate. Coordinate. Take him down.

Moving with infinite care, Adam crossed to the small table. Metal rattled, a match scraped against the side of the box, a flame flared, low and flickering at first, and then steady as the wick caught.

In the lantern's glow, Maggie saw McGowan clearly for the first time. Above the rifle, his battered face was frightening in its implacable intensity. Not a single spark of life showed in his gray eyes. They were flat. Cold. A convicted murderer's eyes.

The click of claws on wood jerked Maggie's attention from the caretaker's face to the shape behind him. To her fury, Radizwell ambled into the hut and hunkered down, as if settling in to enjoy the show.

"Some guard dog you are, you stupid—"

With great effort, she bit back one of the more descriptive terms she'd learned from her father's roughneck crews. It was a mistake to let McGowan see how furious she was, and she knew damn well it was unfair to blame Radizwell. The sheepdog wouldn't view Hank McGowan as an enemy. Hell, the thumping they'd heard a few seconds ago was probably his stump of a tail whapping against the snow in an ecstatic welcome. Still, there were two hides she wouldn't have minded tanning at this moment.

"Who are you?"

McGowan's low snarl brought her eyes snapping back to his face.

"What?"

"Who the hell are you?"

The dog picked up the savagery of his tone and tilted his head, as if confused by this confrontation between humans he knew and trusted.

"Never mind," McGowan continued. "I don't care who you are. Just tell me what you've done with Taylor."

Maggie's mind raced with the possibility that this man wasn't the one they'd tried to bait the trap for. Slowly, carefully, she shook her head.

"I haven't done anything with the vice president."

His mouth curled. "I'd just as soon shoot you as look at you, lady. If Taylor's hurt, you're dead anyway. Where is she?"

"I can't tell you. You have to trust—"

"The first shot goes into her knee, Ridgeway." His eyes never left Maggie's face. "The second into her right lung. How many will it take? How many do I have to pump into her until you tell me?"

As it turned out, the first shot didn't go through Maggie's knee. It came through the open door and went right through McGowan's shoulder. Blood sprayed, splattering Adam as he leaped for the man.

It was the second shot that hit her. The rifle in McGowan's scarred hands bucked. A deafening crack split the air, and Maggie slammed into the back wall of the hut.

Chapter 14

In the curious way time has, it always seems to move in the most infinitesimal increments at moments of greatest pain.

When Adam lunged forward to knock the rifle aside, he felt as though he were diving through a thick pool of sludge. Slowly. So slowly. Too slowly.

His mind recorded every minute sensation. He felt warm blood splatter his face. Saw McGowan's finger pull back on the trigger in an involuntary reaction to the bullet that ripped through him. Heard the roar as the rifle barrel jerked. Tasted the acrid tang of gunpowder and fear as Maggie crashed back against the wall.

Like a remote-controlled robot, Adam followed through with his actions. He shoved the barrel aside. Digging a shoulder into McGowan's middle, he took him down. He rolled sideways, away from the caretaker, and was on his feet again in a single motion. Through it all, every nerve, every fibrous filament, every neuron, screamed a single message in a thousand different variations.

Maggie was hit. Maggie was down. Maggie was shot.

Only after he'd yanked the rifle out of McGowan's slackened hold and spun around did another stream of messages begin to penetrate his mind.

She was down, but not dead. She was hit, but not bloodied. She was shot, but not wounded.

She'd been thrown against the wall and crumpled to the floor, but her eyes were wide and startled, not glazed with pain. A look of utter stupefaction crossed her face, then gave way to one of sputtering panic.

As Adam raced toward her, he heard a hiccuping wheeze and identified the sound instantly. He'd seen enough demonstrations of protective body armor to recognize that choking, sucking gasp. The force of the hit had knocked the air out of her lungs. She was so stunned that her paralyzed muscles couldn't draw more in.

He couldn't help her breathe. She had to force her lungs to work on her own. But he could sure as hell protect her from the two white-suited figures who came bursting through the open door at that precise moment.

Shoving Maggie flat on the floor, Adam covered her body with his. He twisted around, his finger curling on the rifle's trigger as he lined up on the lead attacker.

The figure in white arctic gear and goggles ignored him, however. Legs spread, arms extended in a classic law-enforcement stance, he covered the sprawled McGowan.

Or rather *she* did.

Adam recognized Denise Kowalski's voice the instant she belted out a fierce order to the downed man.

"Don't move! Don't even breathe!"

Keeping her eyes and her weapon trained on McGowan, she shouted over her shoulder, "Ridgeway! Is she hit? Is the vice president hit?"

Before Adam could answer, a savage snarl ripped through the hut. From the corner of his eye, he saw Radizwell rear back, his massive hindquarters bunching as he prepared to launch himself at this latest threat.

The second agent swung his weapon toward the dog.

"No! Don't shoot! Down, Radizwell! Down!"

At the lash of command in Adam's voice, the sheepdog halted in midthrust. Confused, uncertain, he quivered with the need to act. Under his mask of ropy fur, black gums curled back. Bloodcurdling growls rolled out of his throat like waves, rising and falling in steady crescendos.

In the midst of all the clamor, Maggie's feeble cry almost went unheard.

"Adam! Get . . . off . . . me!"

At the sound of her voice, the two agents froze. Then Denise transferred her weapon to her right hand and shoved her goggles up with her left. Keeping the gun trained on McGowan, she risked a quick look at the far end of the hut.

Adam pushed himself onto one knee. With infinite care, he rolled the wheezing Maggie onto her side. She immediately drew up into a fetal position, her knees to her chin and her arms wrapped around her middle.

Relief crashed through Adam when he saw where she cradled herself. The bullet had struck low, below her breastbone. A higher hit might have broken her sternum or smashed a couple ribs.

"Herrera!" Denise snapped. "Get out your medical kit. The vice president's been hit."

"She's wearing a body shield," Adam said. "I think she's okay."

Maggie's awful wheezing eased. "Okay. I'm . . . okay."

Slowly, her face scrunched with pain, she straightened her legs. Adam slid an arm under her back and helped her to her feet. Her knees wobbled, involuntary tears streaked her cheeks, and she kept her arms crossed over her waist, but she was standing.

With everything in him, Adam fought the desperate urge to crush her against his chest. Added pressure was the last thing she wanted or needed now. She'd have a bruise the size of Rhode Island on her stomach as it was.

Incredibly, she gave a shaky grin and tapped a finger against her middle. "What do you know! It...worked."

After their hours together in the snow cave, Adam had been sure he couldn't love this woman more. He'd been wrong. Then, her passion and her laughter had fed his soul. Now, her courage stole it completely. As long as he lived, he would remember that small grin and the way she gathered herself together to shake off the effects of a bullet to the stomach.

A grunt of pain behind them brought both Maggie and Adam swinging around. The caretaker pushed against the floor with one boot, bright red blood staining his worn sheepskin jacket as he dragged himself upright.

"I told you not to move, McGowan," Denise warned.

He sagged against the wall, and he sent her a contemptuous look. "What are you going to do? Shoot me?"

"I'm considering it. And this time I won't shoot to wound."

"Too bad you took down the wrong man, Kowalski."

"I got the right one. The one holding a gun on the vice president."

His lips curled in a sneer. "Are you blind or just stupid, woman?"

"Neither. Nor am I lying in a pool of blood."

Pain added a rasp to McGowan's gravelly voice. "She's not the vice president."

"Sure. And I'm not—"

"That woman is not Taylor Grant."

His utter conviction got through to Denise. Adam saw the first flicker of doubt in her eyes as she threw a quick look at Maggie.

"Come on," McGowan jeered, wincing a little with the effort. "I know you're new to Taylor's detail. But even you must have picked up on the dog's reaction to her last night. She's good, whoever she is, damn good. But she's not Taylor Grant."

The agent's mouth thinned. "Herrera! Search this man for weapons."

She kept her gun leveled on the caretaker's head while the second agent opened the sheepskin and patted him down.

"He's clean."

"Keep him covered."

The agent swiveled on his heels to look up at her. "Shouldn't I patch that hole first?"

"In a minute."

"But—"

"He'll live!"

Her sharp retort wrung a half smile, half grimace from the wounded man. "You're one hard female, Kowalski."

"Remember that, the next time you pull a weapon on one of my—" She stopped abruptly. "On one of my charges," she finished slowly.

Maggie heard the hitch of uncertainty in Denise's voice. Well, the agent might have her doubts, but Maggie had a few of her own, as well. Hanging on to Adam's arm with one hand, she casually slipped the other into her pants pocket. Her palm curled around the derringer.

"Did you—?"

She had to stop and drag in a slow breath. Pain rippled through her at even that slight movement of her diaphragm, but Maggie gritted her teeth and finished. "Did you plant a listening device in my bedroom, Denise?"

The agent stiffened.

"Did you?"

Denise didn't respond for long moments. When she did, her brown eyes were flat and hard. "Yes."

Maggie felt Adam's muscles tense under her tight grip. "Why?" she asked sharply.

"Because it was ordered by the vice president," Denise replied with careful deliberation. "Who isn't you, apparently."

A sudden silence descended, broken a moment later by McGowan's snort of derision.

"Taylor wouldn't allow any bugs upstairs. She doesn't even like the cameras downstairs. That cabin is the only place in her whole crazy world she has any privacy. She'd never authorize you to peep into her bedroom."

"Well, she did." Denise bit the words out, her eyes on Maggie.

"Did she, Kowalski?" Quiet menace laced Adam's voice. "Did she personally order it?"

Denise dragged her gaze from Maggie to the man beside her. She frowned, obviously debating whether to reply. "The order came down through channels," she said at last.

"What channels?" Adam rapped out.

"Secret Service channels. What the hell's going—?"

"Who issued the order?"

Despite the ache in her middle, Maggie almost smiled at the stubborn, angry look that settled on Denise's face. She'd had the same reaction herself, on occasion, to being grilled by OMEGA's director.

"Dammit, what's—?"

"Who, Kowalski? I want an answer! Now!"

Denise responded through clenched teeth. "The order came from the secretary."

"The secretary of the treasury?"

"The secretary of the treasury. Personally. Direct to me. He told me..." Her jaw tightened. "He told me the vice president had authorized it."

"Bingo," Maggie whispered.

Adam's eyes met hers. A muscle twitched in one side of his jaw. The president's friend, he thought. The highest financial officer in the nation. The bastard.

"We may know who," he said, his jaw tight, "but we still don't know why."

"We will," Maggie swore. "We'll get the last piece of the puzzle if we have to..."

A coldly furious female intruded on their private exchange. "If one of you doesn't explain in the next ten seconds what this is all about, I'm going to take action. Very drastic action."

"Better tell her, Ridgeway," McGowan drawled. "If you don't, she'll shoot to wound, and get her rocks off watching you bleed to death."

"Oh, for—" Shoving her hood back, Denise raked a hand through her short sandy hair. "Stuff a bandage in his wound or in his mouth, Herrera. I don't care which. Now tell me—" she glared at Maggie "—just who you are and what the hell's going on here."

Maggie opened her mouth, then closed it with a snap. Slicing a hand through the air for quiet, she cocked her head and listened intently.

In the stillness that descended, she heard the echo of a faint, wavering roar. Her fingers dug into Adam's arm as she whipped around to face Denise.

"Is more—" She gasped as the violent movement wrenched at her middle, then shook her head, as if denying all pain. "Is more of your team on the way?"

Frowning, Denise responded to the urgency in Maggie's voice. "No. There's only Herrera and me. The president wouldn't authorize a full-scale search," she added stiffly.

"So you came on your own?"

Her chin jutted out. "So we came on our own. You are— you *were* my responsibility. We tracked McGowan from the moment he left the cabin."

"Hell," the caretaker muttered in profound disgust. "I'm getting sloppy. Tracked down and gunned down by a female."

Denise ignored him, her sharp gaze focused on Maggie's face. "What do you hear?"

"Snowmobiles," she murmured, moving closer to the door to listen.

"Do you think it's the team that hit you this morning and took down my man?"

"Probably."

"I owe them."

A ghost of a grin sketched across Maggie's mouth. "Me too."

"Listen to me, Kowalski," Adam cut in. "The vice president is safe. She's at Camp David, working on some highly sensitive treaty negotiations. But before she left, she received a death threat, a particularly nasty one, which is why my agent is doubling for her."

"Agent?"

"That's also why the president wouldn't authorize you to institute a search," Adam continued ruthlessly. "We told him not to."

Denise blinked once or twice at the news that the president apparently took orders from the tall, commanding man in front of her.

"Why no search?" she asked, doubt in her eyes, but still tenacious.

"Because we didn't want the wrong people walking into the trap we've set. We want the team that hit us and your man this morning. Badly. And the individual behind them. Are you with us?" Adam asked in a steely voice. "You have to decide. Now."

Maggie saw at once that she wasn't the only one who'd learned to trust her instincts. Denise flicked another look from her to Adam, then back again. Squaring her shoulders, she nodded.

"Tell me about this trap."

"I'll tell you as soon as I call in our reinforcements," Adam said, shoving back his sleeve. "From the sound of it, we're going to need them."

At Cowboy's laconic assurance that he was barely a good spit away and closing fast, the tension in the hut ratcheted up several more notches.

Working silently and swiftly, the small team readied for action. At Denise's terse order, Herrera divided up their extra weapons and ammunition. While Maggie showed the two agents the placement of their rudimentary defenses, Adam propped a shoulder under McGowan and took him into the shelter of the trees. Radizwell trotted at their heels, rumbling deep in his throat until Adam's low command stilled him.

"Christ," McGowan muttered. "He never obeys me like that. Or anyone else, Taylor included. Last time she was home, she threatened to skin him and use him for a throw rug."

"It's all in the tone."

"Yeah, I guess so."

His lips white with pain, McGowan was still for a moment. The distant rise and fall of engines grew louder with each labored breath. "You'd better give me my rifle."

Without speaking, Adam eased his support from under the caretaker's shoulder.

"I didn't mean to pull that trigger," McGowan stated flatly. "Not when I did, anyway."

"I know."

"I would have, though. I would've shot you both if I thought you'd harmed Taylor."

The whine of the engines pulled at Adam. He needed to coordinate a final approach for Cowboy. To check the disposition of his meager forces. To make sure Maggie was secure. But the bleak expression in the caretaker's eyes held him for another second.

"You love her that much?"

A flicker of pain crossed McGowan's face, one that had nothing to do with his wound.

"About as much as you love that woman, I reckon," McGowan said quietly. His gaze drifted to Maggie, a slender shadow against the snow. "They're a lot alike, aren't they? Her and Taylor?"

"Many ways. And nothing alike in others." Adam started back to the hut. "I'll send Herrera out with your rifle."

"Ridgeway?"

"Yes?"

"Good luck. Take care of your woman."

A wry smile tugged at Adam's lips. "She prefers to take care of herself."

It was over almost before it began.

Scant moments after the hut's occupants took position in the trees surrounding the hut, a wave of dim shapes burst into the open meadow. They raced across the snow, throwing up waves of white behind their skis. The first few were halfway across when a Cobra gunship lifted above the dark peaks directly behind them.

Maggie couldn't see the chopper, since it flew without lights, but she heard it. The steady *whump-whump-whump* of its rotor blades drowned the sound of the approaching snowmobiles.

When they caught the sound of the chopper behind them, the attackers swerved crazily. Gunfire erupted, and streaming tracers lit the night sky. The cacophony of noise intensified with the appearance of a second gunship, then a third.

The choppers circled the swarming vehicles like heavenly herders trying to corral stampeding mechanized cattle. Blinding searchlights turned night into day. One of the 50 mm cannons bristling from the nose of the lead gunship boomed, and a fountain of snow arched into the sky.

One after another, the buzzing snowmobiles stopped. Their white-suited drivers jumped off, hands held high, while the giant black moths circled overhead.

Only two mounted attackers escaped the roundup. The first dodged across the snow and headed for the trees behind the hut. The second followed in his tracks, almost riding up the other's rear skis.

From her high perch, Maggie took careful aim. She wasn't about to let even one of these scum get away. As soon as the second vehicle entered the ring outlined in the snow by the scattered brush, neither one of them was coming out. No one in their right mind would drive a gasoline-powered snowmobile though the flames about to erupt.

Her finger tightened on the trigger just as a white shape flew out of the trees. Maggie's shot ignited a flash bomb at the same moment Radizwell crashed into the lead driver, knocking him off his churning vehicle.

Flames shot into the sky and raced around the ring of gasoline-soaked brush. Two drivers and one savage, snarling komondor were trapped inside a circle of fire. Horrified, Maggie saw the second driver jump off his

snowmobile. Lifting his automatic rifle, he spun toward the
dog and his thrashing victim.

In a smooth, lightning-fast movement, Maggie braced her
wrist against the limb, took aim and fired. With a sharp
crack, the driver's weapon flew out of his hand. When another warning shot threw up a clump of snow just in front
of him, he dropped to his knees. Rocking back and forth,
he clutched his injured hand to his chest.

Maggie had shimmied halfway down the tree when she
caught sight of a dark figure running toward the wall of
flames. Bending his arm in front of his face, he disappeared into the fire.

"Adam!" Her instinctive cry was lost in the fire's roar.

By the time Maggie leaped through the fiery wall and
joined him, Adam had the injured driver covered, and
Radizwell had terrorized and almost tenderized the other.
Adam held the straining animal with one hand while the
man scuttled backward, crablike.

"I don't know!" he shouted.

"Talk, or I let him loose!" Adam snarled, as fearsome as
the creature at his side.

"I told you, I don't know who hired us!"

Adam relaxed his grip enough for Radizwell to leap for
the man's boot. Clamping his massive jaws around it, he
shook his head. The driver screamed as his whole body lifted
with each shake, then thumped back down in the snow.

"Call him off! I swear, I don't know!"

Maggie skidded to a halt beside Adam. She watched the
man's frantic gyrations with great satisfaction.

"Have him chew on his face for a while," she suggested,
loudly enough to be heard over the growls and cries. "It will
improve his looks, if nothing else."

Evidently Radizwell had reached the same conclusion. He
spit out the boot and lunged forward. The man screamed

and threw up an arm. At the last moment, Adam buried a fist in the woolly ruff and hauled the dog back.

"You've got five seconds. Then I let him go."

"I don't know," the man sobbed. "Our instructions come to a post office box, unsigned. The money's deposited in an account at the bank."

Adam stiffened. "Which bank?"

"What?"

"Which bank?"

"First Bank. In Miami."

The three choppers settled on the snow like hens nesting for the night. In the blinding glare of their powerful searchlights, a heavily armed counterstrike team rounded up the band of attackers and stripped them down to search for weapons.

A tall, lanky figure left the circle of activity and plowed through the snow toward the ring of fire.

"Thunder? Chameleon?"

"Here!" Maggie shouted.

Leaping over dwindling flames, Cowboy came to an abrupt halt. He pushed his Denver Broncos ball cap to the back of his head, surveying the scene.

A white-suited figure with his hands behind his head stumbled forward in front of Maggie, who covered him with the puniest excuse for a weapon Cowboy had ever seen. Adam knelt in the snow to retrieve a semiautomatic. And a mound of shaggy white perched atop the stomach of a downed attacker, fangs bared. A series of spine-tingling growls rolled toward Cowboy, and he didn't make the mistake of moving any closer.

He shook his head in mingled amusement and relief. "Here I bring the cavalry chargin' to the rescue, and you didn't even need us. You've got your own..." He jerked his chin toward the still-growling creature. "What *is* that thing, anyway?"

"A Hungarian dust mop," Maggie said.

"A Hungarian sheepdog," Adam corrected.

The Hungarian in question snarled menacingly.

"Not exactly a hospitable sort, is he?"

Maggie shook her head emphatically. "No."

"Yes," Adam countered. "Once he gets acquainted with you."

"Well, we'll have to get acquainted some other time. My orders are to get you back to Sacramento immediately. Jaguar's got a plane standing by to fly us to D.C."

"Why the rush?" Maggie asked.

She was as anxious as he to bring down the final curtain on this mission, but she'd thought—hoped—she and Adam would have at least an hour or two at the cabin to clean up and finish one or more of the several interesting discussions they'd started in the past few days.

"Jaguar radioed just before we landed. The vice president's completed those treaty negotiations faster than she or anyone else thought possible. She's flying in from Camp David, and insists on resuming her public persona. Death threat or no death threat, she wants to be at the press conference tomorrow when the president announces the treaty. He's calling you in."

Chapter 15

As it turned out, the entire ragged band flew back to Sacramento with Maggie and Adam.

A grim-faced Denise Kowalski insisted on accompanying her ''charge'' back to D.C. Hank McGowan set his jaw and refused to be taken to a hospital. He wanted to see with his own eyes that Taylor was safe. A medic with the counterstrike team packed and patched his wound on the spot.

To Maggie's disgust, even the dog got into the act. He whined pathetically when Adam climbed aboard the chopper and refused to remove his massive body from a skid. Forced to choose between ordering the pilot to lift off with a hundred pounds of komondor on one track and taking the creature aboard, Adam had opened the side hatch. With a thunderous woof that had half a dozen well-armed counterstrike agents swinging around, weapons leveled, Radizwell leaped into the cabin.

With his odoriferous presence, the air in the helicopter took on a distinct aroma. After a day of strenuous physical

activity followed by a night that had raised Maggie's ner-
vous-tension levels well beyond the stage of a discreet, la-
dylike dew, she wanted nothing more than a bath, a good
meal and Adam, not necessarily in that order. For a few
more hours, though, she had to maintain her role.

With unerring skill, the chopper pilot put his craft down
a few yards from the gleaming 747 that waited for them,
engines whining. The media, alerted to the vice president's
departure by the presence of Air Force Two, crowded at the
edge of the ramp. Realizing that this might be her last public appearance as the vice president of the United States,
Maggie gave them a grin and a wave as she walked to the
aircraft. Luckily, the night was too dark and the photogra-
phers were too far away to record the precise details of Taylor Grant's less-than-immaculate appearance, much less the
blackened hole in the front of her ski jacket left by a 44-40
rifle shell.

The diminutive martinet who waited for her inside the 747
saw it at once, however. Lillian's black eyes rounded as she
gaped at Maggie's middle.

"Good heavens! Are you all right?"

"I'm fine."

Her face folding into lines of tight disapproval, the dresser
scowled at Denise, who entered the plane behind Adam.
"You told me she'd been attacked down at the lake. But you
didn't tell me she was hit."

"She wasn't," Denise said wearily, dragging a hand
through her sandy hair. "Not down at the lake. McGowan
put a bullet through her, or tried to."

"Hank?" Lillian's gray eyebrows flew up. "Hank shot
the vice president?"

The uniformed stewards ranged around the huge cabin
listened with wide-eyed astonishment. All the crew knew was
that a call from the president had cut short the vice presi-

dent's scheduled vacation. And that an "accident" of some sort had occurred just prior to their departure from the cabin for Sacramento.

"It was a mistake," Denise said, confirming the story. "One McGowan's already paid for," she added. "I put a bullet through his shoulder."

"Good heavens!" Lillian repeated faintly.

"She's a damn hard woman," the caretaker stated, panting. He leaned a forearm against the bulkhead to catch his breath. The effort of climbing the stairs had pearled his face with sweat and darkened a spot on the shoulder of the jacket he'd borrowed from Herrera. He'd insisted on coming along, but it had obviously cost him.

The arrival of Cowboy, Herrera and an enthusiastically sniffing Radizwell snapped Lillian into action. In her best drill-sergeant manner, she took charge.

"I've laid out clean clothes in your stateroom, Mrs. Grant. I knew you'd want to shower and change as soon as we took off. Hank, you come with me. I'll look at that shoulder. Steward! Take this animal to the aft compartment. He stinks!"

"The understatement of the year," Maggie murmured.

Unfortunately, Radizwell refused to be separated from his pal, Adam. Maggie suspected the delicious aromas wafting from the galley had something to do with his fierce, growling stance. The hound wanted his share.

So did she. As her nose picked up the mouth-watering scents, her bruised stomach sent out a series of growls very close to Radizwell's in volume and intensity. Suddenly Maggie realized she could fulfill all three of her most immediate needs and still maintain her role.

"Why don't you come with me, Adam?" she suggested. Keeping her tone light, for the stewards' sake, she nodded toward the forward compartment. "You said you needed to contact your people to let them know about our change of plans. You can use my office while I shower and change. Then we can have a bite to eat.''

"Fine."

"We'll serve as soon as we're airborne," the head steward added helpfully. "We've prepared a vegetable quiche for Mrs. Grant, but perhaps you'd prefer a steak, sir?"

"Steak," Adam replied, his eyes glinting. "Definitely the steak."

In the privacy of the well-appointed bathroom, Maggie made free use of various sundries kept on hand for the vice president. It was amazing how much a toothbrush and the prospect of soothing, perfumed lotion after a hot shower could revitalize a woman.

The prospect of the hot shower itself was even more revitalizing. Eagerly Maggie shed her boots and socks, along with the turtleneck and brown pleated pants, now a great deal the worse for their wear. Her movements slowed a bit when it came to removing the bodysuit.

Wincing, she twisted to one side to reach the Velcro straps. Her stomach muscles screamed a protest as the supporting shield fell away. Using both hands, she lifted the hem of her thermal undershirt, then froze. Her jaw dropping, she surveyed the effects of the rifle shell in the bathroom mirror.

A bruise the size of a dinner plate painted her middle in various shades of green and purple, with touches of yellow and blue thrown in for dramatic emphasis. She gulped at the dramatic colorama, then tugged the shirt over her head and bent to push off the bottoms. An involuntary "Oooooch" escaped her when she tried to straighten up.

Realizing that she might have to adjust the scope of her plans for the next few hours or so, Maggie padded to the glass-enclosed shower. Under her bare feet, the floor vibrated with the power of the 747's huge engines. While she waited for the water to heat, Maggie let her appreciative gaze roam the wood-paneled bath.

Air Force Two was a model of efficient luxury. It had to be. It served as a second home for the vice president on her frequent trips around the globe. Just as her predecessors had, Taylor Grant represented the president at everything from weddings to funerals of various heads of state. This duty required extensive traveling, so much so that Mrs. Bush had once quipped that the vice president's seal should read Have Funeral, Will Travel.

Maggie smiled at the thought and stepped into the shower. With a groan of pleasure, she lifted her face to the pulsing jets and let the hot water sluice down her body. Sighing in sybaritic gratification, she dropped her arms to her sides while heat needled her shoulders and breasts.

She was still standing in a boneless, motionless lump when the shower door opened.

"The steward just served your dinner," Adam said, his face grave. "Having experienced firsthand how testy you get when you're hungry, I thought I'd better let you know immediately."

"Thank you," Maggie replied, equally grave, as though she weren't standing before him completely naked.

Through the mist of the escaping steam, she saw that he'd taken advantage of the selection of sundries in one of the other bathrooms, as well. The dark bristles shadowing his cheeks and chin were gone, and he'd made an attempt to tame his black hair. He'd scrounged up a clean white shirt, but wore the same snug jeans and ski boots.

Adam appeared just as interested in her state of dress, or undress, as she was in his. In a slow sweep, his gaze traveled from her face to neck to her breasts. Maggie felt her nipples harden under his intimate inspection, and a twist of love at the sudden pain in his eyes when he saw her stomach.

"Remind me to give the chief of Field Dress a superior performance bonus when this is over," he said fiercely. "A big one."

Maggie was too busy enjoying the blaze of emotion on his face to spare more than a passing thought for the pudgy, frizzy-haired genius who'd produced her torturous corset. A fiery warmth that had nothing to do with the water steaming up the shower enclosure coursed through her belly, and her muscles contracted involuntarily. Maggie ignored the stabbing ache in her middle and focused instead on the ache building a little lower.

Lifting his gaze to hers, he smiled. His eyes held a tender softness in their blue depths that Maggie had never seen before. One that intensified the liquid heat gathering low in her belly.

"Do you want to eat now, or later?"

"Now," she told him with a grin. "And later."

As she watched Adam strip off his clothes, Maggie thought she'd melt from the sizzling combination of hot water and spiraling desire and disappear down the shower drain in a rivulet of need. From a snow cave to a 747, she thought. From under the ground to a mile above it. From an attack beside a frozen lake to a ring of fire beside a deserted shack. Out of all the missions she'd ever been on, she knew this one would always remain vividly emblazoned in her mind.

And when Adam stepped inside and closed the shower door behind him, Maggie knew the expression in his eyes would always—always!—remain imprinted in her heart.

Water streamed over his broad shoulders and down his chest as he buried his hands in her wet hair. Tilting her face to his, he smiled down at her.

"I love you, Chameleon. In all your guises. But I love you in this one most."

His use of her code name gave Maggie a little dart of pleasure, then one of pain. Her personal relationship with Adam was so inextricably bound to her professional one. Yet she knew in her heart that couldn't continue. They'd stepped through the barriers that separated them, and there was no stepping back. Not now. Not ever.

"I love you, too," she whispered, sliding her palms up the planes of his water-slick chest. "In all your guises. Special envoy. Director. Code name Thunder. Plain ol' Adam Ridgeway. But I love you in this one the most."

She wrapped her arms around his neck and brought his mouth down to hers. He tasted of warm, rich brandy. Of smoky fire. Of Adam.

Rising up on her toes, she brought her body into his. She managed to contain her startled gasp when her bruised tummy connected with his, but he didn't miss the tiny, involuntary flinch. Sliding his hands down the curve of her waist, he grasped her hips gently and pushed her away.

She murmured an inarticulate protest.

Guiding her gently, he rotated her slick body until she faced the wall. "Like this, my darling," he whispered in her ear. "Like this. I don't want to hurt you."

Maggie discovered that "this" wasn't bad, after all. In fact, she thought on a gasp of pure pleasure, "this" was wonderful. Adam's broad chest felt solid and strong and sleek against her back. The way he reached around to mold her breasts with both hands sent waves of sensation washing through her. The touch of her bare bottom against his belly was even more electrifying. Hard and rampant and fully erect, he pressed against her.

Bracing her palms on the shower tiles, Maggie arched her back. Her head twisted, and he bent to take her mouth. While his tongue and hers met in a slow, sensual dance, his hands played with her nipples. With each tug and twist, fire streaked from Maggie's breasts to her belly. With each nip of his teeth against her lower lip, she felt the sting of need in her loins.

When his hands left her breasts to brush with a feather-light touch down her middle, her pelvis arched to meet them. Her head fell back against his shoulder as he parted her folds and opened her to his touch and the pelting of the pulsing water. Maggie gasped at the exquisite sensation.

"Adam! I don't think— I can't hold— Oh!"

"Don't think," he growled in her ear. "Don't hold back. Let me love you, Maggie. Let me feed your soul, as you feed mine."

When her soul had been fed, twice, and Adam's at least once, they decided it was time to feed their bodies. While he used one of the fluffy towels monogrammed with the vice president's seal to dry himself, Maggie pulled on a thick, sinfully soft terry robe.

Plopping herself down on a vanity stool, she treated herself to a spectacular view of Adam's lean flanks and tight white buns as she towel-dried her hair.

"Mmm... Nice." Her fingers curled into the towel. "Maybe that steak could wait a few more minutes."

"The steak might, but Radizwell probably won't. I left him sniffing around the office. If we don't get back in there, he's liable to—"

"Adam!" Sheer panic sliced through Maggie. Throwing the towel aside, she jumped off the stool. "You didn't leave that animal in the same room with my steak, did you?"

The terry-cloth robe flapped against her legs as she rushed through the paneled bedroom and threw open the door to the office.

"I'm going to shoot him!"

Hands on hips, Maggie glared at the shaggy creature stretched out contentedly beside the litter of dishes he'd pushed off the table onto the floor, all of which were licked clean. Sublimely indifferent to her anger, Radizwell raised his head, thumped his tail at Adam a couple of times, then yawned and laid his head back down.

"I'll shoot him!" Maggie snarled again. "I'll skin him. I'll—"

"Strange," Adam murmured. "McGowan said Taylor threatened to do the same."

"It's not strange," Maggie fumed. "It's natural. It's possible. It's very likely, in fact, that someone will do so in the very near future. Why Taylor would keep this obnoxious, smelly, greedy beast is beyond me."

"Probably for the same reasons you keep a bug-eyed reptile with a yard-long tongue."

"Terence," Maggie pronounced with lofty dignity, "has class."

Adam laughed and lifted her in his arms. Taking care not to bump her stomach, he carried her to the wide leather sofa at the far end of the office.

"It's not funny," she muttered. "That . . . that Hungarian ate my steak!"

"My steak, remember? Don't pout, Maggie. I'll order another one. I seem to have worked up quite an appetite."

*   *   *

The head steward delivered Adam's second dinner some time later.

By then, Maggie had retreated once more to the bedroom to finish dressing. She couldn't bear the thought of strapping the body shield on over her sore stomach again, and she left it on the dressing stool.

To her surprise, the pantsuit Lillian had laid out fit perfectly even without the tight corset. A size eight, no less! She smoothed her hands over trim hips covered in a soft, pale yellow wool and admired her silhouette in the mirror. Biting her lip, Maggie debated whether she should forgo her half of Adam's second steak, after all.

Nah! Not this time!

She flipped off the lights, casting a last look over her shoulder at her reflection in the mirror.

Maybe next time, though.

They had just polished off their meal when Cowboy rapped on the door. Poking his sun-streaked blond head inside the office, Nate Sloan gave them a lazy grin.

"You two finished chowin' down yet?"

"We're finished," Adam replied.

"About time!"

Nate strolled into the office with his graceful, long-legged gait. Radizwell lifted his head lazily, issued a halfhearted growl, then thumped it back down again. A juicy steak appeared to have the same mellowing effect on his temperament as it did on hers, Maggie thought in amusement.

"Jaguar's been trying to raise you for the last half hour," Cowboy said casually. "Forget to put your transceiver back on, Chief?"

Adam glanced down at his wrist, which was bare except for its dusting of dark hair. "Apparently."

Maggie remembered last seeing the thin gold watch tossed on the bathroom carpet, along with Adam's clothes.

"Jaguar said he could wait, so I decided not to interrupt your...meal."

"I'll go get the transceiver," Adam said, unperturbed.

Maggie, on the other hand, wavered between a grin and a ridiculous blush at Nate's knowing look. She struggled with both while he sprawled with his customary loose-limbed ease in the leather chair opposite her and regarded her with a twinkle in his hazel eyes.

"We were all taking bets on which way this mission would go, you know."

"Is that right?"

"We figured you and the chief would find a way to patch up your differences or come back ready to use each other for target practice on the firing range. Looks like you did some patchin'."

Maggie tucked her legs under her and rested her hand on her ankle. The glint of gold on her ring finger caught her eye. She smiled, realizing that she and Adam would have their forever, after all.

"I'm not sure I'd call it patching," she said, her smile easing into the grin she'd struggled against the moment before. "And we still have a few significant differences to work out. But we will work them out, one way or another."

Nate's eyes gleamed. "He's a good man, Maggie. One of the best."

"*The* best," she replied.

"Hellfire, woman, it took you long enough to recognize that fact."

"I recognized it a long time ago. I just wasn't ready to do anything about it."

"Why not?"

Her smile slipped a bit, but she answered easily enough. "He's my boss, Nate. He's had to maintain a distance, an objectivity, just as I've had to keep my personal feelings separate from my professional ones.''

"And now?"

"Now? Now I couldn't separate them if I tried."

"So what are you going to do about it?"

She hesitated, not quite ready to put into words the decision she'd come to in the shower, but Nate already knew the answer to his question.

"You're going to leave OMEGA."

Maggie nodded. "I have to. Wherever our relationship goes, I have to leave OMEGA. Neither one of us can operate the way we have been. Not anymore."

"Adam might have something to say about that."

A gleam of laughter crept into Maggie's eyes. "I'm sure he will. He usually has a long list of items to discuss with me when I return from a mission."

She stretched, feeling immeasurably relieved now that she'd taken the first step.

"There's nothing to discuss about this particular matter, though. You know Adam's needed more at OMEGA than I am. He has the president's ear. He moves in the kind of circles necessary to carry off his double role as special envoy and director of OMEGA. He's the best man for his job. The only man."

"So what will you do?"

"I don't know." She glanced around the wood-paneled compartment. "Maybe I'll run for office. I could get used to traveling like this. And there are a few issues I'd like to tackle."

"Such as?"

"Such as the distribution by gender of toilets in public places."

Nate gave her a look of blank astonishment. "Come again?"

"You don't think all those long lines outside women's rest rooms are a violation of the First Amendment? Or whichever amendment guarantees us life, liberty, and the pursuit of happiness?"

"Maggie, darlin', I can't say I've ever given women's rest rooms much thought."

"Neither has anyone else," she said sweetly. "That's going to change."

Nate was still chuckling when Adam came back into the office a few moments later. His blue eyes gleamed with a suppressed excitement that didn't fool Maggie for an instant. For once, Adam Ridgeway's cool control had slipped.

"What?" she asked, sitting up. "What is it?"

"I just talked to Jaguar. We've got it, Maggie. We've got the 'why.'"

"We do?"

She scrambled out of the leather chair.

Detouring around a half acre of prone sheepdog, she joined Adam at the vice president's desk. Her eyes widened as she scanned the notes he'd scribbled during his conversation with Jaguar.

"Adam! You were right! First Bank is managing James Elliot's blind trust during his term as secretary of the treasury. That might be the connection."

"They're managing more than a blind trust. Elliot has several accounts with them." Adam smiled grimly. "Accounts he failed to disclose during his background investigation and his Senate confirmation hearing. Accounts that received large electronic deposits from offshore banks."

"Good grief! Drug dollars?"

"It's possible, and very likely. We'll have to dig deeper for absolute proof. The mere fact that he failed to disclose the accounts will cost him his office, however."

Maggie shook her head. "But what does all this have to do with me? I don't have any involvement with First Bank. Why did he go to such desperate—?"

She broke off, her eyes widening. "Luis Esteban! Those phone calls I made for him, hinting at high-level government interest in First Bank! My God, Elliot must gotten wind of the calls and thought I was on to something."

"He thought a nameless, faceless special agent with the code name Chameleon was on to something. He had to flush her out. One way or another."

Chapter 16

"We're here to see the president. I believe he's expecting us."

The White House usher looked a little startled at Adam's cool announcement. A dubious expression flitted across his face as he took in the gaggle of people ranged behind the special envoy.

Maggie couldn't blame the poor man. They constituted a pretty intimidating crew.

After flying through the night, Air Force Two had landed at Andrews Air Force Base just as a weak January sun washed D.C. in a gray dawn. The entire entourage had piled out of the plane and driven straight into the city. Adam couldn't have shaken any one of them if he tried.

Maggie, of course, wanted to be in on the kill.

Cowboy had come along for backup.

Denise Kowalski refused to abandon her post.

Hank McGowan wanted to make sure Taylor was all right.

Lillian insisted that the vice president, who was flying in from Camp David, would need her help to get ready for the news conference scheduled in less than a half hour to announce the historic treaty.

And no one could separate Radizwell from Adam without losing a hand or an arm in the process.

When faced with his newly appointed shadow, Adam had shrugged and stated calmly that the animal had taken down two of Maggie's attackers. He was as much a part of the team as any of them.

The usher swallowed as he looked the group over once more. "You're here to see the president, sir? All of you?"

"All of us."

Radizwell didn't seem to care for this unnecessary delay. He curled one black gum and issued a warning that made the man's face pale visibly.

"If you'll accompany me, sir."

With a measured pace, the usher led the small band through the corridor that connected the White House proper with the semidetached west wing. He stopped before a set of tall wooden doors, one gloved hand on the latch, and gave the uncombed, aromatic sheepdog another doubtful glance.

"All of us," Adam repeated firmly.

"Yes, sir."

The receptionist rose at their entrance. Giving Radizwell a wide berth, she took their coats and supplied them with coffee. Maggie had just taken a sip of delicious mocha laced with dark chocolate when the double doors opened once more. The vice president strode in, followed by the stony-faced senior agent with the half-chewed ear—Buck Evans.

"Adam! You're back!"

Taylor Grant strode across the patterned carpet, hands outstretched. Her broad smile encompassed the entire group, but her first greeting was for the special envoy.

"Buck briefed me on the attacks. Are you all right?"

Adam bent to brush a kiss across her cheek. "We're fine. Congratulations on the treaty, Madam Vice President. No one but you could have pulled it off. You're going to make history this morning."

She could handle this, Maggie told herself, swallowing a gulp of coffee that suddenly tasted like sludge. She could handle the sight of Adam's dark head bent over Taylor's sleek, beautiful one. She could handle it, but she didn't have to like it.

Beside her, Hank McGowan stiffened imperceptibly. Maggie caught the slight movement and darted him a quick look. His battered features showed no emotion, but below the rolled-up sleeve of McGowan's blue work shirt Maggie saw the snarling bear tattooed on his forearm twitch.

She wasn't the only one who caught the tiny ripple of movement. Across the room, Denise Kowalski's brown eyes narrowed as she glanced from McGowan to the vice president.

Her lips twisting, Taylor released Adam's hands. "I understand you're going to make history yourself this morning. You . . . and Chameleon."

She turned to Maggie, and a small shock of surprise widened her eyes when she looked at her alter ego fully for the first time.

Maggie's involuntary diet and rather strenuous activities during the past week had altered her face as subtly as her body. Her cheeks had small hollows under their prominent bones . . . like Taylor's. Her generous mouth had thinned a fraction . . . like Taylor's. She was far closer to a perfect double now than when she'd embarked on this masquerade.

The vice president quickly mastered her surprise and gave Maggie a sympathetic smile. "I understand I wasn't the target, after all. It was you all the time."

"We think so."

"Perhaps we should have reversed our roles. Instead of pouring out my most intimate secrets to a stranger, I could've spent a couple of weeks in the mountains with Adam, acting as your double."

"I *don't* think so."

Taylor blinked at the drawled response, and Maggie saw that her message had been received. No one, not even the vice president of the United States, was going to be spending any weeks with Adam Ridgeway. In the mountains or anywhere else.

Except Maggie.

Smiling, she took a sip of her mocha coffee while Taylor greeted the rest of the entourage. She gave Lillian a quick hug, then gasped aloud.

"Radizwell!"

Maggie swung around to see the sheepdog calmly lowering his leg. Having marked his territory to his satisfaction on the delicate hand-painted eighteenth-century wallpaper, he moved on to explore the rest of the office.

Taylor's violet eyes squeezed shut. "I'm going to skin that animal," she said through gritted teeth. "I'm going to skin him and tan him and use him as a throw rug."

Shaking her head in disgust, she summoned the dog. "Come here! Here, boy."

The komondor ignored her.

Adam snapped his fingers once.

Radizwell obediently plodded to Adam's side and settled back on his haunches with a satisfied air. He'd seen his duty, and he'd done it.

Taylor's auburn brows shot up, but before she could comment, the door to the inner office opened.

The chief of staff stepped out, his eyes widening as he looked from Taylor to Maggie, then back again.

"Madam Vice President . . . er, Madams Vice President, the president will see you now. And you, of course, Mr. Special Envoy. He's asked the secretary of the treasury to join you in a few moments, as you requested."

Adam stood aside to allow the women to precede him. Taylor took one step, then stopped and stood aside for Maggie. "This is your show. You have the honors."

Nodding graciously, Maggie sailed into the Oval Office.

After the gut-wrenching tension and chilling events of the past few days, Maggie would have expected the moment the perpetrator was finally unmasked to be one of high drama.

Instead, James Elliot's face turned ashen the moment he stepped into the Oval Office and saw her standing beside Taylor. When a shaken president confronted his longtime friend with evidence of his failure to disclose ties to a bank with links to a Central American drug cartel, Elliot seemed to collapse in on himself, like a hot-air balloon when the air inside the silk bag cools.

Under Adam's relentless questioning, Elliot admitted everything, including his desperate attempt to silence the woman known only as Chameleon.

Maggie's nails bit into her palms when the man who had wanted to kill her wouldn't even look at her.

"She had to die," he whispered, in a remorseless confession to the president. "That was the best solution. The only solution. I didn't know how much she knew. Just the tiny scrap of information linking First Bank to the frozen assets of the Cartozan drug lord was enough to bring my whole world tumbling down if she followed up on it. She had to die."

"Get him out of here," the president said in disgust.

A grim-faced Denise Kowalski was given the distinction of arresting her own boss. She walked into the Oval Office, flashed Elliot her badge and advised him of his rights. With Buck Evans on one side and Denise on the other, the former secretary of the treasury departed.

For long moments, no one moved. Then the president shoved a hand in the pocket of his charcoal gray slacks and walked over to the tall windows facing south. He stared at the stark obelisk of the Washington Monument rising out of the mists drifting off the tidal basin.

"Christ! Jimmy Elliot!"

His shoulders slumped, and the indefatigable energy that characterized both him and his administration seemed to evaporate.

Adam's eyes met those of the vice president. She gave a slight nod, then addressed the man at the window with remarkable calm.

"You have a press conference in ten minutes, Mr. President. Do you want to go over the treaty provisions a final time, or do you feel comfortable with them?"

The president squared his shoulders. Turning, he gave his deputy a tight smile.

"No, the brief you sent me from Camp David was excellent." He paused, and then his smile eased into one of genuine warmth. "I still can't believe you pulled this treaty off. Good work, Taylor. Whatever the hell bad choices I might have made, when I picked you, I picked a winner."

"I'll remind you of that when you get ready to announce your support for your successor," she replied, laughing.

"You do that!"

Walking across the room, he held out his hand to Maggie. "I'm sorry you had to go through this torturous charade."

"I'm not. The assignment had its finer moments. Besides," she continued smoothly, ignoring Adam's raised brows, "it was all in the line of duty.

"A duty I understand you do extremely well. The director has told me that you're good. Damn good. One of the best."

"*The* best," Adam said coolly.

Maggie flashed him a startled look. His eerie echo of her exact words to Cowboy surprised her, until she remembered the transmitter in her ring. Adam must have heard the entire conversation, including the part about her decision to leave OMEGA!

From the steely expression in his eyes, she knew that this mission's postbrief was going to make all her others seem tame by comparison.

"We'll have to talk about that later," the president said, with a smile for Maggie. "Right now, I have a press conference to conduct. Adam, if you'll stay just a moment, please?"

Some moments later, Maggie stood in the wings beside Adam and Taylor Grant as a composed and forceful chief executive strode to the podium in the White House briefing room. His back straight, he glanced around the packed auditorium. Ignoring the clear Plexiglas TelePrompTer in front of the podium, he addressed the assembled group directly.

"I called this press conference to announce a historic treaty, one that constitutes the first positive step toward eliminating a scourge that hangs over our world."

He paused, his jaw squaring. "But before I give you the details on this treaty, I have another, less pleasant duty to perform. I regret to say that a few moments ago I was forced to request the immediate resignation of James Elliot, my treasury secretary, for reasons I'm not yet at liberty to discuss."

A wave of startled exclamations filled the room. The president waited for them to die down before continuing.

"I can tell you, however, that I've already selected his replacement. Ladies and gentlemen, it gives me great pleasure to introduce my nominee for secretary of the treasury, Adam Ridgeway."

Stunned, Maggie lifted her eyes to the man beside her. She heard the spatter of applause that quickly rolled into thunder. And the hum of excited comments from the audience. And Taylor's warm congratulations. But none of them registered. All that penetrated her whirling mind was the glint in Adam's eyes as he tipped her chin.

"We'll talk about this, among other things, when we get back to headquarters," he promised.

"Our list of items to discuss is getting pretty long," she replied breathlessly.

He kissed her, hard and fast and thoroughly, then strode out to join the president at the podium.

Dazed, Maggie listened to his brief acceptance and the easy way he fielded the storm of questions from the media.

A welter of emotions coursed through her. She couldn't imagine OMEGA without Adam Ridgeway as director. He'd guided the organization and its tight cadre of agents and technicians for so long, with such unerring skill. In her mind, Adam *was* OMEGA.

At the same time, Maggie swelled with pride. She couldn't think of anyone more qualified for a cabinet post than this man.

And she wouldn't have been human if a thrill of excitement hadn't darted through her veins. Adam's promotion meant she didn't have to leave OMEGA. He wouldn't be her boss any longer. What he would be was something they would discuss as soon as they got back to the headquarters. Anticipation and joy leaped through her.

Knowing Adam would be mobbed by the media even after the treaty announcement to follow, Maggie decided to slip away. She wanted to be out of Taylor's skin and in her own when she and Adam met again. For once, Chameleon wanted no guises, no cover, nothing to hide her from the man she loved.

Her pulse thrumming, she turned to leave.

Taylor stopped her with a hand on her arm. "I didn't thank you. For being me when I was the target. Even though it was you . . . Well, you know what I mean."

Maggie's quicksilver grin blossomed. "It gets confusing, doesn't it? Half the time I wasn't even sure just who the heck I was."

The other woman's eyes gleamed. "It doesn't appear Adam had that problem."

"No, I guess he didn't."

"He'll make an excellent secretary of the treasury. And I think you'd make an excellent special envoy."

For the second time in less than ten minutes, Maggie was dumbfounded. "Me?"

"You. We don't have enough women with your rather unique qualifications in leadership positions. I'll talk to the president about it."

"While you're at it," Maggie replied, still astounded but regrouping fast, "you might mention establishing a commission to—"

She stopped, too anxious to get back to headquarters to take the time to explain the public potty proclamation she'd issued at the Kennedy Center.

"Never mind, I'll talk to you about it later. Right now I have to change back into me. I want to be wearing my own skin when I claim my forever."

A smile feathered Taylor's lips. "Your forever? That's nice."

"It's from your ring."

At her blank look, Maggie held up her hand. "The inscription in your wedding ring. *Now, and forever.*"

"What are you talking about? There's no inscription in my ring."

Chapter 17

On the outside, the elegant Federal-style town house on a quiet side street just off Massachusetts Avenue appeared no different than its neighbors. Neatly banked snow edged the brick steps leading to its black-painted door. A brass knocker in the shape of an eagle gleamed in the cold afternoon sunlight. The bronze plaque that identified the structure as home to the offices of the president's special envoy was small and discreet, drawing the attention of few passersby.

Inside, however, the town house hummed with an activity level that would have astounded even the most jaded observer of the Washington political scene.

Raking fingers through hair newly restored to its original glossy chestnut color, Maggie stepped out of the third-floor crew room into a control center crackling with noise. Joe Samuels's banks of electronic boxes buzzed and beeped and blipped continually as the harried senior communications technician fielded a steady stream of transmissions from all corners of the globe. Word of the president's startling announcement had been beamed to OMEGA agents in the field, and they wanted to know the details. All the details.

"Roger, Cyrene," Joe said into the transmitter. "It's true. The confirmation hearings are scheduled for next week. There are going to be some changes around here."

His dark eyes caught Maggie's. "A lot of changes," he added, grinning.

Maggie shook her head at his knowing grin. She'd only been back from the White House a little over two hours. Most of that time had been spent with Jaguar in a closed-door mission debrief, the rest in a fever of anticipation in the crew room, working frantically to restore herself to her natural state.

She hadn't had time to discuss with anyone, let alone the still-absent Adam, any of the several urgent items on her list. Yet OMEGA's global network had already spread the word. There were going to be some changes around here. A lot of them.

Joe answered another beep, then nodded to Maggie over his bank of equipment. "Chief's on the way back from the White House, Chameleon. Be here in fifteen minutes. Think he'll have any news for us?"

Maggie sidestepped Joe's less-than-subtle probe to discover what she knew, if anything, about Adam's replacement. The idea that she might actually be named to head OMEGA was too fantastic to consider. Besides, she had more important matters to take care of right now.

"I don't know," she replied, heading for the elevator. "I'll let you know as soon as I hear anything for sure."

She took the specially shielded high-speed elevator to the underground lab and bearded the chief of Special Devices in his den.

"I need that special lubricant, Harry. Right away."

The scientist pushed his glasses to the top of his shining bald forehead. "Lubricant?"

She waggled her left hand in front of his face. "The one you developed so I can slide off this ring. I want to look at the inscription one more time before you guys remove the device soldered inside."

Maggie had no intention of surrendering the wide gold band permanently. In fact, she planned to put the ring to good use in the immediate future. But she wanted to see with her own eyes the words inscribed inside. Even with the pounds she'd shed, however, the band wouldn't fit over her knuckle.

"We didn't develop the lubricant."

"What? Why not?"

Blinking at her startled surprise, the senior technician hunched his shoulders and slid his hands into the pockets of his white coat. "The chief sent word through Jaguar that it wasn't necessary."

Maggie rocked back on her heels. "He did?"

"Didn't you know?"

She could only shake her head.

"The word came down the same day you left. No, the next morning. Jaguar said something about a bus backfiring and the chief swearing he wasn't going to ever let you out of range again."

"Well, well, well..." she said softly, twisting the ring around and around on her finger. "To think all that was going on behind his oh-so-cool, Mr. In Control exterior."

Maggie's mouth curved in a private smile as she recalled a few other revelations Adam had made during those hours in the snow cave about what went on in his mind. One of which, if she remembered correctly, had to do with locking his office door and throwing her down on the mahogany conference table she always perched on.

It was time to do a little perching.

"Gotta go," she told the still-confused lab chief as she whirled and raced for the elevator.

Her heart was thumping wildly when she stepped out onto the second-floor landing. A quick scan of the video monitors showed no one in the special envoy's reception area except the gray-haired Elizabeth Wells. Slapping her palm against the hidden sensors, Maggie shivered in impatience while she waited for the computers to verify her print.

The moment the titanium-shielded door hummed open, she dashed through the reception room.

"Is the chief back yet?" she flung at Elizabeth.

"No, but—Chameleon, wait!"

Maggie didn't have time for questions or explanations about all the changes coming down at OMEGA. Not now. Not with anticipation thrumming through her veins like heated wine. Not with a long list of urgent items to "discuss" with Adam.

"I'll catch you later, Elizabeth," she called over her shoulder. "I want to wait for the boss in his office."

Actually, she wanted to wait on a certain conference table, but she didn't think the matronly Elizabeth Wells would appreciate that bit of information.

"Wait, Chameleon, there are people in—"

Maggie stumbled to an abrupt halt on the threshold to Adam's office. Jaw sagging, she surveyed what looked like half the population of the nation's capital.

Apparently every OMEGA agent who wasn't in the field had gathered to hear firsthand the amazing news. With their wives. And children. And fathers-in-law.

Helplessly, Maggie looked from the dark-haired, steel-eyed Jaguar to a grinning Cowboy to the conservative, square-jawed Doc...who sported, she saw in stunned amazement, a mane of moussed hair that only Stoney Armstrong's Hollywood stylist could have sculpted.

Before any of them could comment, however, Senator Orwin Chandler strode forward, his unlit cigar clamped firmly in his mouth. "Is Ridgeway with you?" he boomed. "We have to start plotting our strategy for working his nomination through committee."

"Never mind that now, Dad."

Silvery-blond Sarah Chandler MacKenzie pushed through the crowd. Her aquamarine eyes alight, she took Maggie's hands in both of hers. "I can't believe Jake kept you in debrief for so long. We've all been waiting to hear about Adam's nomination. And when you two are going to announce your plans."

"Our plans?"

With a pang, Maggie realized she'd have to drastically revise her immediate plans. She cast a regretful glance at the huge mahogany conference table.

Three scrubbed, bright-eyed faces beamed back at her. Jaguar's adopted children were seated in the plush chairs pulled up to the table, being served a banquet of ice cream by a wiry preteen with a precocious air.

"We wish to know about your plans to wed, mademoiselle," the boy elaborated with Gallic savoir faire. "Did I not tell you when you lie so sick and green faced in Cannes that this Thunder, he has the eye for you?"

"Henri!"

Soft-spoken Paige Jensen admonished the pickpocket who had attached himself to her during her unexpected stint as a high-priced call girl.

"But it is true, Madame Paige! You said to Doc when we fly to this so-cold city last night that these two, they are made for each other."

"So I did, Henri." With a smile, Paige turned to Maggie. "Well?"

"We, uh, haven't quite finalized our plans yet. I was hoping to…discuss a few matters with Thunder when he got back."

The Russian-born, exotically beautiful Alexandra Danilova Sloan gave a low laugh. "Ah, Maggie. The women of my tribe have a saying about allowing men a say in such important matters."

"I'm not sure I want to hear this," Cowboy groaned.

Ignoring her husband, Alex smiled serenely. "At least once each year, it is wise to ask your man's advice about what should be done, but taking such advice is another kettle of potato soup entirely."

Maggie twisted the heavy gold ring with her thumb. "Well," she admitted with a grin, "I've already decided on one or two of the more important— Ack!"

She jumped straight into the air as a yard-long tongue shot out from under Adam's desk and planted a wet kiss on the back of her calf. Spinning around, Maggie saw a blue-and-orange-striped tail whip back and forth in lazy satisfaction. The rest of her pet iguana was firmly ensconced in the foot well of Adam's desk.

"Terence! What in the world are you doing here?"

"I brought him," Elizabeth said from the doorway. "The fool thing was pining away for you. It wouldn't even drink the Coors your father offered him last night before we went to dinner."

Maggie's brows soared. "You and Red went to dinner last night?"

The older woman patted her gray hair with a graceful, feminine gesture. "Actually, dear, we've had dinner together every night since you left. You suggested I call him, remember?"

"I . . . I think so."

The idea of crusty Red Sinclair connecting with this gracious, well-groomed woman who qualified every year at the expert level on a variety of lethal weapons both surprised and delighted Maggie. She started to tell her so, but just then a thunderous boom emanated from the outer office.

Half the people in the room reached for their weapons. The other half froze.

Maggie groaned. "Oh, no!"

A moment later, a shaggy white shape came bounding into the office. When he saw the assembled crowd, Radizwell dropped to his haunches and planted his front paws in an effort to skid to a halt, but his momentum carried him forward. Like a runaway bale of cotton, the sheepdog careened into Senator Chandler.

Arms windmilling, the dignified, silver-maned senator stumbled backward and landed on his duff. He glared at the unrepentant animal and clamped his jaw so tight the end of his unlit cigar broke off.

"Someone grab him before he decides to mark his territory," Maggie pleaded before she turned to face the man who stood in the doorway, surveying the scene with a look of unholy amusement on his face.

"Adam! What's that . . . that Hungarian doing here?"

With a nod to the various occupants of the room, the secretary of the treasury-designate strolled over to Maggie. When she saw the look in his eyes, dread washed through her in waves.

He confirmed her worst fears. "The vice president gave him to us as a wedding present."

"Oh, nooooo!"

Laughing, Adam gathered her into his arms. "Oh, yes, my darling."

"But—"

At that precise moment, Terence and Radizwell discovered each other. Total, uncontrolled pandemonium broke out.

Letting loose with a series of barks that had the resonance and earsplitting volume of an artillery barrage, the komondor danced around Adam's desk. Every time he got within striking distance of the foot well, a long pink tongue shot out and landed a stinging kiss on his face.

At least Maggie thought it was his face. With Radizwell, she was never quite sure.

Squealing with delight, the children jumped out of their chairs to join in the fun. Childish shrieks, adult laughter, and Senator Chandler's blustery admonitions to get that damned hound under control joined Radizwell's booming woofs.

In the midst of it all, Maggie stood cradled in Adam's arms. "What are my chances of convincing Taylor to take him back?" she shouted.

"About the same as convincing me to ever let you go."

Wrapping her arms around his neck, she grinned up at him. "In that case, I guess he's ours. Now, and forever."

* * * * *

COMING NEXT MONTH

Take 4 bestselling love stories FREE

Plus get a FREE surprise gift!

Special Limited-time Offer

Mail to Silhouette Reader Service™

3010 Walden Avenue
P.O. Box 1867
Buffalo, N.Y. 14269-1867

YES! Please send me 4 free Silhouette Intimate Moments® novels and my free surprise gift. Then send me 6 brand-new novels every month, which I will receive months before they appear in bookstores. Bill me at the low price of $3.12 each plus 25¢ delivery and applicable sales tax, if any.* That's the complete price and a savings of over 10% off the cover prices—quite a bargain! I understand that accepting the books and gift places me under no obligation ever to buy any books. I can always return a shipment and cancel at any time. Even if I never buy another book from Silhouette, the 4 free books and the surprise gift are mine to keep forever.

245 BPA AWPM

Name	(PLEASE PRINT)	
Address	Apt. No.	
City	State	Zip

This offer is limited to one order per household and not valid to present Silhouette Intimate Moments® subscribers. *Terms and prices are subject to change without notice.
Sales tax applicable in N.Y.

UMOM-995 ©1990 Harlequin Enterprises Limited

SILHOUETTE®

Desire®

CELEBRATION 1000

is on its way
in April, May and June 1996!

Join us for the celebration of Desire's 1000th book!
We'll have

- Book #1000, *Man of Ice* by Diana Palmer in May!
- Best-loved miniseries such as **Hawk's Way** by Joan Johnston, and **Daughters of Texas** by Annette Broadrick
- Fabulous new writers in our Debut author program, where you can collect **double** Pages and Privileges Proofs of Purchase

Plus you can enter our exciting Sweepstakes for a chance to win a beautiful piece of original Silhouette Desire cover art or one of many autographed Silhouette Desire books!

SILHOUETTE DESIRE'S CELEBRATION 1000
...because the best is yet to come!

As seen on TV!

Free Gift Offer

With a Free Gift proof-of-purchase from any Silhouette® book,
you can receive a beautiful cubic zirconia pendant.

This gorgeous marquise-shaped stone is a genuine cubic
zirconia—accented by an 18" gold tone necklace.

(Approximate retail value $19.95)

Send for yours today...
compliments of ▼ *Silhouette*®

To receive your free gift, a cubic zirconia pendant, send us one original proof-of-purchase, photocopies not accepted, from the back of any Silhouette Romance™, Silhouette Desire®, Silhouette Special Edition®, Silhouette Intimate Moments® or Silhouette Shadows™ title available in February, March or April at your favorite retail outlet, together with the Free Gift Certificate, plus a check or money order for $1.75 U.S./$2.25 CAN. (do not send cash) to cover postage and handling, payable to Silhouette Free Gift Offer. We will send you the specified gift. Allow 6 to 8 weeks for delivery. Offer good until April 30, 1996 or while quantities last. Offer valid in the U.S. and Canada only.

Free Gift Certificate

Name: _____

Address: _____

City: _____ State/Province: _____ Zip/Postal Code: _____

Mail this certificate, one proof-of-purchase and a check or money order for postage and handling to: SILHOUETTE FREE GIFT OFFER 1996. In the U.S.: 3010 Walden Avenue, P.O. Box 9057, Buffalo NY 14269-9057. In Canada: P.O. Box 622, Fort Erie,

---

FREE GIFT OFFER
079-KBZ-R

ONE PROOF-OF-PURCHASE

To collect your fabulous FREE GIFT, a cubic zirconia pendant, you must include this original proof-of-purchase for each gift with the properly completed Free Gift Certificate.

079-KBZ-R

Are your lips succulent, impetuous, delicious or racy?

Find out in a very special Valentine's Day promotion—THAT SPECIAL KISS!

Inside four special Harlequin and Silhouette February books are details for THAT SPECIAL KISS! explaining how you can have your lip prints read by a romance expert.

Look for details in the following series books, written by four of Harlequin and Silhouette readers' favorite authors:

Silhouette Intimate Moments #691
Mackenzie's Pleasure by *New York Times* bestselling author Linda Howard

Harlequin Romance #3395
Because of the Baby by Debbie Macomber

Silhouette Desire #979
Megan's Marriage by Annette Broadrick

Harlequin Presents #1793
The One and Only by Carole Mortimer

Fun, romance, four top-selling authors, plus a **FREE** gift! This is a very special Valentine's Day you won't want to miss! Only from Harlequin and Silhouette.

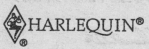

VAL96